SUELLEN

LUCILLE GUARINO

Black Rose Writing | Texas

This is a work of fiction. Names, characters, businesses, places, events, and incidents are either the products of the author's imagination or used in a fictitious manner. Any resemblance to actual persons, living or dead, or actual events is purely coincidental.

ISBN: 978-1-68513-559-1
PUBLISHED BY BLACK ROSE WRITING
www.blackrosewriting.com

Printed in the United States of America
Suggested Retail Price (SRP) $21.95

Lunch Tales is printed in Minion Pro

*As a planet-friendly publisher, Black Rose Writing does its best to eliminate unnecessary waste to reduce paper usage and energy costs, while never compromising the reading experience. As a result, the final word count vs. page count may not meet common expectations.

For all the ladies who lunch

PRAISE FOR
LUNCH TALES

"The winner of A Woman's Write 2023 novel competition, *Lunch Tales: Suellen* is rich and engaging. Embracing powerful issues that snag the lives of contemporary women by addressing Suellen's world of work, love, and a life-changing diagnosis, *Lunch Tales: Suellen* is tough to put down and worth the read. I promise you."
–Kristan Ryan, *A Woman's Write*

"Law office gossip, relationship advice, emotional support... there's nothing that these co-workers won't tackle. But there are some challenges that even the lunch bunch can't fix."
–Gail Ward Olmsted, award-winning author of *Miranda Quinn: Legal Twist series*

"*Lunch Tales: Suellen* is a perfect book for lying on a beach or cozied up in front of a warm fire. Author Guarino draws you into conversations between Suellen and her cohorts over shared lunches so adeptly, moving the plot along with a first-person narrative that makes you feel everything she feels. A charming book and enjoyable read."
–Barbara A. Luker, author of *The Right One*

"How does a wealthy, shopaholic, professional woman with horrible taste in men find love? Wrong question! Lucille Guarino's Suellen turns the question upside down...what will Suellen do when true love finds her?"
–Cam Torrens, best-selling author of the *Tyler Zahn series*

"Lucille Guarino creates an honest, raw, heartfelt journey embedded in beautiful prose, characters you won't forget, and love for the protagonist. Suellen's journey to give and receive love, learn to trust herself and others, and fight through life's obstacles, will touch your heart and you'll swoon for more."
–E.D. Hackett, author of *The Havoc in My Head*

"A tender love story sprinkled with a bit of angst. Slip it into your beach bag and enjoy."
–Linda Rosen, author of *The Emerald Necklace*

"A warm tale of friendship, struggle, and eventually love. *Lunch Tales: Suellen* follows a confident young attorney as she searches for meaning in her career and relationships."
–Kathryn Dodson, author of *Five Tries To Get It Right*

ACKNOWLEDGMENTS

Suellen's story hits close to home for me as I'm sure it will for many women out there, but I wouldn't have been able to tell it without the village of folks who helped bring it to fruition. For an author, feedback is fundamental and foremost. I am as equally grateful for the honest criticisms as the enthusiasm I've received.

To my ever-dependable, ever-candid beta readers: Erica Haraldsen, Gail Dwyer, Jeri Retzlaff, Emery Silva, Cam Torrens, Barbara Korbman, Jessica Pajda, and Johanna Buckley. To Kristan Ryan of A Woman's Write, Pamela Taylor, and Ann Leslie Tuttle for their editorial services. And to the Women's Fiction Writers Association (WFWA) for their wonderful creative workshops and programs – the gift that keeps on giving.

Thank you Black Rose Writing. To Reagan Rothe, the creator, David King, the cover designer, and the entire acquisition and marketing team, thank you for your excitement for *Lunch Tales: Suellen* and for bringing me into your community of extraordinarily talented authors. What an honor!

Most importantly, to my husband, Peter Guarino, for putting up with all aspects of my writing enterprise, from noisy keyboard tapping in early morning hours – "I need to get this down before it flies out of my head" – to hasty, impromptu dinners; for his encouragement when I feel my confidence wane; and for buoying me up during all the emotional swings. He is my sounding board, my long-suffering listener, my rock.

As I mostly write by the seat of my pants, how my stories evolve often surprises me. I guess that's the idea. Robert Frost said it best: "No tears in the writer, no tears in the reader. No surprise in the writer, no surprise in the reader."

"If I cannot do great things, I can do small things in a great way."
–Martin Luther King, Jr.

*"If you love something, set if free; if it comes back, it's yours, if it doesn't,
it never was."*
–Richard Bach

CHAPTER 1

I refuse to die today. A gulp catches in my throat, and I remind myself that breathing is imperative to staying alive. I clutch the thick lap bar with a death grip, white knuckles stiffening with strain as screams detonate in the back of my throat, ear-piercing shrieks that sound as if they belong to someone else. A plummet and twist whip my body from weightlessness to heaviness in just under four terrifying seconds, a dizzying array of visuals catching up to my mind's eye.

Steve flings his dark, wind-whipped hair from his eyes and smirks. "And that's why they call it the rocket."

Dazed, heart decelerating, I step out of the orange train car – the color of Jack-o-lanterns – and breathe out one long sigh of relief as soon as my feet touch the earth.

"Let's go again." I hear him say, even as my brain tries not to let it in.

My stupor waning, I stare into his eyes with an intensity I want to be certain he sees. "Are you fucking kidding me?"

Steve squints in response. He's not kidding. When is Steve ever kidding?

"I drove sixty miles so you could get your adrenaline rush. That's all I agreed to," I say. *We would have to live one hour from the tallest, scariest roller coaster in the world, fastest in North America.* "That's what your coaster enthusiasts group's for."

Steve doesn't hear a word I say. He's walking backward, his eyes riveted on Kingda Ka. We go over to sit on a bench with a panoramic view of the king of all roller coasters, and I pass Steve a water bottle. "So . . . was it everything you hoped it'd be?"

He picks up on my sarcasm. "No, Suellen. Had you helped me 'get off' while we were up there, now that would have been somethin'."

Oh, Suellen . . . Suellen, when did dangerous and exciting turn into such irony? "If only I hadn't wasted seconds screaming my head off. How clumsy of me." *If only I hadn't wasted ten months in an on-again, off-again relationship.* It's a toxic cycle – breaking up, going back for more. Dependable familiarity, thrilling uncertainty.

Steve takes a deep slug of water. "You need to work on your multitasking skills, babe."

I roll my eyes. This is how it goes with us, the back and forth. Which one will top the other? It's getting old.

It's a beautiful, clear September day. The sky is crystal blue. My mother told me it was a day just like this on the fateful date of 9/11, bright and perfect. It's strange that I'm thinking about this right now. I was young when that happened, but I imagine it's embedded in northeasterners how tranquility can turn into calamity with almost no warning.

I didn't go into a relationship with Steve thinking it had long-term prospects. I'm not an idealist. But lately we're fighting more – a consequence of living on the wild side of life, I guess. What I once thought exciting about him infuriates me now. But it's his birthday this week and I'm a sucker for birthdays. I promised I'd celebrate it with him as he saw fit, although I may have had a couple of drinks in me at the time I said it. Steve's wild side is what attracted me in the first place, the beautiful bad boy I couldn't resist. I wish I had.

Lately, even my short-term expectations leave me feeling deflated. While I consider Steve's autonomy a strength, he runs hot and cold so often I never know who I'm with until it's too late.

"Look at that," Steve says. "Those lucky bastards." A green train car does a rollback on the coaster, giving its riders an extra hydraulic launch.

I can't understand his obsession with outrageous adventures, one more thrill-seeking than the next. Don't get me wrong. I can keep up with the best of them. Or used to anyway. Between my twin brother and me, I was the daring one growing up. Simon was cautious and analytical. I was spontaneous – the risk-taker. Simon hated to get dirty; I was the quintessential tomboy. But Steve's fixation on danger is something different. In a maniacal way, death defiance powers him up. It's like a drug to him.

"Can we go now?" I say, trying to suppress a sigh.

Steve stands up from the bench. I still marvel at his muscular twenty-nine-year-old body, his strong stubble-haired chin, his beguiling blue eyes. I have seen them go from a dark iridescent blue to a murky gray within seconds, illuminating the unstable man within. *What will you look like ten years from now, Steve? After years of too much drinking and too much anger?*

We exit the Six Flags Park jungle scene. "I hope you're satisfied," I say.

"Nah. We still have to go bungee jumping."

"I'm never going bungee jumping." I cross my arms over my chest. "That's a solid no."

"Let's stop somewhere for dinner," he says.

Dinner that will consist of several drinks, but I'm driving. "Sure."

I first met Steve Holt a year ago when he pulled me over for speeding. I couldn't have been doing more than ten miles over the speed limit, but Officer Holt begged to disagree. His eyes fell to my lap, and I flushed as I looked down at my bare legs under a short skirt. I squeezed my thighs together. He continued writing me a ticket despite my protests, tearing it off with a flourish. "Thanks," I grumbled. An impervious crooked smile met my frustrated one. I threw the ticket onto the passenger seat and didn't look at it until days later when I noticed it wasn't a ticket at all. It was a page torn from the back of his ticket book. On it he had written, "Call me" with his cell phone number.

I didn't call.

Several weeks later, he spotted me at the Ringside Pub. My co-worker, Carol Bonetti, had invited me to hear her boyfriend's band. I had only been there once before and didn't know any of the locals. Before long, his eyes were laser-focused on me, the new girl with the long, glossy dark hair who never called.

The bartender placed a Tootsie Roll shot in front of me, nodding toward the man at the end of the bar. "It's on him."

At first, I didn't recognize Steve without his policeman's uniform. He was dressed in a hunter-green button-down shirt, his chiseled chest teasingly exposed, long sleeves pushed up on his forearms. Only his sleek black police haircut gave him away.

He shot me a blatant look in total indifference to the blonde woman who was with him at the time. Men and women couldn't help but stare at him when he was nearby, as if drawn to his good looks, and he knew it. Mischief gleamed from his eyes.

I drank my shot and bought him the next one. I wanted to learn everything I could about this brazen, exciting man.

"He's a cop," Carol said under her breath.

"I know. He pulled me over once."

"I see him here a lot, sometimes in uniform with his cop friends, sometimes not. As far as I know, he's unattached and bent on keeping it that way. There's always a different woman chasing him. My instincts tell me you should probably steer clear, but I'm not telling you what to do."

"You just did." I smiled.

Carol scowled, her springy mahogany curls surrounding her face. "He's the trouble type. Just saying."

"He's a type?" I laughed. "I'm a big girl."

Two things stood out. One, he enjoys the chase, and two, he likes to play it tough, so at least he's not the needy type. Couple that with my propensity for going after things I'm told to avoid, and the perfect storm was brewing.

I challenged myself to change the trajectory of this man's dating life by falling back on a tried-and-true method. I threw my hair behind me and turned away from him, engaging Carol in more conversation. I could feel him watching me, but I continued playing hard-to-get, feigning disinterest. When I went to the ladies' room, his eyes followed me. When I returned, he had somehow ditched the blonde and was talking to Carol.

I resumed my seat, Carol giving me her look-who-showed-up-while-you-were-gone stare. With Carol he was cajoling, yet cunning, but his eyes were on me. I knew I was his real target. Carol was blushing, her earlier opinion of him now thrown by the wayside. She giggled so much I wanted to shake her back to her senses. He had her complete attention. *Carol, can't you see what he's doing? He's using you to get to me. Remember what you told me?*

Steve was adding more conflict to the game by luring Carol to his side. I've always been able to think on my feet. I wasn't about to stop now. With clever finesse, I started a dialogue with the guy on the other side of me. Alone and nursing a drink, he was staring up at a basketball game on one of the televisions overhead. "Who're you rooting for?" I asked, turning toward him. Two could play at this game. The chase was on.

By night's end, while Carol helped her boyfriend's band pack up, the guy on my left was slouched over the bar, fully inebriated, thanks to Steve buying him more drinks. Steve and I found ourselves alone.

"You're in no position to drive home," Steve had said. He was buzzed but in control, a man on a mission, his penetrating blue eyes deliberate and clear.

"Good thing I'm not," I said. "My friend's boyfriend is driving." I glanced over at Carol and the band members disassembling instruments. Steve's face fell and my impulsive smile radiated in triumph.

"So, you're a lawyer," he said.

What else did he manage to weasel out of my intoxicated girlfriend?

Steve was not put off. "Did you lose my number?"

"Must have misplaced it."

"Ready to go?" Carol said, her eyes glazed, head swaying.

I looked at the guy still smashed over the bar. Somehow, I felt a little responsible. "Is there room for one more?"

"No," Carol said. "Car's full."

"Okay. I'll be right along." I sighed. "This guy needs help," I said to Steve. "He can't drive himself home."

"What're you getting at?" Steve said.

I ripped a piece of cocktail napkin and wrote on it. "He lives in town. See him home safely, and you can have this."

"What is it?"

"My phone number."

That was ten months ago. Now, after our dinner at the Cloverleaf Tavern, I pull into the driveway of my townhouse, an end-unit in one of Livingston, New Jersey's newest upscale communities. Steve has dozed off, but as soon as I turn off the car's engine, his eyes flash open. He looks over at me with woozy anticipation because he's spending the night.

Steve has two drinker personalities. The one following me inside my house is, I am certain, the I-want-my-birthday-sex one. He hasn't had enough to drink for his other personality, Mr. Hyde, to show up.

My Persian cat, Lucy, darts out of the room when she sees Steve. Lucy usually leaves wherever she's lounging if Steve comes within a few feet of her. Steve doesn't hide the fact he doesn't like Lucy. Feeling's mutual.

I flip the switch to the gas fireplace to take some chill out of the house, the living room's cathedral ceiling challenging the heater. Going over to the kitchen, I drop my purse on the counter. Steve rakes a hand through my thick, long hair, twisting it around his fingers before he grips the back of my neck, turning my face toward him.

"Let me get my jacket off first," I say to no one who'll listen.

Steve yanks it down from my arms and throws it onto the floor then bends me over the kitchen center island. He presses his mouth on mine, heating with whiskey breath and a flickering tongue. Moving with amazing dexterity for someone with so many drinks in him, he unzips his jeans with one hand, the other on my breast. He grasps my hips with both hands and lifts me onto the island, stripping off my jeans and panties and letting them fall next to his on the floor. I'm splayed across cold granite. Foreplay out of the way, Steve pushes inside me, hard, urgent thrusts bringing him to a quick finish. Restrained under the heaviness of his upper body, I'm unable to move.

A small spider scurries across my kitchen ceiling. I watch it for a while, waiting until Steve's off me, thinking only that birthdays can be overrated.

CHAPTER 2

I'm sitting at my desk, staring at my computer screen, when I see the email. "Another pro bono case? Really?" My voice reverberates brasher than I intended, and I imagine a few heads behind their cubicles popping up like jack-in-the-boxes. Since I'm one of the newest and youngest associates at the Bender & Simpson law firm, I'm yet again being assigned a pro bono to handle. Mr. Bender's email is scrolled up to the top. I reread the last sentence. *See me in my office at 2:00 today.*

I remember my last pro bono case from a year ago. Mr. Bender, the firm's top partner, had put his typical judicious spin on it for me. "Pro bono assignments give young lawyers such as yourself a chance to lead a case you might not be ready to do with paying clients. It's a great learning experience." It was a case involving a senior citizen in Newark who'd been living in her parents' home since their death and wanted to sell it to move closer to her daughter and grandchildren in South Carolina. She didn't have a clear title to the house, and her parents had left no will. After a few months of my assistance, she was able to sell the house and be with her family, which was satisfying, but the paperwork had been tedious and time-consuming, and I wished it had been more exciting.

Teagan Quinn, my closest friend and sidekick, appears in my office doorway with her empty mug. "You okay?" she says.

"Mr. Bender wants to see me at 2:00 about another pro bono case." I grab my mug and join her to head over to our floor's pantry room.

"I heard," Teagan says.

"You did? How?"

"Everyone up and down the hall heard you."

"Oh. Right." I sigh. "I get that it looks good for the firm to help clients who otherwise wouldn't be able to pay for capable representation, but my workload is already full without adding another pro bono case to it. Don't get me wrong – working from the heart rather than for profit is as honorable as it gets, but my heart is already full."

As we walk the rest of the way down the hall, Teagan chuckles at my tongue-in-cheek quip while I fume to myself in silence so no one can complain. Just what I need after another unnerving weekend spent with Steve.

"So . . . what else is bothering you?" Teagan says, going over to the coffee bar. She pours coffee into both our mugs. "You're crankier than usual."

For the first time this morning, I study her look. Front blonde strands hang loose below an angular chin outlining deep-set green eyes. The rest of her hair is clipped back in a big tortoiseshell claw clip. "You don't usually wear your hair like that." I side-step her question. "I like it."

I add cream and sugar to my coffee and take a sip before giving Teagan an answer. "Weird, isn't it? The reason I fell for him in the first place was his self-assuredness. He didn't have anyone to pave his way for him." I don't even have to say his name because Teagan knows who I'm talking about as if we're already in the middle of a long conversation. "He had to do it all himself. I thought he was fiercely independent. Turns out, fiercely independent means he doesn't care about anyone but himself."

"Ah, Steve again." Teagan puckers her brows.

"What gets me is he never considers my feelings. I used to think it was because he was afraid to feel, afraid of getting hurt. So he put up this wall to protect himself. But I'm not so sure anymore. He's becoming more volatile."

I know Teagan's stifling an opinion. She's heard it all before, and I know how she feels. Ever since Steve and I hooked up almost a year ago, she's expressed how she can't understand why I put up with his meanness. But all the same, she doesn't judge me. She is quiet and courteous as she stands there, allowing me the freedom to vent for the umpteenth time. Teagan has one of the biggest hearts of anyone I've ever met, a trait typical of her large, spirited Irish Catholic family. I love hearing stories about her family, who are unlike mine. Even though we come from different backgrounds, we get each other and have become fast friends ever since I started at the firm a little over two years ago.

We head back to our offices, and before I turn into mine, I say, "Steve always told me what a cold, heartless bastard his father was and now, more and more, I think about what my father used to say. 'The apple doesn't fall far from the tree.'"

"You're rebellious when it comes to your father," Teagan says with a smirk. "Let's put that out there first."

Sporting pointed-toe flats today when I'm usually in heels, I have to look up at her 5'9" height to meet her gaze. This is one of those times when having an all-too-familiar friend feels akin to a troubling conscience. Teagan turns to go, then swings back. "See you at lunch." It's our interim solution to whatever's troubling us.

I settle at my desk just across the hall from hers on the accounting side, and take a sip from my coffee mug. The man who was first in my life, the one I blame for the detrimental lack of his presence throughout my youth and more formative teenage years, the parent I defied at every turn with every ounce of my body – it's uncanny that my father's voice is the one I hear most often inside my head. Did he leave his indelible mark on me after all? Am I turning into him? Deep down, am I my father's daughter?

•   •   •

Bender & Simpson's lunchroom is akin to a preferred dining room you'd see at a large airport. With its oak tables, lounge chair groupings, and a part-time on-site restaurant, it caters to 124 attorneys, plus staff. Shortly after I joined the firm two years ago, our lunch group began to form. We claimed the table closest to the entrance, and now everyone knows it's permanently reserved for us. Today I claim the chair across from Lynne, my confidante mentor who also happens to be the administrative assistant to Alan Bender. Associate attorneys and staff learn fast that if you want to get in Mr. Bender's good graces, you need to start by getting in Lynne's good graces.

Lynne Turner returned to the workforce several years ago, after experiencing a bitter divorce. Her husband had been cheating on her. She remains as guarded as she is cautionary. An attractive woman in her early forties, her straight brunette bob is highlighted with just the subtlest of blonde. She wears her makeup light and dresses in tasteful neutrals. Today, a silky floral scarf adds a pop of vintage red to her blouse's tan neckline.

I was twenty-six when I was hired as an attorney at Bender & Simpson. Located in northeast New Jersey, just forty-five minutes outside Manhattan, it's one of the most prestigious law firms in the state. Young and idealistic, with a penchant for idolatry, I was assigned my first legal research project on one of Mr. Bender's medical malpractice cases. Standing at the threshold of the firm's inner sanctum, I stopped cold. Mr. Bender's large end office was bright and spacious with an immense glass wall overlooking an immaculately landscaped field of rolling suburban grass hills. In the far corner, he sat at a large, organized desk. Even in his sitting position, you could tell he was tall and lean. He sat straight up, shoulders pushed back so only his head was bent over the papers he was reading. All I could see was a curly cap of hair the color of dark pewter and thin gold wire spectacles resting low on his nose. Above his head, degrees hung in black wood frames – NYU and Columbia Law, my own law school alma mater. I won't deny that attending the same law school as Mr. Bender might have given me an edge in getting my foot in the door, but I'd never say so out loud. Another wall held various plaques of honor and framed newspaper clippings of multi-million-dollar medical malpractice awards. I don't know how long I stood there, trying to take it all in on the spot, but Lynne must have been watching me from her desk because she said,

"You can go in. He only looks scary." Ever since then, I liked her, and that's how she became my first real connection. She was everything I needed at the time – levelheaded, supportive, and protective.

Lynne pops open a can of Diet Coke, pouring it into a glass. "Why the frown? Would it have anything to do with Steve's birthday weekend?"

I grumble an incoherent answer.

"Why don't you just tell Steve you don't want to see him anymore? Seems to me you should end it with him if you're not happy."

"I'm working up to it." I flip my long hairs behind my shoulder and lean over a bowl of today's soup-of-the-day – minestrone.

"Honestly, it surprises me you're still seeing him. It never seemed destined to last."

"It surprises me too. Today's his actual birthday though. He'll be coming over for take-out and cake this evening." I slurp a spoonful of soup and watch Teagan and Carol working their way over to us.

"You're just prolonging the inevitable," Lynne says, stopping it there. I can tell she senses I'm through talking about Steve, a subject that always seems to start and end in the same obvious place – an unhealthy relationship that's run its course and is nearing the end. I'm not deep in. I can break free as I've planned. Just maybe not on his birthday.

"How was everyone's weekend?" Carol says.

Teagan opens her brown bag lunch. "Mine was uneventful unless you count the celebration I'm planning."

"What're you celebrating?" Lynne asks.

"Eight more payments to go on my student loans, and then I'm finally done. I'm thinking about how I want to celebrate it. A mini-vacation perhaps, a full spa day, a shopping excursion? I want to treat myself to something really nice."

"That does call for a celebration," Carol says, nibbling on a fry.

"What a great feeling of accomplishment," Lynne says. "I put away as much money as I could for my daughters' college and Bob contributed, but they're still going to be saddled with some student loan debt. College is so expensive. Good for you, Teagan."

"Why not do all three?" I say. It's my clueless attempt to relate.

"Believe me. I've thought about that. But I don't want to rack up another debt after just paying one off."

Topics like this make me feel guilty. I want to fit in so I'm careful not to divulge too much of my financially-advantaged upbringing. In a weird way, I'm embarrassed by my privilege. My friends can surmise that I come from wealth since they often see me wearing a new designer outfit to work or never-before-seen shoes or handbags. But what they don't know is that I'm a trust-fund daughter. My world's not their world.

I'm proud of myself for landing the job at Bender & Simpson because I made it happen on my own, with hard work and finishing law school in the top ten percent. But I grew up with money. Maids and nannies. And no shortage of material things. There's no other way to say it – I'm a spoiled rich girl.

"You're awfully quiet today," Carol says, staring at me. Her reddish-brown spirals bound around her round face with the same energy as her chipper personality.

"I have a meeting with Mr. Bender. He wants me to take on another pro bono case for the firm." I glance at Lynne. "You wouldn't by any chance know anything about it, would you?"

Lynne shakes her head. "Contrary to popular belief around here, there are some things in this office I'm not privy to."

"Guess I'll find out soon enough." I rise from my chair and go over to the trash can to throw out my lunch carton. "I should head back to my office."

"Cutting out so early?" Carol says, looking disappointed. "You didn't even tell us about your amusement park adventure over the weekend. Did you go on that dreaded roller coaster ride?"

"Yes, I did."

"And?"

"I live on."

"Okay. Suit yourself," Carol says, sounding annoyed. "You know we'll just talk about you when you're gone though, right?"

What connects Carol, Teagan, and me, besides our closeness in age, is we see the satirical comedy of everyday things, particularly at the law office. While Teagan's gift is in being a good follow-up listener, Carol's the comedian of our lunch group.

Before I turn to leave, I give Carol a smirk. "Knock yourselves out."

•   •   •

Mr. Bender sits in his usual straight-backed position behind his desk, focusing downward through half-moon glasses. Of all the good manners instilled in him as a child, sit-up-straight-and-tall had apparently sunk in.

"Suellen," Mr. Bender starts, his eyes moving across the page in front of him, "I trust your weekend was good." He continues to look down at the papers before him.

"Yes, thank you." Don't think he'd agree with a death-defying roller coaster ride as being a fun time, but hey, to each his own.

"Your family – they're well?" He keeps up his friendly dialogue while still reading, a trait cultivated by years of multitasking.

"Yes. Thanks for asking," I say, directing my attention to the 8 x 10 black-and-white of his wife that sits on the credenza behind him, her classic smile a perfect match for the double-looped choker of pearls around her neck. I visualize her greeting her husband when he comes home from a busy day at the office – a Johnnie Walker for him, a martini for her – waiting on their foyer tabletop pending dinner reservations Lynne no doubt made for them. No. I think I can safely say they're not the roller coaster fanatic types.

Mr. Bender looks up at me for the first time. "I'm assigning a new pro bono case to you."

Buckle up. Here we go.

"You'll be appointed guardian ad litem for a seven-year-old girl who's been in foster care for several months now. The foster parent wants to adopt her."

"The child has no living parents?" I say.

"The mother's being sentenced to go to prison for murder."

"Murder?" I sputter.

"She was convicted of killing her husband with his gun while he slept."

I drop back in my chair. "Oh." Is that all? I try not to sputter this time as Mr. Bender studies me closely.

"Her public defender argued she'd been physically and psychologically abused over an extended period," Mr. Bender says.

"And yet she still has to serve time?" *What am I missing here?*

"According to the case notes, the prosecutors argued that unlawful aggression on the part of the deceased was absent since he was sleeping. The woman was aware of what she was doing when she shot her husband in the head."

"So, the battered wife syndrome legal defense didn't have any bearing in this case?"

"An insanity defense would have exempted her from criminal liability but would have required her to be confined to a mental institution. The battered wife syndrome defense was harder to prove since he wasn't violent or threatening her and was asleep at the time."

I have many more questions, but I keep them to myself for now. Mr. Bender must notice my perplexed look.

"Your only focus on this is to advocate for the child. Her mother's case is over. She was charged with murder, but will likely plead to aggravated manslaughter so she could get a lesser sentence. But under the Graves Act, she would still be facing twenty years, ten without parole."

My head is spinning, my heart pounding. And I haven't even begun to work on the case.

"You'll write a report of recommendation to the court based on your research for what you believe to be in the best interest of the young girl. Of course, you'll need to make some home visits as you deem necessary and conduct interviews." Mr. Bender removes his eyeglasses and closes the manila folder, indicating the meeting is over.

I stand and walk over to his desk to take the file from him.

"As you know, Suellen, our firm's still growing. We have a social responsibility to keep up a good image. I'm certain you'll tackle this in the same diligent manner as I'd expect from you. And . . . you'll be continuing to build more skill sets."

"Yes," I say, taking the file from him with a smile intended to impart thank-you-for-this-opportunity. Meanwhile, as I walk down the hall toward my office, I can't help wishing this new *opportunity* assignment was less disturbing, like the last one I handled. *Be careful what you wish for.*

CHAPTER 3

The ringing phone drags me out of a dreamless slumber. It is the night security guard at the front gate confirming permission for Steve to enter my housing community. I check the time on my phone. Twenty minutes past midnight. *Really?* I let out a heavy sigh. "Sure. Let him through."

I cross my arms in a rigid stance inside my kitchen, watching him stagger through the door. "Now you show up. Why didn't you pick up? I left you three messages."

Steve wears an exaggerated smile as his body sways. "When I'm at the bar, I don't hear my cell phone. You know how loud the guys get when there's a game on."

"I thought we agreed you'd come over for dinner at seven. Besides, the Giants game ended at eleven." My grogginess is wearing off faster than expected.

"You keeping time for me, babe? Cause I don't ever remember asking you to. The guys were celebrating my birthday. What was I supposed to do? Tell them I had Thai food waiting?" Steve comes over and wraps his arms around my waist in a clumsy hug. "Come on, don't look like that. I'm here, ain't I?" He slobbers a kiss on my neck, and I push him off.

"Why did you bother coming over at all then? And don't tell me you had your heart set on Thai."

"The time just got away from me, but now that you mention it—"

"Yours is in the refrigerator," I utter, storming off to my bedroom. "I'm going back to sleep." I lay my head down on the pillow and close my eyes.

"Hey, is that cake for me?" Steve shouts from the kitchen.

My lids pop open and I sit up again, wide awake. "Yeah. You can take it home with you."

"Chocolate. My favorite."

The next thing I know, Steve's sitting on the edge of my bed pulling his shoes off. My part-time live-in's wearing me thin. I probably shouldn't have let him through the gate, but I can't make him leave now, not in his drunken state.

"Why do you have to drink so much during the week?" Steve's Rugby shirt is up around his head, his bare chest glistening with sweat. "Police officers aren't immune to DUI arrests."

"Don't worry 'bout me. I can take care of myself," Steve says in a muffled voice, still struggling with his shirt. "I've been taking care of myself practically all my life. Not like you'd know a thing 'bout that."

"What're you even saying?"

"Not everyone's got a rich daddy like you." He gives one final tug on his shirt and tosses it onto the floor.

"We don't choose who we're born to. Am I supposed to feel guilty because your father deserted you?" As soon as it leaves my mouth I want to take it back. But it's too late. A crazed look crosses Steve's face, his eyes going dark. I slither away until my back hits the headboard. "I didn't mean it the way it sounded," I say, recoiling.

Steve flies across the bed, his face inches from mine, forcing me to look into his cold, menacing blue eyes. "Don't mess with me, you spoiled brat." He pokes a finger into my chest. "Who do you think you are?"

I'm not sure which is worse – the hatred in his eyes or the foul odor of alcohol and cigarettes. *Why do I always choose to ignore the warning signs?* There have been plenty in the past ten months. I turn my face away.

"Your father controls you with his money. You're twenty-eight, and he still owns you." Steve rocks backward and falls onto the bed.

"You don't get to talk to me like that because it's just not true," I say. "I work my ass off and you know it."

"It's easy when you have a backup plan. Not many people I know have a daddy who bought them a condo, a Lexus SUV, and anything else his little girl's heart desires. Pretty rough when you have everything handed to you." Steve's knees buckle under him, and his head hits the pillow. He rolls over onto his back, spread-eagle, and stammers, "You don't know a damn thing."

"I know I worry about you sometimes."

"I don't need your worrying. What? Now you're gonna tell me you love me or somethin'? What would you even know about love? You're in love with things. This place is full of your *things*. Love to you is a Gucci bag and a diamond watch."

"Why do you always have to be so mean?" Tears spring to my eyes and I'm angry with myself for allowing him to get to me. I choke back a tear. "Is it so hard for you to believe I care what happens to you?"

"I never hid who I am. You belong to your father. I belong to nobody."

I realize having a meaningful discussion with Steve right now is useless, but his self-centeredness and my fury demand I ask, "Haven't you ever cared for anyone in your life?"

"I never made you any promises," Steve says, his eyelids quivering. "You knew what you were getting, so don't lay that sob crap on me."

"I took the trouble of ordering food for the both of us. It wouldn't have hurt for you to show me some consideration, like any decent person."

Steve lies plastered over the bedspread. "I ain't no decent person," he murmurs.

Seconds later, I hear snoring – loud, throaty sounds that don't exit his mouth. I lift his leaden arm away from my side of the bed and place it over his chest. I know it will be impossible for me to move him off the covers, so I leave him like that – shirtless and still wearing his jeans. I slide back under the covers in the small space left beside him, but I can't fall back to sleep. I hate it when he drinks too much, which has become more often. He's a nasty drunk.

I was intrigued with Steve when I first met him, his good looks, his sly, sarcastic mannerisms. I liked how it challenged me. Now, I never know which Steve I'm going to get. The seductive one or the cruel one. There's no way to know. Unless he's been drinking. Then it's a given the cruel Steve will come out.

Lucy follows me as I move to my other bedroom, his last words rumbling in my mind. *I ain't no decent person.* I also hear my dad reciting one of his favorite sayings: "A drunken man's words are a sober man's thoughts."

•   •   •

Sitting across from Steve in my favorite armchair, I stare at him watching a football game on my big flat-screen TV, looking relaxed and fed. We haven't seen one another since his birthday debacle, a text message here and there, but today, several days later on a Sunday, he turns up wanting to see me again. His last booty call text simply said, "No hard feelings. Only hard for you. Let's hang out."

While Steve expects a lazy afternoon watching football at my place, my motives are more purposeful. I can't put my finger on it, but something's happened to me. I don't want to be this person in this depressing relationship anymore. It's no longer sustainable. Sometimes, when I fear my brain has given up trying to rebuff the advice of many where Steve's concerned, hope pushes through and I have a good talk with myself. *Stop the charade, Suellen. You can't keep on doing this to yourself. Face up to the truth and get on with your life.*

It's time I fully break free of this man.

The cozy, glowing embers in my fireplace are in complete contrast with the all-white walls and mantel, while outside my floor-to-ceiling windows, a deepening gray sky emulates the end of winter rather than the thick of autumn. Dad's impending country club invitation for the upcoming Thanksgiving holiday will no doubt include Steve, but Mister Antisocial won't have to suffer through it. Besides, the mere mention of my dad sets Steve off. But I don't care anymore.

Steve hasn't taken his eyes off the television since he arrived. Our half-eaten Chinese take-out cartons are still spread out over my white coffee table. He reaches for his beer as if guided by radar. I'm grateful for the distracting game on television as I contemplate my exit plan.

Breaking up doesn't have to be messy, I reason. I will be considerate, and wait until the game's over, or maybe during half-time. Of course that might piss him off. It isn't as if I haven't gotten practice at ending relationships. I ended my last one before Steve, and the one before that. What's another blip in my reckless dating life?

Tempted by the smell of food, Lucy comes out of her hiding spot and leaps onto the table, sticking her curious nose into one of the cartons.

"Get outta there," Steve yells and before he can throw something at her, I'm on my feet swooping Lucy into my arms. I sit back in the chair and hold her in my lap.

"It's okay, Lucy," I say, stroking her white Persian fur. "Mommy's got you."

Snuggling together on the chair, Lucy and I eye Steve like sentinels wondering when the next attack will come.

"I swear I'm allergic to that damn cat." Steve bellows like he always does whenever Lucy's near. "My eyes are starting to itch again."

I get up from my chair and set Lucy down gently, then clear off the coffee table and dump the open food containers into a garbage bag. "Well, Steve," I say, doing my best to ensure he knows I'm serious, "you won't have to worry much longer."

"Now you're talkin'." His eyes are still fixed on the game. "Get me another beer while you're up, will ya?" A cocky smile crosses Steve's face. "'Bout time you get rid of that cat."

Sometimes an opening just presents itself. "No, Steve," I say. "Not the cat."

CHAPTER 4

"How's my favorite girl doing?" As usual, Dad likes to call me at my office because he knows Steve won't be there and he can talk candidly. I picture him sitting in his expansive doctor's office behind a large mahogany desk facing a few momentous photographs in gilded frames. A couple of 5 x 7s of me and Simon on our respective graduation days are dwarfed by a larger professional black-and-white headshot of Eve, his new wife.

"I've been doing okay. Work's been busy," I tell him. The leaves on the trees outside my window are showing a hint of new fall colors. Only a couple of weeks ago it felt like we were experiencing a second summer in New Jersey.

"Working on any interesting cases?"

"A few, but not the kind you like to hear about."

"Then don't tell me. My malpractice insurance is high enough. Don't get me started."

"I know, Dad. I tried not to," I say, trying to make sure he understands I care how he feels. Medical malpractice lawsuits are a sensitive subject to my doctor dad. As far as he's concerned, his daughter went over to the dark side. "How are you and Eve doing?" I rush to change the subject.

"We're both well. I know it's still early, but you'll be joining us for Thanksgiving at the club again this year, won't you?"

I wonder if my lunch friends dread getting formal invitations to holidays as much as I do. Or do their families look forward to gathering as a group of indiscriminate individuals each year, rather than caring family members? "Simon and Sarah will be joining us, too."

"Do they know the baby's sex yet?" I ask, shifting the conversation once again to Dad's first grandchild.

"Not yet. Simon thinks they'll know by Thanksgiving."

The remainder of our conversation goes as it always does, like we're stuck in the movie, *Groundhog Day*. Dad says, more with political correctness than enthusiasm, "Your friend's welcome to join us too."

Taking less exception than I once did that my dad chooses not to remember Steve's name, I say just for the record, "You mean Steve?"

Dad never acknowledges that Steve and I are anything other than a passing fling. No matter how many times I tell him marriage never comes up between us, he remains guarded. To my father, marriage, and pre-nup go together like soup and sandwich.

Dad's from a wealthy family of real estate investors, and he's one of several doctors in his family. The money started with my great-grandfather who invested in big-tenant properties in Manhattan, and Dad grew up on Park Avenue. Even before Dad opened his cardiology practice, he had inherited a nice fortune. Since I'm a fourth-generation beneficiary of their wealth, matrimony is looked upon as a contractual obligation, not unlike a business venture. I once told him if he really got to know Steve, he wouldn't be so worried. Now that *I've* gotten to know Steve, I understand why he *is* so worried. Dad and Steve only met a couple of times, but it was enough.

I never understood until now that Dad has the unique ability to diagnose people the same way he diagnoses diseases. As for Steve and marriage? Believe me. The prognosis was never good.

"Can I get back to you about Thanksgiving?" It isn't as if I have a whole lot of alternatives. "If I can make it, I'll be alone. I'm no longer seeing Steve." I imagine the smile on Dad's face.

"Well, that didn't take long." I don't say anything so he continues. "There's still plenty of time, but Eve and I wanted to let you know early." There's another awkward pause before Dad speaks again. "What's new with your mother?"

"Not much. She's still into holistic medicine and yoga. Says she's a hundred percent vegan now."

"Florida seems to agree with her," Dad says.

"Yeah." *Florida and Morris.*

Why my parents ever fell in love has always been a mystery to me. That my conformist Protestant father may have been excited at the challenge of being with my open-minded liberal Jewish mother is not hard to understand. Nor is it that my free-thinking mother may have thought she needed my father, someone grounded in tradition, to balance the scales. They were opposites in every way, but those things that attracted them to each other pulled them apart in the end. Dad would come home late, and they would conduct their nightly fights in strained whispers at first until they no longer cared to go on pretending.

My bat mitzvah and Simon's bar mitzvah were over-the-top celebrations held in New York City. Our party planner was tasked with creating a two-themed event – one for me, the other for Simon. Guests and classmate friends were directed to either a pink-and-white tennis motif or a blue science lab. The waitresses on my side wore tennis outfits and on Simon's, they donned lab coats. A few days later, our parents told us they were splitting up.

After overhearing our parents' explosive battle the day before our milestone birthdays, Simon and I realized that our lavish party had merely delayed their breaking news. When it became real, Simon grew more anxious and withdrew. I became defiant. We craved our parents' attention equally because it was something we never seemed to get enough of. Simon aimed to please, doing everything he could to garner Dad's approval, and his love, achieving top grades, and focusing on pre-med from as early as I can remember. While Dad's high expectations incentivized Simon, I found them intolerable. I turned to negative behavior and was unconcerned with consequences in my teen years. I fought. I rebelled. I challenged him. I didn't settle myself until I went away to Boston College, where I didn't have to prove anything to anyone but myself. In my senior year, I shifted from a liberal arts curriculum to focused paralegal studies. By the time I graduated, I knew

I wanted to go to law school and become a lawyer. *Put that in your Doctor Daddy pipe and smoke it.* I passed the bar exam while clerking for a Superior Court Judge. Then after a couple of years working at a friend of my dad's small firm, I applied to Bender & Simpson and was offered a full-time junior associate position.

Both my parents have since remarried. Dad married Eve, a former receptionist from his cardiology practice, who is eighteen years his junior. Mom eventually took up with Morris, a wealthy Jewish philanthropist from Miami who's heavy into the arts, and they married after Simon and I had left for college.

"Please let us know when you know for sure that you're coming," Dad said. "Won't be the same without you." *I think Eve would beg to differ.*

"Will do."

"By the way, I saw Dr. O'Connor at a hospital dinner the other day. He says you haven't been in to see him in a while."

"I know. I've just been so busy." Another new cyst has surfaced in my left breast. I might need to have this one aspirated like another I once had, so I'm keeping an eye on it. "I'll call his office and schedule an appointment as soon as I get the chance."

"Good girl. Are you still getting those migraine headaches?"

"Not since I changed birth control pills."

"That's good. Eve sends her best. Let us know as soon as you know."

Eve, the planner, hates last-minute responses. I learned that the hard way one holiday when I showed up late and she didn't speak to me the entire time. Truth is, I usually hope for better options. I love my dad but he's a different person around Eve, more formal and less Dad.

"I love you," Dad says. I always feel a little sad the way he says that to me, his tone conciliatory, like he's still trying to balance his life between two camps – Camp Me and Simon and Camp Eve.

"Love you too, Dad."

CHAPTER 5

Destiny Evans and her foster mother, Edwina, sit across from me around an ash-colored Formica table, thin scratches over the surface suggesting years of wear. A 1920s colonial with a small front yard and longer narrow back lawn, Edwina's house is tidy and furnished with usable fixtures that give off a lived-in feeling.

Seven-year-old Destiny hasn't said very much. She's reticent and wary. Who can blame her? In her short life she's already lived through some of the worst traumas a young girl can experience. Her black hair is pulled back from her face in two fishtail braids, her dark eyes are unfathomable, and I wonder how long it takes to pry trauma from a young person's body. My heart breaks just looking at her, knowing what I know. I engage her carefully, asking what sorts of things she likes to do, what are her favorite foods. She dips her last oatmeal cookie in a glass of milk and stares out the kitchen window where a younger boy plays, where she wants to be.

"Finish up now," Edwina says, "then you can go outside and play with Jamar."

Alone with Edwina now, I listen to her story. There's no need for me to go down the list of questions I have for her. Edwina's done this before. She could recite my questions to me.

"I was a foster child myself so I know the good, the bad, and the ugly." She squints behind eyeglasses, the creases on her black face spreading out under a close-cropped head of curly hair peppered with gray. "I've fostered a total of eight children and adopted two of them.

Some have grown and moved on. Destiny's my seventh. The young boy outside makes eight." She leans into the table, eyes steadied on mine. She's reading me, my reactions, my earnestness. "Destiny's a highly sensitive child. She wakes up screaming on many nights and it takes all I got to calm and soothe her back down to sleep. She needs lots of lovin' and stability. Adoption's the only way I can guarantee her that. I've grown attached to her while her mother's been incarcerated. Destiny's in temporary custody of the state, and who knows what will happen to her, how long her mother's sentence will be, if she even gets out before Destiny turns eighteen. This is a girl who can't take much more. She's as fragile as they come, and I've seen a lot in my years. I know when someone's on the edge of unfixable."

I manage to eke out one small question. "I understand Destiny's mother was a victim of her husband's violent abuse, but is there anything else I should know?"

Edwina looks me straight in the eye. "Oh, you don't know, do you?"

I shake my head, already regretting it.

"Her mother came home from work one day and walked in to find her worst nightmare had come to life when the abuse moved on to her daughter. Destiny had been raped by her drunken father. She was six at the time, barely conscious, eyes vacant as a dead person's. Destiny's mother, Shaquana, was a repeated victim of his brutality, but something snapped inside her when she saw her young daughter like that. She covered Destiny with a blanket, then went over to where her husband was passed out on the couch and shot him in the head three times with his own gun."

I squirm on the steel chair's vinyl seat, as a shiver runs down my spine.

"Still raging, Shaquana collapsed to the floor in tears. Her crying subsided only when she noticed Destiny standing over her and taking in the entire scene."

I swallow hard and try to settle the trembling in my body, glancing out the kitchen window so I can watch Destiny playing alongside the young boy, rolling around in leaves that have fallen, plucked out of the horrific scene of her six-year-old self. There are no words to say.

Edwina reaches out to touch my arm and waits while I collect myself. She sees my pained expression and in a soft tone says, "Take your time."

I look down at my legal notepad and scribble two words easier to write than say. *Unspeakable violence.* With a calmer composure, I stand up, my professional detachment hanging by a thread. "Thank you for your time, Edwina. I'll be in touch." I start to leave before I turn back again. "By the way – Destiny's mother – how well do you know her?" I realize I may have to pay a visit to Shaquana if I want to do right by all.

"I know her really well. And Shaquana knows who I am. I fostered another child whose mother had OD'd. Shaquana knew the mother. She trusts me. I write her letters so she knows how Destiny's doing."

I get inside my car and drive a few blocks away from Edwina's neighborhood, pooling tears now stinging my eyes. A few rapid blinks send them spilling down my cheeks.

CHAPTER 6

"It's weird, you know? Steve's scent is still there. And no matter where I am in my house, something reminds me of him. His unpleasant aura just won't go away."

Lynne grimaces from across our lunch table. "I hear you. I still see my ex clipping his toenails in my living room. Never can get that image out of my mind."

I chuckle. "I don't like down time. That's my problem. It's hard having to get used to being alone again. How do you do it, Lynne?" A heartbeat later, I say, "That didn't come out right."

Lynne waves it off. "No harm done. Sometimes I love being alone. When you've lived with two screaming, dramatic teenage girls for as long as I have, it's refreshing to be able to hear yourself think again. But I'm not going to lie to you. It can get lonely. You need a new hobby. Some new thing that'll get your mind off Steve."

"I hope you don't mean I should take up knitting."

"Ha." Lynne chuckles as she gets up to walk over to the water cooler. "Nothing wrong with that." Coming back to our table, she says, "Seriously though, maybe not knitting but some other new hobby. It takes time to get over a relationship."

"Even a bad one," I admit. "Before Steve, I was alone for almost two years. Guess I just need to get used to it all over again." I take a bite out of my cheeseburger. "Here I am talking about my problems when Teagan's having surgery tomorrow. Did you speak to her today?"

"Not yet. I plan to call her after lunch," Lynne says.

"I talked to her yesterday morning. She sounded scared, and I fumbled my words. I didn't know what to say to her."

"Maybe all she needs is for us to listen," Lynne says. "Just be there for her."

I nod. Teagan has been trying to have a baby for several years. Her last checkup before trying in vitro again showed a cyst on her right ovary. She's having surgery tomorrow to biopsy it.

"So, did you happen to catch *The Bachelor* last night?" I change the subject. "That's another good thing about not having Steve around. We never agreed on what to watch on television, and he hated that show."

"No," Lynne says. "I'm afraid I agree with Steve on that one. I can't seem to get into reality shows."

"You should check it out sometime," I say. "It takes place in some of the most romantic places – Rome, Venice, Paris. You should watch it."

"I'll buy a travel guide instead."

"But then you'd miss out on all the romance."

"Suellen, you don't really believe in that stuff, do you?" Lynne says, forking a clump of tuna salad. "I mean, those people will act any way they have to. They're in front of a camera for Pete's sake. It's all hype."

"I know it's all just fantasy, but it's fun to watch the women playing each other. I mean, who's to say two people can't fall in love during the show? It happens to Hollywood stars all the time."

"Look. I don't mean to burst your bubble, but since we're talking about a reality TV show, let's keep it real. There's as much sincerity and truth to it as there is in a daytime soap. It's purely entertainment. I mean, how coincidental that he finds his true love in what . . . eight episodes, is it? What if he can't make his mind up in those eight episodes? What if, by the end of the show, he doesn't like any of them? He still has to pick someone." Lynne scoops tuna salad onto her fork. "It's ratings, Suellen. Just ratings." She swallows the tuna, washing it down with her water.

"But you should see the way he looks at them. The camera doesn't lie."

Lynne rolls her eyes and chuckles. "You can't be serious. Normal people don't fall in love because they're on a TV show together, and they have to be a little nuts to be on that show in the first place. It doesn't fly. But then, I'm the exception. Apparently, it has a lot of appeal to all the hopeless romantics out there."

"More like just hopeless in my case."

"Now, now. I wouldn't exactly say you were hopeless. You just need to steer away from the Steve types. They only break your heart."

"You want to know something crazy? I didn't love him. I cared about him in a . . . tragic sort of way. I might have even felt sorry for him."

"Ouch. That's never a good sign," Lynne says.

"I know. My bad."

"I get it," Lynne says. "You thought you could help him . . . change him maybe? Not the first person who's ever tried to do that." She raises an eyebrow, not in a sarcastic way, but in a matter-of-fact kind of way. "And now, you've accepted him for the person he is. Looks to me like the one who did any changing was you."

Lynne's real-world view on life astonishes me. Her kind of practicality would take most people a lot more years to cultivate than her forty-four. "Yeah. Guess I have changed." A scene plays in my mind when Steve likened us to one another. *We're alike, you and me. Users.* It was a low blow, even for him. He often vilified himself to me, but grouping me into his nefarious fold? That was the nail in the coffin. He never really knew me. "Wish I had more of your good sense, Lynne. It would have saved me a lot of trouble."

"And where do you think it comes from? Life experiences, that's where."

"He could be so hurtful, you know? We broke up a few times, but then we'd go back within a few days. I get the feeling he thinks this is another one of those times. It felt unsettled when I asked him to leave. I mean, he cursed me off and all. But while I stood there holding my cat, he leered at me from the doorway, like he knew I'd be back." I roll my shoulders. "I think maybe he knows this time is different."

"Good. He's where he belongs – in queue with your other crushed ex-boyfriends." Lynne gives me a sly grin. "You know I love you, which is why I have to ask, do you see a pattern here? I mean, why do you think you went back with him each of those times?"

"Not really sure. Or maybe my brain's trying to protect me." I chuckle. Lynne doesn't.

"Take a stab at it," Lynne says, not relinquishing. "Why'd you go back?"

"Crazy good sex? Rebelliousness? Boredom? I'm a glutton for punishment," I say, embarrassed. "It was a phase I was in."

"Was?" Lynne says.

"I'm getting too old for it now. What did it all prove? I'm through with making bad choices."

"Then it wasn't a waste, was it?" Lynne gives me an encouraging smile.

"You want to know something even crazier?" I say. "I've never been in love. Never fallen for anyone. Ever. Does that sound strange to you?"

Lynne shakes her head. "No. It sounds honest."

"I never told anyone that before. I don't mean to get all serious on you, but seeing *The Bachelor* again gets me thinking. Maybe I should try out for the next one. I'll be the bitch everyone loves to hate."

Lynne swats my shoulder with the back of her hand. "I can't see you cast in that role."

"I could do it," I say. "When the cat fights start and the girls' claws come out, that's when the show gets really good. I'm hooked."

"Hi, guys." Carol strolls over to our table, accompanied by a twenty-something girl in a fitted pink turtleneck with bouncy golden-brown hair. "I'd like you to meet Rachel Finch. Rachel, this is Lynne and Suellen."

"Hello," Rachel says. She waits until Carol sits down with us and then takes the seat next to her.

"This is Rachel's first day," Carol says. "I've been showing her around a little."

"Oh," I say. "Where do you sit?"

"Second floor. I'll be working for Mr. Campbell."

"That's right," Lynne says. "I heard Fred was looking for someone. Did you answer an ad or was it through an agency?"

"It was the online ad." Rachel opens her plastic take-out container.

"Did Carol tell you the firm hires on-site caterers for lunch? So the food's not too bad here," Lynne says.

"Where're you from Rachel?" I ask.

"I live in Verona, but I grew up in Livingston."

"Livingston? That's where I'm from," I say. "What year did you graduate?"

"2011."

"A year after me. I thought you looked familiar. Do you know a guy by the name of Tommy Matthis? He lived on our block. I think he was in your year."

"Sure. I know Tommy. And Donnie, too."

"You know Donnie?" I say. "How do you know him?"

Rachel takes a bite of her sandwich; I notice there's no ring on her finger. "I dated Donnie for a year."

"Really? Seems you and I have something else in common. I also dated Donnie back when I was in high school."

Rachel's mouth stops chewing. "Did you hear he moved to Arizona?"

"No. I didn't know," I say. "I lost touch with him."

"Then you must also know Pat and Guy. They were always together," Rachel says.

"Yeah. Guy was as crazy as they come," I say.

"Pat was all right though. We went together for a short while sometime after Donnie and I broke it off."

"You went out with Pat, too?" My voice is tinged with skepticism. Pat was the star of our high school football team. "When was that?"

"In my senior year. We met at a party when he was home from college. We hooked up for a while."

"Wow," Carol says. "That's already more boyfriends than I've ever had."

"What a small world," I say in a tight voice. "Not only do you and I come from the same town but apparently we dated the same guys." The competitiveness in me starts stirring. I'm not sure why, but something about Rachel rubs me the wrong way. Am I looking at a different version of me? I notice Lynne looking at my hands, and then she looks straight at me. We're both thinking the same thing. That my claws are starting to show.

Lynne says, "Where did you work before coming here, Rachel?"

"I worked at the Mantel Horvitz firm."

"In Newark," Lynne says. "We have a few cases with that firm. An attorney by the name of Jankowski comes to mind."

"Oh yes," Rachel says, "that's Drew."

"Don't tell me," I say, gritting my teeth. "You dated him too."

There's an awkward silence before I say, "Just kiddin'." *Not.*

"You going to Todd's farewell party on Friday?" Carol says, changing the subject.

"I was planning on it," I say. Todd's one of Carol's and my favorite people at the firm. He's one of the nicest lawyers I've had the pleasure to work with, always willing to help and offer guidance. He'll be missed.

"I'm going," Carol says. She turns to Rachel. "Todd is an attorney here. He's going to the Attorney General's office."

"Their gain, our loss," I say.

"Rachel, why don't you try to come too? It's a great way to get to know people in the firm," Carol says.

Who made Carol social director?

Lynne gets up from her chair. "Work calls. I want to call Teagan too," she says. "Nice meeting you, Rachel."

"Same here," Rachel says.

When Lynne walks off, Rachel turns to Carol. "She's very nice."

"Yep. Try to come this Friday," Carol says. "You'll get to meet more nice people. Outside the office environment."

"Maybe I will," Rachel says.

Carol turns toward me to be sure. "See you there then?"

I stare into Carol's eyes, squinting. "Don't worry," the cat in me says. "I'll be there."

•   •   •

"So now you know," I say to Lynne in a hushed voice. "The motivating reason behind Teagan's check-up in the first place was to get her doctor's go-ahead to do in vitro again. She's still trying." I shake my head and blow out a frustrated breath. "She doesn't want everyone to know, but says it's okay to tell you. She was asleep when you phoned. Says she'll get back to you."

"I'm just glad the news is good," Lynne says, "and that she's feeling okay."

"Yes. It was a benign tumor, so they didn't have to remove her ovary, but the matter of in vitro is closed for at least another six months." My phone is on silent, but I can see a call coming in from Steve. I let it go to voicemail.

"How old is Teagan?" Lynne says.

"Thirty-one. She's been trying to get pregnant for the past four years."

"Has she tried in vitro before?"

"Five times. Didn't take."

"I'm so sorry," Lynne says. "I didn't know she was going through all that."

Lynne's desk phone rings and she goes to answer it. "See you at lunch later?"

"Yeah. See you down there."

I leave Lynne's office and return to mine and listen to the voicemail message Steve left me. His dour voice drones on. *Whatsamatter? You don't return phone calls anymore? I also left you several text messages. I want my stuff still at your house. I'm missing a couple of shirts and my favorite jeans. I'm sure there are other things I'm forgetting. I'd like to see for myself. And I want my beer stein.*

I envision the bag containing the last remnants of his clothes that's stuffed inside my hall closet. Before I text him back, I weigh my options. I can't ignore him anymore. I know Steve. He won't give up, and I don't want to make him angrier than he already is.

I text him to come at the end of the week.

The thought of seeing Steve again fills me with dread. I've seen his dark side and it's enough to make me nervous. I kicked him out three weeks ago, so I'm sure he's not going to be in a friendly mood and I'm tired of fighting with him. Still, I rationalize, better to cooperate with him. Better still, I'll have someone there with me when he comes over just in case he tries to start something. I'll invite my neighbor, Gladys, over for tea.

There were a few times when I thought Steve was close to striking me, especially when he'd been drinking. Each time, I rejected the idea, but I don't want to find out I was wrong.

CHAPTER 7

My extra workload keeps me late at the office, but I don't want to miss Todd's send-off gathering. Heading for the Star Tavern, I turn on the car radio only to be assaulted by a Christmas song. *Already? We didn't even get to Thanksgiving yet.* But then a dispiriting thought swoops in – I'll be alone again for the holidays.

Images of my family exchanging extravagant Christmas gifts in front of a big stone fireplace at my dad's snobbish country club don't inspire me. I envision us sitting around a giant evergreen tree embellished with gold ornaments and white lights. It's quite magnificent, but all the elaborate holiday accouterments in the world are what I don't need. Simon and Sarah will make their typical excuse as to why they have to leave early – so they can spend part of the day with her family. At least they have a good excuse. I wish I could come up with a valid one.

I don't enjoy being with Dad as much when Eve's there, which is pretty much always. Watching him walk on eggshells around her is not fun. Eve was never married before Dad and is very possessive of him. Simon and I are annoying byproducts she barely tolerates. Eve didn't want children. She just wants it to be about her and my dad. They've already traveled the whole world together. In fact, immediately after Christmas, they'll depart for their annual two-week holiday cruise. Eve gets to live in the world of the one-percenters and have Dad all to herself. It doesn't get any better. For her.

Mom's already wheedling me to pay her and Morris a visit in Palm Beach during Hanukkah. As usual, I'll wind up going for three or four days, just as I've been doing for the past six years. It's all so predictable. Mom, coaxing me to join her and her girlfriends in a game of Mahjong. Morris, fifteen years my mother's senior, strutting around his private dock in Bermuda shorts and designer sunglasses, a Cuban cigar dangling from his mouth.

I heave a sigh and turn off the radio. An abrupt prickliness in my left breast sends my fingers to it. I slide my hand under my blouse to scratch it, and feel the lumpiness underneath the skin. *Damn cyst. Is it that time of month already? Wait. My period isn't due for two more weeks.*

A hurried look in my rearview mirror tells me the Jeep behind is at least three car lengths away so I pump the brake and signal before cutting over to make a sharp left. When I look back in the mirror, I notice the Jeep – the same as Steve's – also turning off the main road and still following at the same distance. It's dark and the headlights are blinding.

I press my foot too hard on the accelerator and leap forward, pulling away fast, then hang another left into a side street. When I look back, the Jeep is no longer there, and I deride myself for being paranoid and find a parking space along a side street as the tavern's lot is already packed.

As I walk back toward the tavern, the strange feeling of being watched returns. Instinctively, I squeeze my purse under my arm and pick up my pace when I hear my name being called.

Carol waves to me outside the front entrance. Rachel's with her, lighting up a cigarette, and while I haven't warmed up to Rachel yet, they are both a welcome sight.

"What happened to you? I thought you changed your mind and weren't coming," Carol yells down the street to me.

Coming up to her I say, "I stayed a little later at the office to finish up some work."

"It's a full house in there," Carol says.

The screeching sound of a vehicle as it speeds past diverts our attention. In a split second, I glimpse the rear end of a dark blue Jeep just before it disappears down the road.

Carol crosses her arms around the tan coat she's wearing, her eyes trying to make contact with mine. "What's wrong? You look like you've seen a ghost."

"The car that just flew past," I say. "I think it was Steve's."

"Are you sure?"

I shake my head. "I don't know. Maybe I'm just imagining things."

"If he's stalking you, that's gotta creep you out."

"One of my old boyfriends did that once," Rachel chimes in. "Used to drive past my house all the time to see if I was home."

I want to say, *so . . . would this old boyfriend happen to be someone else I know?* But I'm not in the mood. I pass through her exhaled smoke to the front door. "I'm going in. See you both inside."

The din inside is almost deafening. Working my way toward the bar, I spot Todd at the far end with a tight cluster of people around him. He sees me and holds up his hand. I wind my way toward him, squeezing in between a couple of guys clutching beers to get up close. "All this just for *you,*" I say and plant a kiss on Todd's cheek.

"Glad you could make it," he says.

"I'm going to miss you," I shout above the noise. "But I'm happy for you."

"I'll miss you too, but I think it's time to move on."

"Timing's everything."

Todd turns to the two men he was talking to. "Suellen, I'd like you to meet a couple friends of mine – Craig and Adam. Craig and I go way back – all the way to high school. And Adam I've known since college."

"Hello," I say. "Nice to meet you both."

Craig gives a nod then takes a swallow of his beer. Adam says nothing at first, only stares, as if his eyes aren't sure what they're seeing.

"Can I get you a drink?" Todd says while he has the bartender's attention.

"A Bloody Mary."

"Suellen . . . Suellen Atkins? I can't believe it. It's Adam Isaacson."

I look back into Adam's eyes – a warm, soothing brown. His dark hair has a wavy look, but the shortness has tamed the locks. "Adam Isaacson? From Mrs. Haberman's fifth-grade class?"

"The same." Adam grins.

"No way. I don't believe it."

Todd pushes my drink into my hand. "You guys know each other?"

"We went to the same elementary school," Adam says. "I had a secret crush on Suellen back then."

"You did?" I say. "I would have never guessed."

Adam grins, yet again. "That's the story of my life."

"What's that supposed to mean?" Craig says.

Todd says, "He's still single, ain't he?"

I let out a little laugh and look into Adam's face. The lip bar and retainer are all gone and in their stead is a row of straight, white teeth. "You were, like, a math whiz if I remember correctly. I copied off your test paper once. Well, maybe more than once."

"I know," he says, smiling. "You look terrific by the way."

"Thank you. So do you." The leggy, geeky boy has filled out and turned into a hottie. *Top-notch, fairy godmother!* "So how do you know Todd?" I say before taking a sip from my straw.

"Todd and I went to Syracuse together," Adam says. "He's going to be working with me at the AG's office, in the Criminal Justice Division."

"That's right," Todd says. "Adam was the one who recruited me. We're going to fight crime together."

"So you're the one who's responsible for taking Todd away from us," I say, handing my drink back to Todd and shedding my jacket. "Phew! Is it hot in here or is it just me?"

In unison, Todd, Craig, and Adam say, "It's definitely you," and clink their glasses.

Adam takes my jacket. "Suellen Atkins," he says in a singsong voice, as if he needs to hear himself say it again. "I still can't believe it."

More well-wishers are trying to make their way toward Todd as the crammed-full tavern continues filling up. Moving out of the way to let more people through, Adam and I head over to the old wooden phone booth in the back where it's quieter.

When Carol, Rachel and some of the others find us, we join the rest of the party with reluctance, heavy now with loud conversation and laughter. Then Rachel brings her face up close to Adam's, which is next to mine. In a breath that smells of nicotine and too much alcohol, she says, "What I want to know is how someone who looks like you got away for so long? I don't see any ring on your finger." She flings her long brown hair off her shoulder and gives him a flirtatious smile.

Adam throws back his head and laughs, but he's not flirting back. An embarrassed look crosses his face, a vestige of the shy fifth grader I knew. He looks over at me, smiling, and I'm at once touched.

Oh no, Rachel! This one's mine.

Then Adam does something that catches me by surprise. He leans over and speaks into my ear. "I don't think Todd would mind if we left. Do you?"

"Todd who?" I hear myself say.

That is all Adam needs. He swipes my jacket off the back of a chair and hands it to me. "Let's get out of here."

•   •   •

When we leave Todd's farewell party together, it's already getting late. Thankfully, I don't see Steve's car anywhere, so I chalk it up to my overactive imagination.

From spending an hour at Todd's party to hanging out at the local diner for over two, the night turns into something unexpected. We talk about some of the teachers and kids we remember, and it astonishes me how much it all comes back to me.

"Remember the fifth- and sixth-grade production we put on about ancient Egypt?" Adam says.

"I do."

Adam grins. "When I heard you were playing Cleopatra, I tried out for Caesar."

I shake my head, smiling. "So, which part did you get?"

"Remember the mysterious mummy played by question mark in the playbill?"

"You mean the one at the end of the show who ran up and down the aisle startling everyone? No one ever found out who it was."

"That one," Adam says, his face breaking into a sly grin. "No one knew it was me except Mrs. Haberman. She got the idea from the movie *Frankenstein*. Boris Karloff was never mentioned in the credits. The monster part was listed as a question mark to keep it spooky."

"That was you? Wow! The audience loved you." I throw back my head and laugh. It's easy around Adam. "You must have been dying to let that secret out."

"I'm a free man."

"I haven't thought about that memory in, like, forever."

"So, are you seeing anyone right now?" Adam says, coming out with it.

Now's the operative word here since I only officially broke it off with Steve a few weeks ago. I hope Steve's gotten the message. We were on and off so much, he might've thought I was just having a bad day. "No," I say, "no significant other. You?"

"No one."

I can't tell if the sigh I hear is coming from him or me.

It's getting late and there's still so much we want to say, so when Adam asks if we can get together again on the following evening, I say yes without hesitation. We plan to meet at The Yankee Doodle Tap Room in Princeton. I look forward to continuing our banter, without the usual sarcasm or contention I had with Steve. It feels good for a change.

•   •   •

The first thing Adam says while we wait to be seated in the dining room is, "I'm glad I bumped into you after all this time. I still can't believe it. But I have to ask you something, and I want you to level with me."

"Sure," I say. "What is it?"

"Did Kevin Flynn really see you in your underwear?"

Some of us change a lot when we grow older and lose our baby faces. Not Adam. His face is manlier, but his eager and whole-hearted smile is as recognizable as it was in his youth. I'm still laughing when the hostess comes to seat us and long after the waiter leaves with our cocktail order.

"Kevin snuck inside the girl's locker room," I say, smiling at the memory. "We were changing into gym shorts. If he said he saw me in my panties, then I guess he saw me." I'm amazed Adam remembered this. It must have left quite an impression on a fifth grader.

Adam gives a long sigh. "Kevin Flynn. That was probably the highpoint of his sex life. Had to be all downhill for him after that," he says with mock sympathy, and we both laugh. "And how's your brother? You and he are twins, right?"

"Simon followed in our dad's footsteps and went into medicine. Orthopedic surgery, sports medicine. He's been married a year now. They're expecting their first kid. He's finishing up his residency at Hackensack Medical Center."

"Say hello from me. We were in the same accelerated math program," Adam says. He leans back in his chair, allowing some time to pass before he says, "So Suellen. What have you been up to these past seventeen years?"

I smile at the way it sounds because what I hear is 'Where have you been all my life?' "The condensed version – my parents got divorced when I was fourteen. Dad remarried a couple of years later. Not one of my favorite people, but Dad's happy. Eight years ago, Mom remarried. She lives with her new husband in Florida. Morris is a character of sorts, but he's all right. To him, the sun rises and sets on Mom."

"I remember your mom. She was at our school more than some of our teachers," Adam says. "I don't remember a single event she wasn't at."

"That would be her. She hasn't changed. Mom was active in the PTA. She came to every one of my school concerts and pep rallies, but that wasn't enough for her. She got just as involved in my education. It was because of my mother that our school started the accelerated math and science program. She believed public schools could be as good as private schools if given the right tools and funding. She also believed education was the answer to everything."

I sip my drink and roll my eyes. "Mom became an environmentalist when I was in junior high. She started on the Beautification Committee, then the Environmental Committee, and then ran as an independent for Councilwoman and won. Don't get her started on global warming or organic foods and pesticides."

"Those are all legitimate concerns," Adam says in my mom's defense.

"You don't know my mother. To most people, those are just issues. For Mom, they're religion. She was a charter member of the Essex County Concerned Citizens and fought the development of that huge incinerator for years."

"I remember that incinerator," Adam says. "There was a big article in the paper about a march. Didn't your mother get arrested?"

I laugh at the memory. "So you *do* remember my mother."

"I remember a lot about you and your family. Whatever happened with her charges?"

"She pled guilty to a petty disorderly trespass and became a folk hero in Livingston politics."

Adam lets out a laugh. "How did your dad take to all this?"

"He was embarrassed, and they fought a lot. I don't know if he was jealous of the attention she was getting or just angry about the attention he *wasn't* getting. I was just a kid; I didn't understand it all. I do remember the big fights they had over my education." I sigh. "Dad wanted me to go into medicine, too. He was indifferent to my legal studies. Just another thing my dad views as me living up to my wayward daughter persona."

The waiter returns to our table. "Are you ready to order?"

"Not yet." Adam answers him. "Could you just give us another minute?" He leans into me with genuine interest. "How about your mother? Did she see you that way?"

I'm moved by the way Adam asks me questions, like he needs to know the answers. "As you can probably guess, Mom encouraged independent thinking, so she was less critical. But then, my parents never seemed to be on the same page, so there's that. When I was young, Mom used to tell me that with a mouth like mine, I should be a lawyer. Guess you can say she inspired me without even realizing it." I roll my eyes. "My poor mother. I drove her nuts. Of course there were the required teenage battles I had with both my parents, but Dad wasn't around as much, so he didn't have to deal with it like Mom did."

"What teenage battles would you be talking about?" Adam says.

"Boyfriends mostly. But that's a whole 'nother matter. Enough about me, let's talk about you. What do *you* think about me?"

Adam points his finger at me. "Bette Midler. *Beaches.*" We both laugh.

"I'm a big movie buff," I say.

"Me too. Old, new, sci-fi, comedy, westerns. I like 'em all."

"Quick," I say. "Give me three of your top favorite movies."

Adam spouts, "*Inception, Shawshank Redemption,* and *Top Gun.*"

"Not bad. I don't think I could have come up with mine as fast."

Adam and I force ourselves to glance at our menus and order, then resume our catch-up conversation where we left off.

"Seriously though," I say, "what happened to you after sixth grade? It was like you disappeared after the summer."

"My family moved down to the shore. Not the easiest thing when you're starting junior high in another town and don't know a single person."

"That had to be rough."

"It wasn't too bad. I did make a lot of friends after a while and school was much more laid back."

"So, what made you go into law?"

"I was doing high school math in the fifth grade. Thanks to the accelerated classes your mother helped start." Adam grins. "By the time I got to high school I was already taking college level economics classes." Adam takes a sip of his drink and then continues. "I got a degree in accounting but I didn't want to just work with numbers. Actually, back then, I was considering the FBI. But it was harder to get in with just an accounting degree, so I went to Seton Hall Law School for my JD. A friend of mine talked me into joining the Attorney General's office instead. So here I am, prosecuting white-collar criminals. Then I recruited Todd. We've been friends since law school. And here we are . . . all thanks to your mother."

I almost spit out my drink. "How crazy is that."

After we stop laughing, I manage to ask, "What kind of crimes do you prosecute? Embezzlement, credit card theft – stuff like that?"

"Stuff like that. Insider trading, forgery, insurance fraud. Pretty much every crime that's associated with greed."

"You must be very busy. The world's full of greedy people."

Adam pulls himself up straighter in his chair. "I'm here to defend truth, justice, and the American way, Lois," he says in a Clark Kent voice.

I lean forward and look close at him. "What happened to your curly hair?"

"Not sure. Guess after a zillion haircuts, it gave up trying. I like how long your hair got."

"This is turning into a trip down memory lane," I say.

"It's as if we found a time capsule that was meant to be opened now, and *we* were inside it. We just burst it wide open."

"Wow," I say. "Does your mind often go off in sci-fi like that?"

"It's been known to."

My eyes wander to the emptied restaurant. With fewer distractions, I notice the walls lined with century-old Princeton grad photos from the time when this place had been an all-male students' drinking club. One remaining bartender is clearing off the bar in front of the Norman Rockwell mural depicting Revolutionary War people.

"We're the only two people here," I say.

"I know," Adam says with a gleam in his eyes.

"No," I say, catching his meaning. "I mean literally." I had finished my last beer over an hour ago and have an hour's drive to get home. "I didn't realize the time. I should probably go."

When we move to Princeton's sidewalks and the street where my car's parked we are still laughing.

"I've had a wonderful evening." Adam comes within inches of my face and I realize he may kiss me. My lids fall. When it seems like seconds pass between us, my eyes flutter open to see Adam staring, a faint smile on his lips. He's kissing me with his eyes, penetrating and intense, as though he's looking inside my soul. It sends a slight shiver through me. I pull back but I can't stop staring at his eyes. In a soft voice, he says, "I've kissed you so many times in my mind I want to be sure this isn't a dream." It's the most beautiful thing anyone's ever said to me. When he presses his lips to mine, I make sure he knows it isn't.

He waits while I get into my car and closes the door, then taps on my window. I lower it. "You want to know something else I haven't told anyone?"

"What's that?" I say.

"I was always envious of Kevin Flynn."

CHAPTER 8

The morning after Adam's passionate kiss, I find myself longing to see him again as scenes play in my mind like favorite reruns. I think about him while lying in bed on this lazy Sunday morning, his soulful laughter, his warm, infectious smile. Lucy's curled up on the foot of my bed, her long, soft fur caressing my leg. I give her a gentle foot stroke and continue gazing at the ceiling.

My cell phone goes off to the chorus tune of "The Trouble With Love," a sound that once made me race to answer it. Now, I dread it, since it's Steve's ringtone. Lucy's feelers are up too, her yellow eyes wide open and alert. I reach for my phone, wishing my imagination was taking over and Steve was on another planet because I'm fully aware of how far I've moved on – away from Steve, away from the tribulation that was Steve's and mine. "Steve," I answer.

"No. It's the gas man."

Same old Steve. Mocking and gauche as usual.

"Did you forget?" Steve says.

Actually, you were the last thing on my mind this morning. "No . . . no," I hear myself say. "You want to pick up the rest of your things. I didn't forget." *Although I was hoping **you** would.* "When do you want to come by and get them?"

"Now. I'm already here."

"What?" I say, my voice shrill. I come up to a sitting position and swing my legs over the bedside. "You're here now?"

"Standing outside your door, babe. Don't act so surprised."

"I'm not dressed," I say. Lucy and I bound out of bed together. *How did Steve get through the gatehouse? I'll need to talk to Sam.*

"Ain't like I haven't seen you without clothes on before."

"You should have called first. I'm just waking up."

"Late night last night?" Steve doesn't bother to disguise the irony in his voice. "I called your phone twice yesterday. Not my fault you never picked up."

I remember now. I'd turned my phone off on purpose when I was with Adam. "Left it in the car by accident," I say, making up an excuse to ward off any suspicion. "Just give me a second and I'll open up," I say before slapping my phone down on my nightstand.

Darn. I don't even have time to call Gladys over like I'd planned. This shouldn't take long. Anything belonging to him is in my front hall closet. I'll just hand the bag over and send him on his way.

I throw on a robe, hurry to the bathroom, and splash my face with water. I start to rub a little toothpaste on my teeth with my finger and then stop. Better if my morning breath keeps him at a safe distance. Lucy follows me, leaps onto the vanity, and watches. In the mirror, I can see the nervousness in her eyes. "You're not happy about this visitor either, are you?" I say as I head to the front door. At the last second, I throw my cell phone into my robe's pocket.

"Well, well, well." Steve blocks my front entryway, his hand raised and leaning on the doorframe. Under a police bomber jacket, he's dressed in uniform. That explains how he got through the gatehouse.

He doesn't wait to be invited in. Taking a few steps inside my front hall, he does a deliberate scan of me standing there in bare feet and a bathrobe, vulnerable to the core.

"How are you, Steve?" I say, sounding confident. I make a conscious choice to ignore any meaning his ominous, cobalt eyes impart. A prudent impulse sends Lucy dashing back to the bedroom.

"'Bout time I caught you home," Steve says, a shock of black hair descending on his forehead.

I realize this calls for a careful lie. "Work's been so busy." I'm already working my way toward the hall closet, my mind focused on the mission. I reach for the bag on the closet floor and drag it out. "Your jeans are in here – and everything else that's yours," I say, but when I turn to hand it to Steve, he's moving toward my living room.

Holding the bag out in front of me, my feet planted on the cold, hard marble floor, I try to appear unaffected and composed while Steve meanders about my living room. "Your beer stein's in here too. I wrapped it in bubble wrap."

Steve doesn't say anything so I go on. "I checked the condo twice. No need to bother." My voice is starting to betray me.

"Mind if I see for myself?" Steve advances toward the living room sofa. "My iPod adapter's missing."

"I didn't see it. I'm sure it's not here."

"I can't find it, and this is the only place it could be."

"Whatever." I drop the bag of Steve's belongings near the front door and join him in the living room. He's checking under the sofa cushions. I cross my arms and force back a sigh. "Look around for yourself, but I'm sure Isabel would have found it by now during her weekly cleaning."

"Really." Steve's voice drips with grating sarcasm. He stands up straight. "And why should I believe you? Fact is . . . you probably tossed it away already, like everything else you have no use for."

"That's really not called for."

"It's true and you know it. You're a spoiled brat who thinks she can do away with guys the way she does her things. We're users, you and I. Only difference is I can admit it."

"I'm nothing like you," I say. "I have a heart. You're—" I stop myself.

Steve turns toward me, tempting me. "What? A cold-hearted bastard?"

That one's pretty good, but how about an arrogant, egocentric sociopath? My right brain can't help itself, so I make a left-brained decision to keep my mouth shut for once.

"Go ahead – say it." His eyes challenge me.

"I don't want to fight with you, Steve. It doesn't matter what I think. Let's just leave it at that."

Steve advances toward me, the flecks in his pupils picking up the black in his jacket, two dark coal eyes bearing into me with all their hatred. It's not the first time I've wondered when the malice inside him will catch up to his outward appearance. He's angry and he needs to pick a fight with me. "You and I have some unfinished business."

"What unfinished business? Relationships end, Steve. There's nothing unfinished about that."

"Your story maybe. But not mine. No one makes a fool of me. Especially some rich, conceited bitch who thinks she can toss me away just cause she feels like it. How easy it would be for you if I just went away quietly. You'd like that, wouldn't you?" Steve stands before me square on, his eyes narrowed and mean-looking. "Tell me – why should I make this easy for you?"

His threat frightens me, but I try to conceal it. I move a few inconspicuous inches away, slowly enough so he can't tell I'm fearful, my eyes not straying from his stare. In a firm, unwavering voice, I say, "You need to leave, Steve. Now."

"What? Things ain't going according to Suellen? You didn't care very much when you fucked me over though, did you?"

I run a shaky hand through my hair. "I didn't do anything to you. You and I both knew it was over between us."

"Princess wasn't having fun anymore? So who's the newest victim?"

"I don't know what you're talking about."

"Come on. It's me. I know you. Remember? That little Lexus of yours has been putting on a lot of mileage since you threw me out."

My mind does a swift flashback to the night I spotted the Jeep following me. I realize now it may not have been paranoia on my part after all. It *was* Steve's jeep.

"I think you're through here," I say in a tight voice.

"Oh, I don't know," Steve taunts, his face darkening. "Am I?"

I look away from his eyes when my cell phone goes off inside my robe pocket. I'd forgotten I threw it in there. It startles us both. In one fell swoop, my hand delivers it to my ear. "Hello."

"Good morning, Cleopatra."

There's a three-second void before I realize my face has broken into a nervous smile. My eyes jump back to Steve. The dangerous gleam is still in his eyes. His senses are tuned into me with such precision it makes my skin crawl.

A couple more seconds pass while I clear my throat. "Hell … hello," I stutter, self-conscious under Steve's gaze.

"I'm sorry. Did I wake you?" Adam's voice flows through me like a cup of warm milk.

"No, no," I say. "I'm up."

Steve shifts his weight onto his other foot, his eyes never leaving me for a second.

"I went to bed thinking of you," Adam says. "I wanted to call you late last night, but I talked myself into waiting 'til morning. I can't seem to remember if I told you how much I enjoyed being with you yesterday."

There's so much I want to say, but Steve's scrutinizing stare holds me back. "You did tell me. I remember."

"I wanted to be sure," Adam says. "This morning, going over yesterday in my mind, it was the one detail I couldn't seem to remember. Kissing you goodnight – that detail I remember." Adam pauses, waits to see if I have anything to say, but since I remain silent, he says, "Oh-kay. This is either the part where you tell me to back off or 'Sorry, wrong number,' and I don't mind telling you I hope it's the latter."

The stillness that ensues jolts me into action, my mind working fast to come up with something – anything – to say, so Adam won't be left feeling deflated. "No, no." I hear myself start. "You have it right."

Steve pulls on his chin, his eyes narrowing, showing his suspicion. He's intent on watching me, and I recognize that a conversation between Adam and me is impossible right now. I make a hasty decision.

Speaking into the phone I say, "You'll be here when? Ten minutes?"

"Ten minutes? Not unless it's by laser beam." Adam lives an hour away.

Steve peers at me through dark slits.

I go out on a desperate limb. "Steve's here with me now, Teagan. He's picking up the rest of his things."

"What?" Adam says, sounding confused.

The effect on Steve is daunting. He flinches, easing his gaze.

I persist. "I'm getting ready to jump in the shower," I say into my phone looking down at my bare feet. "Steve was just getting ready to leave."

"Steve who?" Adam says. "Are you okay?"

"Yes, I think so."

"You can't talk."

"Right," I say in a stilted voice.

"I guess that explains the cryptic conversation we've been having."

"Okay. See you real soon, Teagan." I end the call and force myself to look right into Steve's eyes. Teagan's impending arrival has taken some of the edge off his anger. "As you can see, I'm kind of busy. And now I'm running late."

Steve lets out a rough breath and gives me a calculating look. Realizing he's been beaten, he turns to leave. "Let me know if it shows up." Keeping my face blank I say nothing, only follow him to the door. "My adapter," Steve snarls, as though he needs to remind me.

I play along. "You know what? I may have thrown it out accidentally. I'll buy you a new one and mail it to you."

"Forget it," Steve says. He starts to head out the door.

"Aren't you forgetting something?"

Steve frowns at me over his shoulder.

"Your stuff," I say, thrusting the bag at him. "That is what you came for, isn't it?"

Steve gives me a hard look and snatches the plastic bag from my grip.

When I've bolted the three locks on my door, I pull out my phone and retrieve Adam's number. He answers on the first ring. "Adam," I burst out, my heart still racing.

"Is everything okay?" His earlier upbeat tone is missing.

"Yes." *Now that Steve's gone.* "I'm sorry about that."

"Well, how about that for timing?" Adam says.

"Your timing was perfect." I exhale a breath. "Look. I know how this must look to you, but it's not what you think. Steve was my old boyfriend. He just stopped over—"

"How old?"

"What?"

"You said he was an old boyfriend. How old of a boyfriend is he?"

"Oh. A few weeks." I'm not sure if the groan I hear comes from Adam or from inside my own head. "He just stopped over to get some things he'd left here."

"What kind of things?" The suggestion of apprehension in his voice is disheartening.

"A beer stein, his iPod . . . a jacket." A disquieting silence. "It's over between us, Adam. It's been over for a long time. I only made it official a few weeks ago, so there were still some loose ends to take care of."

It's impossible to gauge a person's reaction through cell phone frequency, but in my mind, I picture Adam reflecting on what he's hearing with an agonized frown. I imagine him pacing the floor and running his fingers through his hair. Then Adam says something I didn't expect. "You seemed nervous."

"It was kind of awkward, that's all." I'm as truthful as I can be without adding stalking concerns to the whole drama. "I mean it when I say we're totally through." I pause to let it sink in. If I'm being honest with myself, I'm not so sure it's fully sunk in for Steve. "It was a toxic relationship, Adam. I needed to leave it, and I did. I finally did." I wish Adam would say something, but he remains quiet while I attempt to explain it away. "I'm in an emotionally good place right now. I'm not rebounding, if that's what you're worried about. I'm just . . . free."

"Okay then," Adam says, giving nothing away.

"You believe me, don't you?" I ask, just to be sure.

"If you say you're free, then you're free." Adam's voice hasn't returned to its initial cheerful tone, but I'll take what I can get.

. . .

I scan today's lunch choices, seeking comfort food. I use my card to pay for it and make my way over to the lunch table, joining the others.

It's been nine nerve-wracking days since I heard from Adam. I'm still not sure what he's thinking. What he isn't saying. If we continue to see one another, the subject of Steve will come up again. It has to.

I hope Adam wants to see me again. I want to see him.

"Lost two pounds this week," Lynne says, sounding casual to the women around our table. "So what if I have salad growing out of my ears." She stabs with her fork at the few remaining lettuce leaves in her garden salad.

"Good job," Teagan applauds her.

I pop open a Diet Coke, then place a small bag of chocolate chip cookies to the right of a heaping pile of macaroni and cheese.

Lynne stares at me in amazement. "I can't remember the last time I ate a generous, guiltless helping of macaroni and cheese. Now, even as I gaze at it, I feel as though I'm packing on the weight and have to force myself to look away. I don't know how you do it."

"Do what?" I ask.

"Stay so thin."

"Burn it off I guess. High anxiety will do that."

"When I was in my teens, I could eat a whole extra-cheese pizza all by myself," Teagan says. "The word 'calories' was not in my vocabulary." Today is Teagan's first day back after her surgery, two weeks earlier than her doctor recommended.

I scoop a spoonful of macaroni and cheese into my mouth, chewing it as if I'm in a race. "How long did it take you? I once ate a pie in under an hour – my brother bet me I couldn't do it." I talk as fast as I eat until I notice everyone watching.

"I wouldn't have taken that bet if I were him," Lynne says, and we all laugh.

"It might have taken me a little longer than an hour." Teagan puts down her tuna wrap and takes a sip of her water. "I don't remember exactly. I took those things for granted. I took a lot for granted then," she muses. "I didn't know it could change."

"If I were you, Suellen, I'd get down on my knees every day and thank the Lord for giving you an amazing metabolism," Lynne says.

I shrug and guzzle some more soda to wash down the macaroni and cheese.

Rachel – the turkey club sandwich – chimes in with, "I've never had a weight problem. I always stay within a five-pound range. It just takes discipline."

"Learning to adapt is about as disciplined as it gets for me," Carol says. "I was chubby most of my life. I've adopted my mother's mantra – 'you're what's called pleasantly plump, dear,'" she mimics her mother's coddling voice. Carol laughs at herself, the dimple in her right cheek deepening. Admitting she may never be a one-digit size comes easy to someone like Carol. She's one of the rare few who prefers acceptance to agonizing.

"Do you think men talk about their weight as much as women do?" Lynne says knowing the answer.

We all shake our heads and frown. "Course not."

Carol shoos her hand at a group of male associates sitting around a table on the other side of the lunchroom. "Men," she grunts. "They're the reason, the problem and the target all wrapped up."

Teagan rolls her eyes. "Ain't that the truth." She tucks a strand of her shoulder-length blonde hair behind an ear. "So, who ever said life was fair?"

I meet her eyes, catching her subliminal meaning. Ever since I've known Teagan, she's wanted to be a mother. Her two older sisters have five kids between them. She puts on a good front, but I know how much it distresses her that she hasn't gotten pregnant.

Carol looks over at me and blows at a springy curl that has fallen into her eye. "Why the high anxiety, Suellen? You're usually pretty chill." Carol never misses a beat. She's like an acoustic searchlight when people are all talking. It's a real talent, how she knows what to zoom in on so she can flesh it out.

All eyes are on me as I shift in my seat. "I think Steve may be stalking me," I say.

"Have you told anyone about this?" Lynne says. "If you believe he's stalking you, shouldn't you report him?"

"Yeah," Rachel says. "I'd let the police know."

"He *is* the police," I say.

"Oh. Wow."

"He can get in a lot of trouble," Lynne says.

"I don't want to jeopardize his job for him. I just want him to leave me alone."

"Look," Lynne says, "I may not always be a good judge of character, and who am I to talk, but stalking's a cruel obsession. It should worry you."

I know where Lynne's coming from. She returned to the workforce after her husband had left her for another woman. "Cruelty . . . cheating. It's all the same thing in my opinion," Lynne says. "On that, I can speak from experience."

"If you're worried, it must be for a good reason," Teagan says. "You can't be too careful."

"He came by my place just a few days ago. He got through the gate because he was in uniform and said he was on official business."

"Ooohhhh. He's a sly one," Lynne says, shaking her head.

"I've alerted the security guard not to let him through, at least not without checking with me first. I'm taking care of it. I don't know. Part of me thinks I'm just being paranoid."

"An old boyfriend stalked me once," Rachel says. "Then one day my neighbor spotted his car cruising down our street really slow and called the cops on him. That pretty much put an end to it."

This is one time I don't feel like being in competition with Rachel. I hope Steve will just move on.

Carol elbows me in the side as Lisa, a fellow attorney, enters the lunchroom. "Look who just walked in," Carol trills, tipping her head in Lisa's direction. Gossip has it Lisa's having an affair with Jeff Simpson, the firm's number two partner, making it the office's biggest scandal to date. There are also rumors going around that the next senior associate invited to become an equity partner may be another woman. Lisa wants nothing more than for it to be her.

She's wearing a form-fitting, slate-gray suit over a silky white blouse, two top buttons open to reveal a sparkling diamond heart pendant that rests below the hollow of her throat. Her confident, late-thirties look is striking, as usual.

She saunters over to the refrigerator and our table falls silent as we watch Lisa's every movement. She bends over into the refrigerator, pulls out a can of complimentary unsweetened iced tea, then reaches in one of the overhead cabinets and grabs a glass. A flick of her blonde hair reveals a sideways glance in my direction before she walks over to me.

"Suellen, can we get together sometime this afternoon?" She flashes her perfect-straight-white-teeth smile. We've been assigned to work together on a case.

"Sure," I say. "I'll come over to your office."

Lisa and I pretend to like each other, but it couldn't be further from the truth. Although she started at the firm a couple of months after me, she's an experienced litigator with ten years under her belt. We keep it coolly professional. Apparently, Lisa's career stratagem changed with her divorce a few years ago. Results- and power-driven, she's added sex to her arsenal. "'I'm a free spirit,'" she once said to me. "'I'll always be a free spirit. It's who I am. My marriage was merely a brief lapse in judgment, serving only to prove I'm not meant for that kind of thing. It's far too limiting.'"

"See you later," she says. "Enjoy the rest of your lunch." She walks out, leaving a trail of very expensive perfume behind.

Carol breaks the tension. "What's the name of the perfume she's wearing? I have to know. Not like I can afford it."

I can't resist. "Baccarat Rouge 540." I try to be careful not to impose my wealthy background on them, but sometimes it slips out.

Everyone's eyes are fixed on me. "Francis Kurkdjian. The famous perfumer? It so happens I have it too." I roll my shoulders nonchalantly. "A Christmas present one year from Eve, my dad's wife."

"I wonder how much time Lisa spends getting ready each morning," Carol says.

"Well, I can tell you one thing," Lynne says. "Mr. Bender would not approve of what's been going on with her and Jeff, even if Jeff *is* a partner."

"She looks a little lost without Jeffrey. He's out of the office today," Carol, who's Jeff's administrative assistant, says. "I swear she's in his office more than her own. And that's not all . . ." She pauses for effect and leans her head over the table, drawing the rest of us in like magnets. She lowers her voice. "I've seen them go off together for two-and three-hour lunches. Mrs. Simpson phoned looking for him during one of those lunches. When he didn't pick up his cell phone right away, she tried him at the office. I can tell you, she wasn't too pleased." Carol rolls her eyes for emphasis. She's in her element.

"Why am I not surprised?" Lynne says. "I wouldn't put anything past her. She's a power-driven cutthroat and frankly, I don't like her."

It goes without saying Lynne is biased since it was a woman like Lisa who broke up her family. I get it. But I sense an undercurrent of a double standard going on here. The focus shouldn't all be on Lisa, who's single, the last time I checked. Jeff's the one breaking his vows.

"I wonder what Mr. Bender would do if he knew Lisa and Jeff were hooking up on company time?" Teagan says.

"Yeah. While the rest of us have to make sure we clock in before 9:00 or get docked, an employee having sex with one of the bosses gets a blind eye. No one's going to tell me that isn't way up there on the not-to-do list."

"Oh, give me a break," I say. "Jeff's the number-two guy in the firm. Who's going to tell him he can't have an affair with one of his associates if he wants to? Are you going to tell him he's breaking the rules?"

"No. But it just makes me so mad. Lisa's such a bitch. She's never nice to me, and she acts like she's better than everyone else," Carol says.

"Look. I'm not a fan either, but her sex life's *her* sex life." I get up and throw out my used lunch container, through with the subject of Lisa already. "I've got to get back to work."

"Wait up. I'll walk with you," Teagan says. "There's never a dull moment, is there?" she says as we get onto the elevator.

Not in this place. Not in my life. "Never is."

My phone dings a message and I instantly start to feel better. Adam wants to know if we can get together again this coming weekend.

CHAPTER 9

"When you come down in February, remind me to give you some books on vegetarian cuisines and holistic living." My mom sings into the phone as I glance at the platter of flour-coated chicken cutlets sitting on my stove.

"I haven't joined the Vegan Society like you, Mom. I'm still very much a cantankerous carnivore." My cell phone is tucked snugly beneath my chin, my hands busy grating chocolate while I speak into it. I empty the grated chocolate into a bowl with sugar, cocoa, and salt and mix it all up.

"I'll make a believer out of you yet."

"I won't fault you for trying."

"I miss you, honey. You'll have to come with me to Yoga class. You must meet my new instructor. I've already mentioned you to him. He's gorgeous, thirty-two, and unattached. In the meantime, I'm going to send you some wheatgrass."

I'm glad Mom can't see my eye roll. "Can't wait."

"So, what else is new? Things well?"

"No complaints," I say. I do not tell her about the curious lump in my breast that I've been watching. My breasts are very dense and cystic. The last two lumps I had went away after my period. I don't want to worry Mom. She'll call me every day, twice a day even, until I have it checked out. I also don't want her to go into another one of her diatribes about therapies containing herbs like sheep sorrel and slippery elm or the enormous health benefits of transcendental meditation.

"Do you want tablets or powder?" Mom says.

"What?" I blow away the flour that's spilled over part of my recipe.

"The wheatgrass I'm sending you."

"Oh. Either one's fine."

"I'll send you both. It comes in a drink, too."

"I don't have an electric mixer," I say out loud, though I'd only meant to think it to myself.

"Something must be wrong with my hearing. I thought I heard you say something about an electric mixer? What do you need with an electric mixer?" Mom sounds as though I've spoken a foreign language.

I place my phone down on the counter and put it on speaker. "I'm baking a chocolate silk pie," I say. Adam's favorite.

"You're baking a pie? Sue . . . Ellen, are you sure you're feeling all right?"

There are only two reasons why my mother utters my name as if it were two: when she would scold me as a child or when she's in a state of total disbelief. The last one fits. Dad wanted to name me after his mother, Susan. Mom wasn't having it. Another thing they fought about. It wouldn't surprise me one bit if I had remained unnamed days past the time they brought me home from the hospital. Although she never said so, I imagine that, in a weak moment of postnatal depression, Mom partly succumbed, but only by joining the two grandmothers' names together to form one.

"I couldn't be better. I'm not sure how this pie's going to come out, but you know this baking thing's kinda fun." I scan my kitchen for the first time since I started my new venture and let out a laugh. There are chocolate shaving trails, flour, and sugar everywhere – on my counters, on the floor. My kitchen has never looked more productive. "I've been missing out," I say. A downside reflection to growing up privileged.

"You sound different," Mom says. "What's happened to you?"

Adam's what's happened. His influence on me has made all the difference. But to Mom, I ask, "Different how?"

"You sound . . . do I dare say . . . happy?"

I let out a hearty laugh.

"See what I mean? Okay, Suellen. Who is he?"

I learned a long time ago that trying to fool my mother was useless. She's a human lie detector when it concerns my brother or me. "His name's Adam. I'm making dinner for him."

"I knew it. Well, that didn't take you long. Glad you came to your senses about the other one you were with. Does Adam have a last name?"

"Isaacson."

"Jewish," Mom says.

"We were in elementary school together. Would you believe it?" I decide not to tell Mom everything I've learned about him. Too much. Too fast. I can withhold information from her. I just can't lie.

"So, what does Adam do for a living?" Mom says, not wasting any time.

"He's a lawyer. A Deputy Attorney General."

I continue reading. *Whisk the meringue until peaks start to form.*

"Is it serious?"

"We're still getting to know each other. So the answer's no. Not yet. Could be."

"You should bring him with you when you come down for Hanukkah. I'd love to meet him."

"I'm not sure that's a good idea. We're still in the developmental stage. Wouldn't want to rush things."

"Who's rushing? It's a trip to Florida."

"It's a trip to meet my mother and her husband."

"Has your father met him?"

"Goodness no. We're not even there yet."

Lucy leaps onto the kitchen counter, and I scoop her up with my floured hand, returning her to the floor.

"So, you're making this chocolate pie for Adam?"

"Mm hmm. And for dinner I'm making piquant chicken piccata."

"I admit I'm amazed at your sudden foray into the kitchen. You don't hold it against me that I wasn't the stay-at-home, cookie-baking mom, do you?"

"Not at all. Look at it this way. You've always encouraged me to be my own person. Well, I am. Anyway, you wouldn't have baked cookies." I laugh. "It would have been more like sprout brownies."

"I guess you're right about that. Anyway, I'm FedExing the wheatgrass to you overnight."

Snail mail would be better. "Say . . . Mom, when did you get the screening test, you know, the genetic test for the breast gene mutation?"

Mom's feelers are up. "Why?"

"I'm thinking about getting it, too. I mean, since Grandma Ellen died of breast cancer, it's something I need to think about."

"Oh. It was around eight or nine years ago I think. It came back uncertain."

"Hmmm."

"You know they keep on perfecting it for gene mutations that aren't even discovered yet. You should do it. I should also test again," Mom says.

"Yeah. We should." I glance at my kitchen clock. "Well, I have to go. Adam will be here soon and I have to get ready."

"Love you sweetheart."

"Love to you and Morris," I say before ending the call.

Making dinner may have been too ambitious for someone with as little practice as I have, but I want to try. If it doesn't work out, I can always order something in.

I take in all the scents. It smells so good in here, like what probably smells like holidays for most folks. Smells of cooking and baking and one more thing I almost forgot. I go over to my living room and light the cinnamon candle on the coffee table. When I return to the kitchen, Lucy is rolling in the flour that's spilled on my floor. I don't know who's having more fun – her or me.

•   •   •

Adam and I sit on my couch, sipping the wine he brought over. Dry. French. Lucy curls up on the rug next to us, purring in her sleep. I prop my feet on the coffee table and lean my head back.

"How do you like it over there in Trenton?" I ask. "Do you and Todd work close together? We all miss him at the firm."

"Yes, we're in the same department. I think he's a good fit."

"Say hello to him for me, will you?"

"I will. I told him I was seeing you this weekend."

"You did? What did he say?"

"He said something about you being a sassy one who'll keep me on my toes."

"He said that?"

Adam shakes his head and laughs. "Okay, so it might have been me who said that and he agreed with me."

I slap him on the arm. "Really, what did he say?"

Adam grins. "He said he thought he witnessed the bolt of lightning flash between us when we first saw each other at the Star Tavern."

I chuckle out loud. "That definitely does *not* sound like Todd. I can see I'm not going to get an honest answer from you, am I?"

"Okay, I'm being serious now. He gave me the thumbs up," he says with a wide grin. "That's guy language for 'way to go, man.'"

"That I can believe," I say.

"So, what kind of cases do you work on at your firm?" Adam says.

"I'm mostly assigned to work on medical malpractice cases. Recently, I've been appointed guardian ad litem for a young girl. It's a pro bono. The foster mother wants to adopt her. It's heart-wrenching. The girl's mother shot her abusive husband dead while he slept and is being sentenced to serve time for it. The details are horrific."

"Wow. Sounds pretty heavy," Adam says, shaking his head.

"It is. I want to interview the mother before I write my report of recommendation. I have to go to Clinton on Monday, where she's being held in the women's correctional facility's maximum compound." I lose my breath for a moment. "I'm not going to lie. It kinda creeps me out. I've never been inside a prison before."

"Are you going alone?"

"Yeah. It's my case." I take in a breath. "The guy was a monster of the worst kind. I have nightmares from what he did to his wife and daughter."

Adam looks into my eyes, holding my gaze. "Well, the experience of visiting a prison is not a very pleasant one. Just be sure to get there a half hour early. There'll be some paperwork, and you'll be searched and have to go through a metal detector. They may even pat you down, so don't wear any kind of jewelry."

I nod, then take a sip of my wine. Lucy jumps up onto the couch and steals over to Adam's lap. "Wow," I say. "I think she likes you."

"You seem surprised," Adam says.

A flash of Lucy running from Steve flits through my mind. "It's just that she's kind of picky."

"You know, I appreciate that you went to all the trouble of cooking dinner for us tonight," Adam says, stroking Lucy's head softly. "I had wanted to take you out. But I will say, there's something sexy about watching you work in the kitchen, your sleeves all rolled up."

I wince. "It wasn't too terrible, was it?"

"You're a woman of many talents," Adam says, grinning. Lucy leaps onto the coffee table and then back onto the floor to do more exploring.

"Hold that thought. You haven't tasted the pie yet," I say. "The meringue looks burnt. I should have stuck with a brownie mix."

"You're a natural," Adam says, his expression now quite sincere. "Maybe you've missed your calling." He slides my feet off the table and brings them over to his lap.

I laugh. "You should've heard my mother when I told her. I don't know which horrified her more – that one of my meal's ingredients was animal or the fact I was doing the cooking."

"Are you more like your mother or your father?" Adam says in his typical way of wanting to learn more about me.

"A little of both," I say. "I have my mother's chutzpah and my father's willfulness. At least, that's what my mother would tell you – that I get my stubbornness from my Anglo-Saxon side."

Adam laughs lightly while he massages my feet. "She'll also say it doesn't really matter because in spirit, I'm Jewish and that's what counts."

With a warm smile, Adam says, "It had to be hard for you when your parents split up."

"Yes and no. After a while, I just wanted the fighting to stop."

"Reminds me of a famous Woody Allen line. 'My parents never got divorced, although I begged them to.'"

"I can relate to that." I stare at Adam, the spark of intelligence and wit igniting his face. *I could really like this guy. There's no toxicity like with Steve.* "How do you do it?"

"Do what?"

"Remember famous movie lines and pull out jokes appropriate for every situation."

"I don't know. Guess it comes naturally," Adam says modestly. "Like your cooking." I smile to let him know I appreciate what he said. "Say, did I tell you about the new sushi bar that just opened? It caters exclusively to lawyers. It's called Sosumi."

I slap Adam on the arm. "And I thought I'd heard all the lawyer jokes."

"I'm not joking," he says. "I just ate there last week."

"You haven't changed," I say, but I can't tell by the look on his face whether he's kidding or not. Being a human lie detector was not one of the gifts I got from my mother.

A slow grin creeps across his face and he takes my empty wine glass and puts it on the coffee table next to his. He dips his head toward me and studies my mouth, tracing over it with his finger in a perfect blend of sweet and sexy, interchanging with the lightest grazes from his lips, touching my cheeks, my chin, then gliding down my neck and across my shoulders. I quiver.

"Okay," I murmur, my head falling back on the couch, "maybe you have changed a little."

I close my eyes. When Adam has me where he wants me, he kisses my mouth with all the nuances of someone who's really into it. I do not remember when making out ever felt this good. I think Steve and I skipped over this part.

Feeling languid after his kiss, my lids still closed, I can't seem to erase the vision of floating dots as they transform into little clouds – meringue-like with brownish peaks.

I really, really like this guy.

CHAPTER 10

I feel like I stepped into a dark medieval city, locked away from the outside world. Beige-colored buildings are confined inside strands of doubled-over razor wire and watchtowers. I enter the maximum security compound where New Jersey's most dangerous women reside. Grey concrete walls. No windows. Stale air.

"I'm an attorney," I say to the tall female security guard who greets me with austerity. "I have an appointment to see Shaquana Evans." She takes my ID and searches through the rest of my belongings. I turn in my keys, my jacket, and my cell phone. A woman visitor ahead of me gets patted down and I cringe inside. But after I come through the metal detector, another armed female guard leads me straight to a room with two chairs across a table, a room as drab as it is small. With my hair tied back, I tug on my turtleneck and focus on the one distracting accent in the room – the door.

A different guard – this one male – brings Shaquana into the room, but before he leaves I say, "You can remove the handcuffs." After doing so, he closes the door behind him and I watch Shaquana settle into the chair across from me. The twenty-four-year-old face that looks back at me is etched with years of torment and beatings. A crooked scar runs down the left side of her lip. Her uniform's the same gloomy beige color as the building and walls around us. Her dark skin and short afro contrast the colorlessness of everything else. I give myself a moment to regroup before I start. "Do you know why I'm here?"

"I know who you are," she says. "You're the lawyer who's going to save my daughter."

Her blunt answer shocks me. "How will I do that?"

"Destiny's in a good place with her foster mother. I want to make sure she stays there –where she's safe and happy. For as long as possible."

"So . . . you're saying you don't object to her being adopted by her foster mother?" I scan down the list of questions I outlined for her.

"I'm saying I want to do what's best for Destiny, and that's what's best for her. Her foster mother's a good woman. She's what Destiny needs. I can't do nothin' for her while I'm locked up. I already done what had to be done."

My eyes shoot up to meet hers, conveying more meaning than any words could imply.

"Okay then," I say.

"I'll still be in her life, even when I get out of this hell hole. She don't need to be movin' around with me while I figure out *my* life."

"I see. Guess we're through here then. That's all I needed to know. Is there anything else you want to tell me?"

"Yeah. It was her birthday last week, and I couldn't get her a gift. Can you help me, please?"

"Why, yes. Yes, of course I can. What does your daughter like?"

"She likes mermaids and unicorns. And she likes to draw." I catch a glimmer of joy in Shaquana's eyes for the first time and give her a reassuring nod. "I'll take care of it. What does she call you?"

"Mommy. That's what she calls me. Cause I'm her mommy." There's a hint of sorrow laced with pride in the way she says it.

When I pull my car out of the vicinity of the prison compound, I breathe a sigh of relief. Besides the dreaded Thanksgiving holiday coming up in a couple of days, I think about the work piled on my desk that's waiting at my office. This will be a short week and deadlines are coming up fast. First, I want to write up my recommendation report to proceed with the adoption of Destiny while it's still fresh in my head. Hopefully, it can all be wrapped up by year's end.

It's a quarter to twelve already, and I could make it back in time for lunch. My stomach's gurgling. But I've already decided to skip it for today. I turn off in a direction away from the law office to a couple towns over where I once saw this quaint toy shop. Jabberwocky I think it's called. A place I wouldn't mind escaping into after my previous scenery.

•　•　•

Teagan and I head over to our lunch table after the Thanksgiving break. Lynne's already there and has brought along Catherine, a fellow associate who's just returned from a two-month maternity leave.

"Hey," Carol says, bringing Rachel with her. They take two empty seats and open their lunches. Our table fills up rapidly. Carol notices Catherine sitting with us and raises her eyebrows. "Catherine, to what do we owe this honor?"

"Can't I have a bite to eat with friends once in a while?" Catherine works on a lot of Mr. Bender's cases and Lynne is also her assistant.

Carol wastes no time. Unwrapping her sandwich and popping open a can of Diet Coke she starts, "So, how was everyone's Thanksgiving?"

"Mine was good," Catherine says. "Had Thanksgiving at my house. It was a first, but it was easier staying home for a change and not having to bundle up the twins."

My fingers fly across my cell phone keypad as I text my brother.

Me

I still haven't forgiven you for leaving me alone with Dad and Eve for nearly two hours. Have I given you enough crap about that?

Catherine's still talking when I look up again. "My mother did most of the cooking. Jim's parents came over too. Mom made her incredible sweet potato soufflé, and my mother-in-law baked an apple pie. I thought I'd never want to eat again but . . . here I am." She forks a tomato slice from her salad into her mouth.

"We had twenty-two people this year," Carol says. "Our dining room was so tight my mom ordered everyone not to move once they were seated – except for my sister and me. We were up and down, collecting dishes and pouring wine. And that was just the lasagna course. We hadn't even gotten to the turkey yet."

My phone dings.

Simon

Sarah and I have to divide our time between her family and mine now. That's how it is when you're married.

"I wound up having two Thanksgiving meals that day," Rachel says, nibbling on a carrot stick. "Once at my house and then again at my boyfriend's. I'm on a strict diet for the next two weeks."

Teagan and I exchange a skeptical look. "Good luck with that," I say.

I text Simon back.

Me

Maybe next time you could warn me.

Simon

LOL

"What about you, Suellen? What did you do for Thanksgiving?" I can always count on Carol.

I shrug, take another bite from my turkey sandwich, chewing it at a snail's pace before swallowing it.

"How can you eat turkey again?" Carol says to me. "I'm all turkeyed out."

"I didn't have turkey on Thanksgiving," I say without looking up. "That's how. I went to my Dad's country club and ordered a steak."

Carol's eyes grow wide with exaggerated wonder. "How can you *not* have turkey on Thanksgiving? Even my Italian family has turkey."

"Funny. That's what my stepmom said to me too," I say, my eyes cast downward. "My dad and Eve are real big on the 'how-can-you's.'" I frown. "How could I ever have been with someone like Steve? How could I have chosen to go into law? How can this be and how can that be? I guess you could say I'm from the 'How-Can-This-Be?' family."

The lunch table falls silent as everyone's eyes fixate on me. I let go of my sandwich and look each of them in the eye. "Sorry. I don't much like holidays. They're always so full of hype, and then it's over."

"Do you always do that? I mean, say exactly what you mean?" There's a tinge of flattery in Rachel's comment.

I roll my shoulders. "Why mince words?" I can't pretend to like the holidays. My friends know I'm often direct, even if it comes off prickly, and it doesn't help that I'm feeling lots of angst today.

I haven't told anyone about Adam yet. I didn't get to see him, although he's been texting me. He already had big plans with his family. Apparently, he's one of the rare few who come from a family who enjoy doing things together. He spent the holiday weekend with his immediate and extended family in New Hampshire at a long-planned reunion. I missed him, but I used the time to catch up on work from home.

I let go of an exasperated sigh. I know I've made some pretty bad choices, especially in the boyfriends department. Adam's one of the good guys, and it scares me. I don't deserve him.

"Was your Dad really upset with you for becoming a lawyer? My parents would have thrown me a big party or somethin'," Carol says. "I mean, I don't get it."

"That's been my life's story." I scrunch my face. "Dad was always pushing medical school on my brother and me, overseeing our course selections, making certain we were taking calculus and chemistry in high school. I remember after I got off the phone with him one day after enduring one of his lectures, I was stewing. I was so mad. In my mother's typical way of overriding him, she said 'Don't let your father get to you.' Then she tried humor. 'You know what Grandma Ellen would say if she were here? Don't *become* a doctor . . . better you should marry one.' To which I'd snark back, 'How'd that work out for you?'"

"Ouch," Teagan says. "How'd your mother react to that?"

I shrug. "I don't remember. I think she just gave me one of her usual long sighs and walked away."

"Wow. Not my mother," Carol says. "She would have yelled, 'I brought you into this world, I can take you out.' Only she would have said it in Italian."

"It's the mothers who set the tone for how a family runs," Lynne says. "I was just thinking about what you said, Suellen. How yours is the 'How-Can-This-Be' family. It got me thinking about mine. I think I can safely say mine's the 'I'll-Drink-To-That' family."

I can't help but smile.

Lynne looks at Catherine. "What about yours?"

"My family? Hmmm. Okay. Here goes. I'm from the 'You'll-Never-Guess-Who-Did-What-To-Who' family."

"I like that," Lynne says, then turns to Rachel, who shakes her head.

"Oh come on," Lynne says. "You can do it."

"Okay, guess you could say I come from the 'Play-Those-Numbers' family."

Carol slaps both her cheeks. "You just took mine."

Lynne says, "You fit right in at this table."

Teagan's up next. "All the good ones are taken. Let me think for a sec. Okay, how about 'You-Gonna-Eat-All-That?' I have a really big family. We never outgrew our food insecurities."

"That could just as easily be my family too," Carol says.

"You're not getting off that easy," I say to Carol, enjoying myself now.

"Every one of yours could describe my family," she says, taking a few moments to think about it. Then a slow smile lights her up from inside out. "I've got it. I'm from the 'If-You-Don't-Like-It-You-Can-Go-Fuck-Yourself' family."

We're all laughing so hard we don't care if everyone else in the lunchroom seems to be looking over at our table. For a little while, I've even forgotten about my gripes and concerns.

"This is why I like sitting at your table," Catherine says.

I glance around the table at each of the women there. My other flawed family – Lynne, who's dealing with teenagers' angst; Catherine, balancing a legal career and recent motherhood; Carol, who's learned to laugh at herself; Rachel, the newbie who's trying hard to fit in; and Teagan, my bestie, who has to suffer through christenings and birthday parties for everyone else's babies. There are all kinds of families out there. I'm so grateful for this one.

CHAPTER 11

I'm dying to tell Teagan about Adam, but she's been in a funk the last few days. I stare across the hall to the accounting side of the office when I glimpse Catrina – the lady who takes care of all the lovely foliage throughout the firm. She's inside Teagan's office watering a hanging fern. I wait until Catrina walks out, and decide to go over to talk to Teagan anyway.

"Hey," I say, stepping inside Teagan's office. "Got a minute?"

"Sure. Just a sec," Teagan says.

While her fingers continue tapping on the keyboard, I survey Teagan's desktop. On one corner a framed photo of her and Mike in front of the Victorian Inn in Cape May and a candy bowl filled with Hershey's Kisses. The rest strewn with a bookkeeper's bedlam of checks and invoices. It stresses me out just looking at it.

I plunk down in the chair in front of her desk and lean forward as I catch two words on her computer screen, which is tilted to the side. Adoption agencies. Suddenly, I forget why I came.

Teagan's fingers finish grazing the keyboard, and she swings her chair around to face me.

"You're wearing my favorite outfit," she says. "Chanel, right?"

I shift in my seat and glance down at the dark chocolate skirt as if I'd forgotten what I put on this morning. "Huh? Oh. Yeah."

"I love that suit. It no doubt cost more than my entire winter wardrobe, but you've got good taste. It looks great on you." Teagan fingers a long, chain necklace. "You seem fidgety. Steve isn't still bothering you, is he?"

"Ugh. Steve didn't take too well to my kicking him out. He's not going to go away so easily. The last time he came over to get the rest of his things, he made me a little uncomfortable."

"Suellen—"

"I took care of it. I told him you were on your way over, and he did an about-face."

"That man needs to get a life. You shouldn't have any more interaction with him. If he doesn't let up, you need to tell someone."

"I'm not going to let him bother me. I can handle it." *I'm more scared of ruining it with Adam than I am of stalker Steve.* "I don't want to talk about Steve anymore," I say. "I'd rather talk about someone else."

Teagan raises a brow. "Who is he?"

"His name's Adam." As I fill her in on our history, I brush my hair back and smile warily. "I'm afraid I'm going to blow it with him. I have to remind myself I need to take things slowly."

"Wow. This one must be different – I've never known you to take anything slow before."

"Adam's different."

Teagan squints like she's trying to peer into my mind. "You're really into him, aren't you?"

"You know how I usually dread the holidays? Adam makes it exciting for me again. I haven't told anyone else about him, but I just had to tell someone."

Teagan folds her hands together and rests her elbows on the desk. "I'm flattered you chose me. I'll keep it a secret if you want, if you're not ready. Aren't you planning on going to see your mom in Florida for Hanukkah?"

"Actually," I say, "I weaseled my way out of it this year. I told her I was cramming in lots of hours on an important case coming up for trial. I had to promise her I'd go for Morris's birthday in February." I reach for one of Teagan's chocolate kisses. "I don't want to get my hopes up, but maybe Adam will go with me then. We'll see."

"I don't think I've ever seen you like this," Teagan says.

"Like what?"

"Like someone who's been swept off her feet. It's a new look for you."

I grin. Teagan's seen me through my dating whims with guys ranging from tedious to narcissistic. But none of them imposed a real risk to my happiness. With Adam, the stakes could not be higher.

"He's everything I need. He's the real deal. That's what makes it so scary." I glance over at Teagan's monitor again.

A distracting question lurks in the back of my mind and keeps pushing forward. "Teag, I can't help noticing."

"Noticing what?"

"The websites you have pulled up on your screen."

"Oh. How's that for scary?" she says. "It's weird when I think about it. I'm googling a baby."

"You'd be such a great mom."

"Whoa. Adopting a baby is still a distant maybe."

"What's the cost?"

"Private domestic adoptions can cost anywhere between thirty and sixty thousand dollars according to my research. I don't even know why I'm still searching. I don't have that kind of money."

"It's a start though," I say. *Wow. It seems easier when the State is controlling the whole process, like with Edwina.*

"It's a start to more disappointments, you mean. I'm still paying off my in vitros. International adoptions are a little less, but it's still a lot to think about."

"There has to be some type of financial assistance available. I'd keep exploring. Who knows what you might find."

"It's just web surfing," Teagan says. "I haven't even discussed adoption with Mike yet. I don't think I can do in vitro again. It's taken such an emotional toll on us both. I don't know what Mike's going to say about it. It's different for him. He's always telling me I'm enough for him. It's not like that for me. I don't feel complete without a child. And I'm not getting any younger."

Carol's standing in Teagan's doorway. "Got one for you." She drops a check into Teagan's inbox. "It's a retainer for a new estate matter. Wrote the client number on it. See you both at lunch today?"

"Yep," I say, getting up from the chair.

A very pregnant administrative assistant from the real estate division pops in to drop a check in Teagan's inbox, her eyes straying immediately to the candy bowl.

"Please," Teagan says, "help yourself."

"You twisted my arm." She takes a couple and waddles out of the office and I catch Teagan's eyes following her. I realize Teagan's smile has tightened up so much it looks like it's stuck.

"Why is she still working in her condition?" Carol says. "She looks like she's about to have that baby any day now."

"A condition I wish I could catch," Teagan mumbles.

Silence lingers in the air, thickening until it seems to rise above the clacking keyboards and thumping noise of Catrina's plants cart as she wheels it down the hall. Carol and I look at one another. There isn't anything either of us can say. There are at least three pregnant women at the firm now. Somehow, the contagion missed Teagan.

•   •   •

Adam is coming over shortly. I'm so excited since he'll be staying the night, and we're planning on spending tomorrow in the city to go to the American Museum of Natural History. I didn't want us to go to a local place for dinner this evening and risk bumping into Steve, so I suggested take-out and a movie at my place instead. Today, I set a new record for rushing out of work on a Friday.

I dry myself off after a quick shower and spread lotion all over my body. I don't know what's going to happen tonight. So far, we've only kissed, but I want to be ready. A thrill goes through me as I envision what the weekend could lead to. Standing topless in front of a full-length mirror, I look with a discerning eye at the shape of my breasts – youthful firm, side-set B cups with space in between, pointy nipples.

They're not perfect, but I like them okay. I wonder if Adam is a boob guy. I turn around to look behind me in the mirror, more pleased with the look of my shapely butt in a lacy thong. Maybe he's more of a butt guy, I think with a giggle.

Remaining braless, I throw on a pink, pajama-like lounge set, the fabric brushing over my left breast alerting me to its sensitvity. I apply more moisturizer, which seems to soothe it, move closer to the mirror, and lift up my top. I can still make out the nick of a scar on the outer side of my breast from more than a year ago, although it's hardly visible now. I hope I don't need to have another cyst aspirated as I roll my finger over the small nodule I feel near the nipple. Hopefully, the lump and tenderness will go away after I've had my period, which I'm due for in a few days.

When Adam steps inside my foyer, he doesn't hide that he's looking me over. He plants a kiss on my lips and then pulls back so I can see the brightness on his upturned face. "I missed you," he says, and just to be sure he means it I reach up to hold his face and kiss him long, his passionate response stirring me. My legs weaken as the wine bottle he's carrying presses up against my back.

"I didn't order yet." I take the bottle from him. "I wanted to wait until you got here."

"I'm told Riesling goes well with Thai food," he says, removing his jacket.

I phone in our order and we move to the living room. Lucy jumps up on the couch and rubs up against Adam's leg, purring. The contrast with her fight or flight response whenever Steve was over, is astonishing.

"We could start a movie now or wait until the food gets here. Have you seen the new Matt Damon movie yet?"

"No, but let's wait." Adam settles back on my couch and takes in a deep breath. "I mean it when I say I missed you." His questions start out light. "How's your pro bono going? How do you usually spend Christmas and Hanukkah?" I can tell he's in the mood to talk. He's still learning who I am, who I've become since our childhood days. Then he segues to what's really on his mind and his questions shift in a more serious direction. He's bent on learning more about my last relationship as though he wants to safeguard his heart. He wants to know if his timing is fail-safe or if it's too soon. Except for Thanksgiving, we've been together every weekend since we met, and our feelings for one another continue to grow.

He finally comes out with what I'm sure he's wanted to know for some time. "Remind me again, how long you were in your last relationship?"

I give it to him straight. "It was ten months."

Adam takes a drink from his glass of wine and gazes into my eyes. "What happened? Why did you end it with him?"

"I . . . " I want to say I didn't love him, but in truth, I didn't even like him. "Steve was not a very nice person. And he also drank a lot, which made him meaner."

"Was he aggressive? He didn't hurt you, did he?"

"No." *But he sure came close a couple of times.*

It's out there now. Except for the ugly parts. He doesn't need to know I still harbor suspicions Steve might be stalking me. I have no proof really, only a strong feeling. I wish I knew what Adam was thinking.

The sound of Pachelbel's Canon tune goes off on my end table and I retrieve my cell phone to answer it. It's Sam at the security gate. "Our food's here."

I watch Adam as he ponders everything I've said, giving him room. I don't know how he feels about all this. Lucy leaps onto the coffee table and I lift her up into my lap. *Why couldn't I have met you a year ago? You would have saved me from myself.*

Adam doesn't want to get hurt, and I don't want him to get hurt either. I feel it coming. The hesitation . . . the mistrust. I wouldn't blame him. It's a lot.

I lean back and exhale the breath I was holding. I want to ease his concerns. "Adam." I look steady into his eyes. I'm falling in love with his eyes – dancing, tender brown eyes under dark lashes. But I'm seeing more than just the color of them. I see intelligence and a sharp wit. "It's okay," I say. "We're just friends for now. That's all this needs to be."

My doorbell rings letting me know our take-out food has been left at my front door. I start to get up as Lucy leaps to the floor, but Adam tugs me back down. "Come here." He cups my face and looks into my eyes. He kisses my forehead, his lips gliding over my lids, my cheekbones. He does it with such tenderness I feel my eyes well up with tears. Then he takes me in his arms and holds me to him. When he pulls back to look at me, he says softly, "You must realize it's far too late for that." And then his lips meet mine.

CHAPTER 12

"Happy Birthday," we all cry out. I join Lynne inside Teagan's office. We're not only celebrating Teagan's birthday but on Saturday, a few of us are getting together for lunch for our annual Secret Santa event. The end-of-the-year holiday bashes are just getting started.

Carol leans over Teagan's desk as she slips a big lavender envelope into her hand. Teagan rips it open and Carol says, "Out loud. You have to read it out loud."

Teagan reads: "*It's your birthday, and I think it's great we're friends who can grow old together.*" She opens the card: "*You go first.*"

She chuckles. "I think I'm older than you by a couple years, so I guess that gives me a strong head start."

"How old are you?" Carol, the gossip wants to know.

"Don't you dare tell her," Lynne says, returning with small paper plates in her hand. "There's a Chinese proverb that says a woman who tells her age is either too young to have anything to lose or too old to have anything to gain. So, I figure you fall somewhere in between and it's no one's damn business."

Teagan shrugs it off. "Thirty-two."

"Go on, read mine." I urge, moving it along.

Teagan slides her finger under the envelope flap and pulls out a card with a cartoon of a woman lounging in a chair and drinking a cup of coffee. She reads out loud: "*A good friend knows how you take your coffee.*" Then she opens up the card. "*A great friend will add booze.*" She breaks into a broad grin. "Good one."

Just then, Lisa strides into Teagan's office and we all stop what we're doing. The effect she has on us astounds me. She's wearing a tailored, black tweed skirt suit and sporting a new, blunt haircut that makes her hair look blonder and has that just-stepped-out-of-the-salon look. She's so well put together, it makes some of the women feel self-conscious. Immediately, I tally up the cost: haircut, color, and style $200; designer suit – Armani, Claiborne, Klein? – $400, maybe $500; shoes by Luca Valentini, $150.

"I need an accounts receivable report for a client," Lisa says. She surveys the office. "Am I interrupting something?"

"It's Teagan's birthday," Carol says.

"Help yourself to a brownie," Teagan says.

"No thanks. The client's Hartshorne. Jeff needs it before noon. On second thought," Lisa says, "maybe I'll take one over to Jeff since I'm headed there now." She puts a brownie on a paper plate and pirouettes on her four-inch-heeled pump. "Oh, happy birthday," she says over her shoulder.

Lynne raises her eyebrows and makes a humph sound. "Off she goes, indulging Jeffrey."

Teagan hums softly. "She looks like someone who feels like a million bucks."

Hmmm, more like a grand.

I still remember my impression of Lisa on her first day. She'd worked for another law firm before coming to Bender & Simpson. I had just been with the firm for a couple of months. Riding the elevator with me and Lynne on her first morning, a leather attaché case in one hand and a Louis Vuitton bag over her other shoulder, she said to Lynne using her most professional-sounding voice, "Good morning. Do you know if Alan's in yet?"

Lynne gave her a slow, I'll-humor-you-just-this-once smile. "*Mister* Bender usually gets in around eight, but he doesn't like to be bothered until after nine or ten. Since you and he seem to be on a first-name basis, perhaps he'll make an exception." The sarcasm was unmistakable. I had to stifle a laugh that Lisa had managed to get on Lynne's bad side on her first day.

"I don't understand her attraction," Lynne says.

"To Jeff?" I ask, puzzled. At fifty, Jeff Simpson is one of the leading product liability trial lawyers in New Jersey. He married into wealth but also made it in his own right. Aside from being one of New Jersey's super-lawyers, he's the best-dressed male at the firm. "What's not to find attractive?"

"I wasn't talking about Jeff. That's not hard to figure. Though he is married, so there *is* that."

I have a personal prejudice against women who break up families, having lived through it with my father and Eve. My twenty-eight-year-old self has rationalized it, now that Dad and Eve have been married for fifteen years. But my thirteen-year-old self may never let it go. Still, I judge Lisa no different than I do Jeff.

"Lisa's not looking to be his wife." Carol reminds Lynne. "Just his equity partner."

"That's the attraction I'm talking about," Lynne says. "If someone told me I'd have to work harder, bring in more clients, collect the cash, and no longer have a life, I'd say, 'no thanks', but everyone's different. Don't get me wrong. I realize it's a status thing and some perks go along with becoming a partner. Even so, is it worth it?"

"It is when you're married to your job," Teagan says.

We start breaking up and Carol reminds us not to forget our Secret Santa gifts tomorrow. "By the way, I have an idea how we can add more zing to the game." She gives us a mischievous twinkle. "This one's called Dirty Santa."

"However do you come up with them?" Lynne says.

"I'm full of good ideas," Carol brags.

I look at Lynne and then at Teagan. "Did she just say she's full of it?"

·   ·   ·

"Did you know couples without children are more likely to divorce?"

I glance over at Teagan for a fleeting moment, my hands clutching the steering wheel as I drive us to Luigi's Restaurant for our end-of-the year lunch gathering.

"Did you know couples where one partner's unfaithful to the other are more likely to divorce?" I say impassively, staring straight ahead at the road in front of us. "Shall I give you some more reasons?"

"No, seriously," Teagan says. "I'm not making this up. I'm quoting from actual studies. The absence of children in a marriage is a common cause of divorce."

"What about the stress the presence of children can bring into a marriage?" I ask, playing devil's advocate. "Did you look up the study on that one?"

Teagan laughs. "Okay. I appreciate what you're doing. But—"

"But nothing. They may be cold, hard facts, but what it comes down to is whether or not the two people in the marriage want to throw it all away. Marriages go through all kinds of changes and disappointments. It's how couples deal with the stress and changes that can make the difference."

"I didn't know you were such an advocate for staying married," Teagan says, drumming her fingers on the wrapped present in her lap.

"I'm not for staying together if it's no longer working. Believe me. I lived with parents who couldn't stand to be in the same room together. But we're not talking about just any marriage here. It's you and Mike we're talking about. I know you. And I know Mike. You're crazy about each other."

"What if it's not enough?"

I realize it's going to take some doing to get her out of this somber mood. "It oughta be everything," I say. I want it to be true. Maybe Lynne's right. Maybe I *am* a hopeless romantic deep down.

I turn right onto the next street. The houses along the way are bedecked with Christmas wreaths and front lawn holiday scenes. Everything looks serene on the outside, but behind the exteriors are people with unrealized hopes and expectations of their own. All of us are just trying to live the best way we know how. And a little luck never hurts. Though the winter so far has been mild, the inevitable cold, gray days are sure to come.

We ride in silence until I slow the car to a stop at an intersection. I put my hand on Teagan's arm. "Don't do anything hasty. You can always get a divorce if that's what you want, but you might not always be able to save your marriage."

"We hardly have sex anymore," Teagan blurts out. "Lovemaking has turned into the business of baby-making."

My heart aches for Teagan. I let her talk it out.

"The stress of our barren marriage changed us both. Mike's refocusing all his energy on his family hardware store. He's putting in ridiculous hours. Hours that don't translate into more money for us. It's just more time away from me."

Teagan's marriage has been stuck in winter for some time.

A narrow bend in the road causes me to hit the brakes, slowing my car down. In my rearview mirror, I notice a police cruiser following two car lengths behind and I squint to get a better look, worried it might be Steve.

Coming out of the turn, I look out my window and glimpse the driver. Steve grins back at me – a look of spiteful vengeance – as my stomach does a flip. I might as well be on the Kingda Ka roller coaster ride. I take in a breath. *Don't let him mess with your head. That's what he wants.* Steve's wrath causes me concern, making me think about Shaquana, the battered woman, who lived in fear for her life every day.

"Sorry. I just need to vent," Teagan says.

"What? Oh. That's okay," I say, tuning her back in.

Luigi's Restaurant is coming up, and I put on my right blinker and slow down before turning into the parking lot. Steve's police car speeds past.

"I always get weirded out around my birthday," Teagan says.

"I get it." *Listen to me giving relationship advice. With my self-perpetuating pathology of meaningless, reckless relationships, I'm not exactly the person to emulate. And now, with Steve, it's coming home to roost. My recklessness went a little too far with him.*

"Thanks again for being my designated driver."

"Of course," I say, finding a parking spot. I'll need an early drink to calm my nerves though. *I wish I had never met Steve.*

I grab my gift bag and we head over to the restaurant's entrance.

"I can't believe I picked your name for the grab bag gift," Teagan says. "What do you get the woman who has everything?"

Everything does not equal happiness.

"I got you two dating books – *The Dating Charade* and *I Had a Nice Time and Other Lies.*"

"Now you've ruined my surprise," I say. "It sounds like I could have written the second one. You know Carol's changing the game rules though, right?"

*   *   *

"Can we have another margarita over here?" I call out to the waitress.

"Are you trying to get me drunk?" Teagan says.

"I got your back."

"When's the last time you got wasted?" Carol asks Teagan.

"On my twenty-first birthday," she says with a livelier timbre than on the ride here. "It was at that martini bar on 46. Everyone was buying me drinks. My girlfriend's boyfriend had to carry me out to the car."

"I'm picturing you thrown over a guy's shoulder and being carried out of a bar drunk. Now that's funny," I say.

"Speaking of boyfriends," Carol says, twirling a springy strand, "maybe it's a wild guess, but I think Joe's getting me an engagement ring for Christmas." Her finger lets go of her hair, leaving a coiled lock where she played with it.

"You're getting engaged?" Lynne says.

"We were shopping at the Short Hills Mall for Christmas presents when Joe stopped us in front of a jewelry shop. Normally, I'm the one who steers us there. Joe looked inside the glass display and pretended to be interested in a necklace. Outa nowhere he asks me if I know the four gemological characteristics of a diamond. I was stunned. Before I could even answer him, he said, 'carat, clarity, color and cut.'"

"Holy shit," Rachel says. "That's definitely suspect."

"Joe's a great guy," Lynne says. "How long have you two been together now?"

"Three years, four months, seven days . . . my mother thinks if a guy's in his thirties and hasn't proposed to you in a year, it's time to get out."

"You told me even your dog likes Joe. That has to count for something," Rachel says.

"Animals are instinc—" A sudden hiccup interrupts Teagan. "Instink-chew-al."

"By my mother's account, I should have left Joe two years ago," Carol says.

"That's fourteen in dog years," Teagan says, her words slurred.

"I think someone's carrying Teagan out of here today," Lynne says.

"You know," Carol starts, "I used to think the odds were good for finding a husband at Bender & Simpson. Until I realized the goods were odd."

We all break out laughing.

"This calls for a toast," Lynne says.

Carol puts out her stop hand. "I don't want to jinx it."

"How about . . . to diamond ring shopping and the 4 C's," I say.

"I'll drink to that," she gushes.

I clink my water glass with theirs and we down our drinks in synchrony.

"By the way, Suellen," Carol says, "You remember Dave – the guy who sings in Joe's band? He's taken an interest in you. Now that you're free and all."

I start to say "No, thanks" but Teagan jumps in with, "He's already too late."

Oh shit.

Everyone's eyes turn toward me. I turn my gaze to the striking red poinsettia plants lined up on a long picture window ledge.

"You move on faster than anyone I know," Carol says. "So who's your next mark?"

Swigging my water that I wish wasn't, I roll my eyes. "You already know too much."

"You go, girl," Lynne shouts.

"Wait a minute. Is it that guy from Todd's farewell party, the one you left with?"

"*That* guy happens to be an old friend from my grammar school."

"Well, he sure ain't in grammar school no more." Rachel gives Carol a high-five.

"You can give me all the details at lunch on Monday," Carol says, her hungry-for-more expression igniting her face.

If I wasn't the designated driver, this would be a perfect time to order a drink.

•   •   •

I sit next to Edwina inside Judge Montalvo's courtroom on the eighth floor of the Essex County Courthouse awaiting the sentencing phase of Shaquana Evans' criminal trial. The courtroom is more than half full. Some of Shaquana's family members are also here. Edwina tells me she doesn't see anyone from the victim's family. The Public Defender reads his family's Victim Impact Statement into the record, which basically says that if Shaquana had not killed her husband, he most certainly would have killed her eventually. "Not even his family is sorry he's gone," Edwina says in a low voice.

I wanted to be here. I'm invested in this one. I guess this is what they mean by 'working from the heart.'

"How's Destiny?" I say to Edwina. During the Thanksgiving break, I had dropped off the birthday toys I'd bought on Shaquana's behalf. I might have gone a little crazy. Art supply kits with colored pencils and crayons, drawing pads, rock and shell paint sets, puzzles and books, mermaid bracelet-making kits, and a unicorn necklace. I remembered the young boy who was at Edwina's house and picked up some toys and games for him as well. Then I had them all wrapped up with glitter paper and decorative bows.

"Playing with her new things," Edwina says with an appreciative nod.

The public defender and prosecutor have made their arguments for an appropriate sentence based on the seriousness of Shaquana's crime. Now it's in the judge's hands. Shaquana's guilty plea bargain should assure her a lesser sentence. Shaquana stands to face her punishment. It's as somber as it is tense in the courtroom now. I swear I can hear my heart beating.

The judge addresses her. "Shaquana Evans, you have pled guilty to aggravated manslaughter. Under the plea bargain, the lowest term of imprisonment I can give you is ten years, three to be served without parole. Is there anything you want to say before the court imposes sentence?"

"Yes, Judge, Your Honor, I just wanna say, 'I was the one who was aggravated!'"

The courtroom erupts in riotous laughter. "Let's have order, please." The judge tries to gain back control of his courtroom, pounding his gavel, but even he can't hide a slight smile.

I squeeze Edwina's hand. "With good behavior, work credits and time served, she should be out in less than three years," I tell her.

The overwhelming empathy for her situation is heartwarming.

Adrenaline waning, heart slowing, I wonder, after being immersed in this criminal case, how I'll ever be able to go back to the other cases I'm handling with the same amount of zeal. I'm on such a high. I text Adam the news and then shoot off a group text to my lunch ladies.

Me

What do you say we go out for lunch today? I'm in a really good mood. (I know. Rare for me.) Lunch and drinks are on me.

CHAPTER 13

I'm standing with Lynne by a window wall that overlooks the banquet hall's expansive grounds. A manicured lawn dusted with snow is adorned with statues and fountains and brick walkways. Big evergreen trees are all lit up with white lights. The end-of-the-year office holiday party is underway. A waitress comes over with a plate of croissants topped with bruschetta. "I love these little things," I say.

"And there she goes," Lynne drones, looking past me.

"Who?" I follow her gaze across the large hall to where Lisa is crossing over to the bar. She's not dressed in one of her classic designer suits. Today she's a vision in red – a long, flattering wrap skirt with a side front opening and cashmere sweater, a Burberry purse hanging on her shoulder. "Mr. Bender still has no idea about her and Jeff?"

"If he does, he hasn't let on." Lynne takes a sip of her drink, leaning slightly, her shoulders aligned below a graceful neck. Her face shows little signs of her true age. She isn't wearing her eyeglasses, and I can see speckles of amber light in her brown eyes, giving off a warm glow.

"You look really nice today," I say. "You've done something different with your hair."

"Do you like the highlights? I was in the mood for a change."

"I like it a lot." I cock my head. "When are you going to tell me about him?"

Lynne opens her mouth as if she's about to act surprised and then shuts it. "Is it obvious?"

"You seem happy."

"There's not much to tell. A lonely girl meets a lonely guy, and as they say in Hollywood, 'and now a word from our sponsor.'"

"How long?" I ask. Lynne doesn't get to minimize it. This is huge for her.

"We're three dates in. A record for me. Tomorrow he's taking me into the City. Some shopping and dinner, then over to Rockefeller Center to see the tree. It will be the longest time we've spent together." I can see the panic setting in on Lynne's face.

"No quick escapes you mean."

"I haven't been with a man in over five years. I'm a little rusty."

"You're not rusty. The Tin Man's rusty."

Lynne laughs. "Suellen, if I had had a daughter at the age of sixteen, I'd want her to be you."

Now I laugh.

A text comes in on my phone from Adam. It's a line from the classic movie, *As Good As It Gets*.

Adam

"You make me want to be a better man." Can't wait 'til tomorrow.

My heart flutters.

"Was that a text from him?" Lynne says.

"Yeah. We're both movie buffs. Now and then he throws out one-liners from movies we like."

Adam's office holiday party is today too. I won't see him until tomorrow, and I'm counting the seconds until then. We never made it to the Museum of Natural History. In fact, we never left my townhouse. Pad Thai and Tom Yum grew cold outside my front door. The last thing I said to him was, "'How hungry are you?'" He answered with a grin and we fell onto each other. Food was the furthest thing from our minds that weekend.

Teagan and Carol spot Lynne and me and work their way over. We take turns complementing one another on how nice everyone looks and then Carol says, "I can't believe it's been a whole year already."

A new year, a new beginning, with someone I'm falling hard for. I can't believe I could be falling in love.

•   •   •

Plates filled with desserts cover our table. Assorted cookies with sprinkles and icing, miniature pastries, and chocolate-covered strawberries. We pass them around to share.

"Has anyone seen Lisa?" Carol says.

"I think she left the party with Jeff," Teagan says.

Carol rolls her eyes. "Jeff looked pretty wasted."

"You mean more than in previous years?" I take a sip of my coffee.

Teagan cuts a kiwi tart in half. "Have half of this with me, won't you?" She pushes the plate nearer to me.

"Okay. But then I do have to be on my way. I want to pick up some groceries for tomorrow before it gets too late."

Carol looks down at a plate of finger desserts as if something's missing. "I didn't get any truffles."

"You're going to have a great time tomorrow," I whisper in Lynne's ear while Carol goes off looking for truffles, keeping her out of the loop for now. "It's going to be a good day." Lynne gives me a thankful smile. "Carpe diem, Lynne. Seize the day."

"What are we seizing?" Carol has returned.

"Season," I say. "We were talking about the holiday season and all the shopping we've yet to do. Speaking of which, I'm off to do just that."

Lynne shoots me a grin. "See you on Monday."

The unattended coat room is dim. I enter it and think I misplaced my coat because it isn't where I thought it was. As I rummage through the coats on the rack, I hear a moaning sound coming from the back of the room. My eyes are trying to adjust to the dim light. In the farthest corner, it looks like there's a tumble of clothes lying on the floor moving. I can make out a man's dark suit jacket, a Bruno Magli dress loafer, and a Burberry handbag on its side. It looks like Lisa's handbag. Jeff wears those designer loafers. A gasp escapes my throat. My brain already registers what my eyes can't believe. Right there on the coat room's carpeted floor, Lisa and Jeff are going at it like two high school kids whose parents aren't home.

Unable to move, I stand there staring, my mouth agape. I'm slightly horrified, but I can't seem to tear my eyes away. I fling myself between the coats, hiding between wool and leather. I'm so embarrassed. For me, for them. I start to plan my escape when the matter of my coat stops me. I convince myself I have more right to be here than they do. Jeff and Lisa are the ones getting laid in the coatroom. All I did was hang up my coat.

I want to go home. I need my coat. I flip through the coats until I find the dark blue wool that must be mine. I yank it off the hanger just as Lisa turns her head sideways, and our eyes meet for a split second. I dart from the coatroom and race to find my car.

Driving to the grocery store, I can't stop thinking how I just witnessed Lisa screwing her way to the top right before my eyes. As I turn the steering wheel to exit the restaurant parking lot, I turn on my radio, hoping to erase the visual of Lisa and Jeff from my mind. An itch in my left breast persists. I open my coat and slide my hand under my bra, rubbing out the itch. The pea-sized lump is still there. I think I feel it move under my fingertips. That's what I tell myself. A year ago I had one aspirated, but was grateful it was benign. Time to make that doctor's appointment I've been putting off. A resistant tug pulls under my arm and I look down my coat sleeve, realizing the shortness of it.

"Oh no," I shout, slapping the steering wheel. *This is not my coat!*

CHAPTER 14

Lisa's gait is confident, her eyes unwavering as I pass by her on my way to Mr. Bender's office. Everything about her exudes haughtiness. I thought she wouldn't be able to face me today, but she looks more self-assured than ever.

I happen to know the first partner's meeting of the new year is coming up. A vote will be taken to decide who should be invited to become the next partner of the firm. I wouldn't be surprised if Lisa has already ordered the new stationery with her name under the partners' column. I reach Mr. Bender's office threshold and give a light tap on the open door. He nods for me to come in. I take a seat across from him, pull out my notes folder from the Rojas file, and wait.

"Andrew will be joining us," he says, clearing his throat. "I want you to fill me in on the Rojas case, and I want him here too."

Andrew's the paralegal assigned to this case because he's handled similar birth injury cases for the firm. We work well together.

Mr. Bender checks his watch. Andrew's four minutes late. I realize I'm bouncing my knee up and down. Although he doesn't raise his voice, Mr. Bender has a way about him, an authority that makes everyone at the firm toe the line. Just as I think about ways to distract him, as if I could, Andrew screeches to a stop at the doorway. He enters Mr. Bender's office, head lowered, and emits one long breath. "Sorry."

Mr. Bender folds his hands over the papers on his desk. "What stage are we at now, Suellen?"

"I think the Rojas case is ready to be put into suit," I say.

"What are the long-term deficits?"

"Our male toddler client's brachial plexus nerves were ruptured I believe during birth. The nerves in his right hand and arm were severely affected, resulting in Erb's Palsy. He has no muscle control in them. The injuries are devastating."

"What evidence do you have that the doctor was negligent and that negligence was the proximate cause of that baby's injuries?"

"All the research I've conducted so far points to a series of wrong decisions made by the doctor who did the delivery. I've had a telephone conference with Dr. Litchfield, our medical expert, who will have his written report for us within a few weeks. Basically, he said that an infant of Carlos' large size was a high risk, and a planned cesarean section may have been reasonable in his case."

"I'm already drafting the pleadings," Andrew says.

"When we have Dr. Litchfield's findings in our hands, the papers will be ready to go," I say.

"Our instincts were right then," Mr. Bender says.

"I felt it in my gut," I say.

Mr. Bender's intercom buzzes and he presses the button. "Yes, Lynne?"

"Mrs. Rojas and her son have arrived," Lynne announces.

"You can send them in."

•　　•　　•

Carlos Rojas shows all the signs of an independent, active toddler. When Nydia Rojas lifts her son up onto her lap, the dark curly-haired boy squirms to get down and scrambles off to survey Mr. Bender's roomy office. When Nydia starts to go after him, Mr. Bender tells her to let him roam. She sits back down on the leather couch.

We watch him as he totters about the office, his balance and step unremarkable for a child his age. He's a happy boy. Except for the arm that hangs limp by his side, he's a normal, curious little boy who has no inkling he has suffered an impairment that will affect the rest of his life.

"Can he have a cookie?" Mr. Bender asks his mom.

She nods and I volunteer to go get it from the nearest pantry. When I return, Mr. Bender is explaining to Nydia that her son's case is ready to be put into suit but that it will be quite some time before they see the inside of a courtroom. "As you can see from the various clippings, we're not afraid to try cases here." He points behind him to the wall of testimonies showing that the firm has obtained multiple verdicts over millions of dollars.

Carlos starts to lose his balance, swaying back and forth a few times before falling to his bottom. He does not look to his mother for support. Instead, he rolls over onto his side and grabs onto a nearby chair with his good hand. While he pulls himself up, the limp arm does nothing to help.

"I don't baby him," Nydia says. "The therapist said he has to learn to compensate."

Lynne sees Nydia and her son out while Andrew and I remain so Mr. Bender can give us some final notes and observations.

Jeff Simpson pokes his carefully groomed head inside Mr. Bender's doorway. "Oh. I see you're busy. Hello, Suellen . . . Andrew," he says looking at us and giving a nod. "I can come back," Jeff says to Mr. Bender. "I just wanted to tell you I've postponed the Glatzer depositions scheduled for Thursday. I'll be leaving for San Antonio."

Mr. Bender looks up from his papers and removes his reading glasses from his face, his curiosity piqued, it seems to me.

Jeff comes inside the office and drops something on Mr. Bender's desk. "Take a look at this report," he says. "The finding on the brakes is significant. SUV rollovers aren't the only thing they have to worry about. It appears the dual exhaust pipes in some of these models were rubbing against the brake lines."

Mr. Bender lets go of the article in his hand. "Causing the brakes to leak fluid—"

"Increasing the risk of a crash," Jeff says, finishing Mr. Bender's thought. He slides his hand inside the pocket of a beautifully-tailored, pin-stripe suit and beams a litigious expression. "That would explain the severe shimmying and shuddering during braking. I'm going to view the assembly plant and then add a couple of days for R and R."

Jeff oversees the firm's product liability cases, which explains Lisa's relatively recent involvement in them. I suspect she will be going along as well and not only for the business portion of the trip, though Jeff doesn't say it, of course.

"Will Rebecca be joining you?" Mr. Bender's poker face leans in but the spine stays straight.

"No," Jeff says. "The women's luncheon to raise money for the Maureen Fund is that weekend."

"Ah, yes," Mr. Bender says cupping his chin in his large, lean hand. "I'd forgotten. My wife plans to attend. She told me Rebecca's chairing it."

"Yes, her schedule's even busier than mine."

Mr. Bender's disciplined lawyer's face reveals nothing. "Be sure to thank Rebecca for the wine gift basket," he says. "That Chardonnay happens to be my wife's favorite." The wiser, judicious man looks at his much younger, stealthier partner for a few moments. "We should all do dinner sometime soon."

"Yes, I'll have Carol check our schedules," Jeff says, choosing his words carefully, his reckless alter-ego hiding behind a polished persona.

I've never been very good at putting on a poker face. I turn away and stare out the window instead.

•　　•　　•

"Mind if I chew your ear off?" I pause at the threshold of Teagan's office.

"What's up?" Teagan says.

"Just that the annual attorney dinner meeting is this Friday night. That's all."

"Where to this year?" Teagan says.

"Mr. Bender's country club again."

"You get to wine and dine in elegance. What could be so wrong with that?"

"Do you want to go in my place?"

"I would but I don't have an ESQ at the end of my name. Whatever do you lawyers talk about at those things anyway?"

"The usual boring stuff such as retainers, hourly rates for partners, associates and paralegals, policies for the new year. Mostly, it's a drinking party." She sees me pout, looking frustrated.

"So why the face?"

"It's not fair they have this thing on a Friday night. I could be spending it with Adam."

Teagan's desk phone rings. "Hi, Lynne," she says, putting the call on speakerphone.

"Did you hear today's forecast?" Lynne says. "You'd never know it was January. I'm telling you, I'm all for global warming. Maybe we can eat outside under the pergola. I left a message on Suellen's phone too."

"Suellen's in here with me right now," Teagan says.

I pick up a crystal paperweight on Teagan's desk, turning it around so I can read it. *Be true to your work, your word, and your friends.*

"Talk it over and let me know. Gotta go. My other line's ringing," Lynne says.

I put the paperweight back down on a mound of papers on Teagan's desk. "I like what that says," I say, my annoyance momentarily mellowing. "The problem is, I can't even cut out of the dinner early," I say. "We're expected to stay the entire four hours. Oh, the injustice."

"I'm sure there are others who feel like you do." Teagan taps her desktop with a pen. "Look, you're part of an elite club around here. Guess you'll just have to suck it up."

I cast my typical look-to-the-heaven frown. "I don't have much choice, do I?" I say, already walking out and taking purposeful steps in my Prada boots.

After grabbing water from the pantry room down the hall, I head back to my office. I know by the time Friday evening rolls around and after I get a couple drinks in me, I won't even care. I'll be sure to Uber to and from the place. It's not so much about my displeasure as it is about getting it off my chest, and that's where my best listener friend comes in.

When I reach my office, Teagan's there, her face cringing as she leans over my desk, staring at my monitor. Looking frantic, she slides out my keyboard shelf.

"Teagan?"

She screams.

"Are you looking for something?"

She raises her shoulders in a timid shrug. "You scared me. Y-yeah. Your lawyer's diary."

"Well, you're looking for it in the wrong place." I reach across my desk to the cabinet overhead and pull the big, red-bound book from the shelf. "Here you go."

Teagan's focus is still on my monitor as she reaches for the mouse. Then I see it. Smack in the center of the screen is a personal interoffice message glaring at me like a neon sign in the middle of Times Square.

EVER FEEL LIKE SCREAMING? SUELLEN WAS JUST IN HERE THROWING ANOTHER ONE OF HER HISSY FITS. THIS TIME IT WAS ABOUT HAVING TO ATTEND THE LAWYERS' DINNER FRIDAY EVENING. WHAT WOULD A GIRL WHO'S THAT WELL-OFF EVEN KNOW ABOUT UNFAIRNESS?

I reel back in shock as a crazed Teagan uses the mouse to delete the message that was up on my screen. With my head tilted sideways, I look into Teagan's eyes, her look of deep regret meeting my confused one. An instant of reckoning freezes me in my spot. We use popup messages in our office when communicating a quick note to the intended recipient. But I wasn't her intended recipient. I was the subject. I'm speechless.

A mouse cursor hasn't been invented yet that can zap away the hurt and shock I feel.

•   •   •

"You're not joining us downstairs for lunch, why?" Lynne pokes her head inside my office.

"I'd rather not say. Let's leave it at that."

"Okay. Look. Teagan told me what happened, and she feels terrible. Try to let it roll off you. You know better than any of us the stress she's been under. Good friends don't let one infraction get between them."

I pull a face and shrug. "Obviously, I've been a complete burden to her."

"Suellen, you can be so stubborn sometimes. I mean, what's the big deal? There are worse things than being called a compulsive complainer, which everyone knows you are." Lynne laughs at her weak attempt at humoring me. "She could have called you a pain in the ass. Look, I know it was wrong of her. She messed up."

I don't look at her, preferring to talk to the Shop-Til-You-Drop statuette on the edge of my desk. I feel wounded and right about now I'm thinking I could use some retail therapy. "I'm leaving work early today for an appointment anyway," I say to Lynne. "I know you're trying to be helpful, but I just can't right now. Sorry," I say, putting an end to it.

"We'll miss you."

I lean back in my chair and cross my arms in a show of resolve. Lynne lets out a frustrated breath and walks off, shaking her head.

I'm taking work home with me again today since I'm cutting out early. Dr. O'Connor ordered a screening mammogram and ultrasound for me. He thinks the lump in my breast may be a fibroadenoma and not a cyst, which would need to be excised.

I push my medical appointment aside so I can think about something I'd much rather think about. I'll be seeing Adam again on Saturday night. He's become my refuge, my safe place. I like who I am whenever I'm with him. He doesn't judge or criticize. He sees the best in me. Sometimes I wonder, when doubt rears itself, if he's even seeing me at all.

Why does it matter to me now when I never seemed to care before?

CHAPTER 15

I'm able to let go all the small stuff when I'm with Adam. And the worrying stuff. Being with him helps take my mind off my inconclusive mammogram results. A biopsy procedure is being scheduled. It isn't my first, but it's always unnerving.

With my Steve feelers still up, I choose an Indian restaurant for dinner in a cultural hub a few towns over. "You're going to love it," I promise.

Adam laughs. "You're talking to a meat and potatoes guy."

"Seriously? We're going to have to do something about that."

"Others have tried and failed." His eyes sparkle with amusement.

"I need to know what I'm working with here. Tell me, what's the most adventurous food you've ever eaten?"

"That's easy. Fried rattlesnake. Down in Texas."

"First, ewwww! And second, what were you doing down in Texas?" I find myself wanting to learn everything I can about Adam.

"I went on a month-long cross-country road trip with a couple of guys in between college and law school."

"That must have been cool. You're not opposed to adventure then."

"Life adventures, no. On foodstuff . . . the jury's still out on that one."

"You'll just have to put your complete trust in me then," I say. "I won't kill you. I swear."

"It can't be too bad if I'm sharing a meal with you. I wouldn't mind going that way."

Warm lighting bounces off a crimson wall behind him as Adam's eyes glimmer with energy and lightheartedness.

Sitting in a sari-upholstered chair, he looks up from his menu and says, "I'm not seeing New York strip steak with baked potatoes anywhere here. Must be an oversight."

I order a fiery-hot south Indian seafood and coconut dish for myself. When the waiter looks toward Adam, he says with a wink to me, "I'll have what she's having."

I let go a snort, catching his meaning and then shake my head at the waiter. "No. Scratch that. He'll have the butter chicken."

"The lady doth protest too much." Adam turns to the waiter and nods. "What she said."

"The butter chicken's light on the heat. You can try mine too, but I want to go easy on you since this is your first time. Trust me. Okay?"

Adam reaches across the table and takes my hand, his face emanating warmth and tenderness in the restaurant's exotic atmosphere. "I trust you." He interlaces his fingers with mine, his dreamy eyes stirring things in all places of my body. "I love knowing you, who you are, what you love, what you hate. I want all of it."

"I have to warn you then, I can be somewhat complicated."

"I'm all in," he says, looking intrigued.

Could Adam be more adorable? It's hard not to jump out of my seat and kiss his face.

The scent of poignant cumin and cinnamon wafts from the kitchen as our waiter comes through the swinging door with our entrees.

"This is going to wow your taste buds." I watch in hopeful awe as Adam takes his first bite of authentic Indian food. His reaction comes slowly, cautiously. I wait for it.

Adam nods. "You know what? This *is* good."

"You're not just saying that?"

"No. I mean it."

I break a piece of naan and dip it into my curry sauce, passing it to him to taste. I feel such a strong desire to please him. Adam leans in closer, opening his mouth for me to slip it through. Eating with all our senses is intoxicating. The aromatic smells, the looks, and the feel of different textures. After our dessert of *gulab jamun*, a doughy ball made with flour and berries, Adam says, "There's only one thing that can surpass this." The glow in his eyes is hypnotic as he reaches under the table and strokes my thigh.

We're of like minds. Adam pays the tab and we grab our jackets.

•   •   •

It's an unseasonably mild January, so Adam leaves his jacket in his car while I carry mine inside my townhouse. We make a beeline for my bedroom as we shed our clothes. When I sit on the edge of the bed and start to unzip my ankle boots, Adam says with a smirk, "Leave those on."

Adam slides my black lace thong past the boots and lays me down, a sensual glint lighting his eyes. "God, you're beautiful," he says.

I am Brazilian waxed and ready as Adam draws my legs up by the heels of my boots, stimulating and teasing me until my back arches and I whimper, "Adam". Somehow, when he slides inside me, I know it's different. It's not sex for its own sake. It's deeper. He's making love to me, slowly and rhythmically, kissing and fondling and gazing. He spreads my arms out over my head and clutches my hands with his, eyes open, watching me watch him. *Those eyes of his.* I am every bit as into this as he is, discovering and pleasing him. Unlike loveless sex, what I'm feeling is transformative, and romantic. It startles and thrills me. My lids close over the emotional tears forming, and I'm transported by an intense surge of exquisite joy.

Feeling safe and warm, I curl up inside Adam's nakedness, when an elusive moment of happiness startles and frightens me. I remind myself I'm in the early stage of a new relationship, the safe period where I'm always at my finest. I'm awesome at beginnings. Until I end it. It's always me who ends it. Maybe this time, with Adam, everything will be different. It already feels different.

For once, there won't be any need to self-destruct.

· · ·

Adam

See you when I get back from D.C. Can't wait to find out what's next on your foodie bucket list.

Adam's text message warms my heart. He's leaving for a convention in DC and I already miss him. I let out a quiet sigh and hang my coat up on the back of my office door.

"I wish you and Teagan would just make up already." Carol's brisk entrance into my office makes me jump. It's not even nine o'clock in the morning yet.

"You guys are ruining lunch hour." Wearing an exaggerated disgruntled look on her face, she sits down in the chair across from my desk. "How much longer are you two going to keep this up?"

"I'm sorry," I say, taking my seat behind my desk. "But she betrayed our friendship. I can't just forget it."

"Teagan said you won't accept her apology." Carol plays with her new engagement ring with her thumb. "She knows she slipped-up, and now she thinks you wouldn't have lunch with her if she were the last person on earth. Is that true?"

"That's a bit of a stretch. I'm just not ready yet." The itchiness around my breast's nipple returns. I should have kept lotion with me. I rub it with my arm.

"Teagan isn't coming down to lunch either, preferring to eat alone in her office. Our lunch group's dwindling." Carol places her hand to her throat, her two-carat solitaire ring catching the fluorescent light.

"Your diamond is blinding me," I say, changing the subject. "It's such a beautiful ring. Did I tell you how happy I am for you?"

"You did. Several times." Carol puckers her brows and wrinkles her forehead while she crosses her arms, and it dawns on me why she's in my office. What she misses. Our lunch hours' worth of talking and sharing and venting.

"So, tell me," I say, "How are the wedding plans coming along? Have you set a date yet?"

Carol's face softens. "I may go nuts before that day ever gets here. *If it ever gets here.* My future mother-in-law already gave me her invitation list – thirty more people than I planned for. When I asked Joe who Margery Glatz was, he said, 'Margery who?' Come to find out, Margery's a woman his mother met at her book club."

"I've never had a wedding, so I'm no expert, but you can't sweat the small stuff. Don't let the little things become a distraction from what's important. You and Joe love each other and are getting married. That's all that matters." *Did I just say that? Earth to Suellen.*

"I know. Of course, you're right. If only I could relax. I just want it to be perfect."

"That's your first problem right there. When does anything ever go smoothly one hundred percent? It's the unexpected things, the things you'll laugh about later, that will give it character." *I'm on a roll.* "When my brother got married," I say, "his best man got so drunk that by the end of the night, he was dancing on the head table, knocking over glassware, and getting his foot stuck in the floral centerpiece. It took three guys to get him off the table. It went from panicky to comical. The whole place broke out laughing. Except maybe for my dad's wife, Eve, who thought it was the most obnoxious thing she'd ever witnessed." My brother and I still laugh about it.

Carol chuckles just as Teagan arrives at the office and passes by my doorway. Hearing Carol's laughter, she glances inside, and for a fleeting second, our eyes meet and I can swear I see a glint of longing in them. That vanishes with a toss of her head as she continues down the hall to her office.

"Tell you what," I say. "Since you're taking me to my outpatient appointment Friday morning, let me treat you to a massage at my favorite spa. I'm going on Saturday. Come with me. Adam's in DC all weekend. What do you say?"

"A deep tissue body massage? The last time I had one was excruciating."

"It shouldn't have been. Your muscles might feel sore but that's to be expected. The therapists at my spa are terrific. They provide other services if you'd rather."

"I'll let you know," Carol says, and then she does a one-eighty. "Are you worried about the lump in your breast?"

"I experience fibrocystic breast changes all the time. It's usually worse right before my period. This one's not going away and needs to be excised. So I'm taking care of it."

"Good thing you're on top of it. I have to keep reminding myself to do self exams."

Rachel swings by my office, still wearing her coat. Seeing Carol with me, she steps halfway inside. "Did you say you weren't going to be in on Friday?" she asks Carol.

"Yeah. Why?" Carol says.

"One of my friends opened up a pizzeria. I thought we could go there for lunch and check it out. It's like ten minutes from here. You too, Suellen."

"I'm busy that day. Perhaps some other time."

"Oh. Right. I forgot you're having a minor procedure done that day." Rachel steps inside my office. "It's no biggie. I had the same thing done. I was home in under two hours. I can't even see the scar anymore."

I want to ask her if she was able to feel her lump move a little, if her breast ever got itchy, did she have a mammogram, and was it inconclusive, but she has already turned her attention back to Carol. "Put it on your calendar for the following Friday then."

"Consider it done," Carol says.

I push my chair away from the desk and stand up. "I need a coffee."

"I'll walk with you," Carol says as Rachel turns to leave us. "Sorry. I might have mentioned to Rachel why I was taking Friday off."

When did the word sorry become such a lame word? "It's fine. But are you sure you can do this? Eve and my dad won't be back from their chartered cruise yet or I'd ask one of them to drive me to my appointment. It's silly I can't drive myself. They won't even be putting me under, but its hospital protocol."

Carol and I walk out into the hallway, the hum of the early morning grind getting underway.

"Yes, I told you, I also have some other personal things to take care of later that day. Besides, you promised you'd take me bridal gown shopping in the city one of these days. There's no one I trust more to help me pick out a dress than you. It'll be like having my own personal shopper with me."

As Carol and I make our way over to the pantry, we notice Jeff Simpson's wife coming toward us. She carries a glass of water in one hand, and a winter white coat is draped over her other arm. She's dressed business casual in winter-white slacks and a navy cashmere pullover, an attractive contrast to her short-coiffed, dyed-blonde hair, but Rebecca Lieberman-Simpson's usual relaxed persona appears strained today. Though her steps are determined and steadfast, the stiff contour of her back looks unnatural to me.

Since most of the Lieberman family members are clients of the firm, there's no telling what new personal or corporate matter has arisen – a deal gone sour, a contract breached, a partnership split-up, another tax appeal. Even a sexual harassment case within one of the Lieberman-owned companies. It could be any number of things.

We want to say hello, but she walks past with quick strides and doesn't look interested in office cordiality. She heads straight toward her husband's office.

"Why is she here now, when Jeff isn't in the office?" Carol says. "He's at a breakfast meeting all morning."

"Does she know that?" I say to Carol.

"I guess not. I should go tell her."

Just then, our attention turns to Lisa who comes dashing down the hall in our direction all of a sudden, looking confident wearing a charcoal-gray tweed lawyer suit and puffed-up smile.

Lynne leans over a file cabinet in the hallway, her elbows propped on it. "Somebody's happy today."

"You would be, too, if you were about to make partner," Carol says under her breath.

Our eyes follow Lisa as she passes and then disappears around the corner that leads to Jeff's office. Then it hits me.

I cup my chin in my hand and look back at Lynne and Carol. "That's strange."

"What's strange?" Carol says.

"Jeff's not here. You said so yourself. And his wife is in his office now."

Lynne, Carol, and I stare at one another for a few seconds, our eyes doing all the communicating.

"Are you both thinking what I'm thinking?" Carol says.

"For a minute there, I was afraid you'd lost your touch," I say.

Behind Carol's eyes, her wheels are spinning. "Exactly *why is* Rebecca Simpson here when her husband isn't? I'd better get back to my desk. If something's going down, I want to be the first to hear it."

"And she's back," I say, turning to Lynne as we watch Carol recede. "Is Mr. Bender even in today?"

"No. He's attending a bar association breakfast." Lynne curls her hands around her coffee mug and faces me full-on. "You may want to reconsider doing lunch today. Something's brewing. And if anything's up, Cindy Adams will know."

I laugh at Lynne's reference to the famous New York gossip columnist. Carol's idol. My split-second answer surprises me. "Wouldn't miss it for the world."

CHAPTER 16

"I can't thank you enough for doing this, Lynne," I say. "Since Carol's mother pulled her back out yesterday, Carol's doing everything for her. She thinks her mother's going to need traction."

"Happy I could help," Lynne says. She pulls her car out of my condo parking lot and drives me to the outpatient facility where I'm scheduled for fibroid surgery.

"Really. I feel bad you got stuck doing this. The mall's not far from there. I could call you when I'm done."

"Thanks, but no thanks," Lynne says. "I don't want to go within fifty feet of a mall. I brought along Colleen Hoover's latest book. Don't worry about me. I'll be fine."

"Okay, but I'm treating you to lunch afterward."

"Fine," Lynne says. "So, when . . . how did you discover the lump in your breast?"

"I felt it during a shower. It seemed to have popped out overnight."

Lynne shakes off an impulsive shudder. "I'm due for a mammogram. I really do need to make an appointment." She lets out a sigh.

"I want to get this out of the way," I say.

"As you should," Lynne says. "You're taking care of it and that's what's important."

"I know." I gaze out the window at the winter sunlight endeavoring to warm up a bitter cold day. "Adam and I are making plans."

"What kind of plans?"

"Adam's away at a convention in DC and won't be back until Sunday night, but in a few weeks, he wants to come with me to Palm Beach to visit my mom. He's trying to talk me into an extra week for ourselves in Fort Lauderdale."

"Wow. Things are going *that* good, are they?" Lynne says, keeping her eyes on the road.

"Yeah. I'd say so. After my mother meets Adam, she'll be on a mission to get me married. I'm twenty-eight. It's all my mother talks about."

"You're so sure your mother will like Adam?"

"What's not to like? Adam's a good person. He's as passionate about helping people as my mother is about the environment. He not only donates his money, but he also gets involved. Ever hear of Habitat for Humanity?"

"Of course. Jimmy Carter."

"Well, Adam helps build houses for poor people."

"Wow. I'm impressed."

I let go of a little laugh. "I keep waiting for the alter-Adam to appear. But it seems he's a man with humanitarian principles and an all-around good guy. I'm still trying to get used to it."

"Well, *get* used to it," Lynne says.

"Sometimes we wind up in these deep conversations about things I don't usually think of. It's strange."

"Are you saying you'd rather go back to shallow Steve?"

"No way. It's just that, well, honestly, I got Steve. I don't always get Adam."

"Not necessarily a bad thing," Lynne says, grinning.

"You sure you and my mother never talked?"

"Don't have to. We belong to the same club."

"Speaking of mothers," I say, "I told Mom I'd phone her as soon as I was through but she may get anxious and call. Since I can't carry my cell phone, can you keep it with you?"

"Sure thing," Lynne says. "And what about your father?"

"Dad's still not home from his two-week cruise. He's returning on Sunday."

"So he doesn't even know?" Lynne says.

"No. Dr. O'Connor and my dad are old colleagues so it's as if I have two fathers anyway. Mom said she'd fly up but I didn't see any reason for her to do that. I've been through this before. And according to Rachel, there's nothing to it."

"You don't really like Rachel much, do you?" Lynne says with a sideways glance.

"Am I that transparent?"

"You were never good at hiding your true feelings."

"It always gets me into trouble."

"If you give Rachel half a chance, she's not so bad really."

I look straight at Lynne. "She's a miss-know-it-all. Doesn't it drive you crazy when she goes on and on about herself, always trying to outdo everyone?" I gaze back out the window. I wonder if we'll get more snow. Adam wants us to go skiing again.

"Look, all I'm saying is that while she may never be the kind of friend who you'll want to bare your soul to, a one-hour-lunch-sharing friend seems tolerable."

The mental picture of Adam and me frolicking in the snow shatters. "Huh?"

"I'm just saying it isn't so bad if she has lunch with us. It's just lunch."

"I'm warming up to her a little," I say, "if it's any consolation. Just don't expect us to be great friends any time soon."

Lynne chuckles. "Speaking of best friends, when are you and Teagan going to get around to making up?"

"I was wondering when you would bring that up. You are one cool cucumber, Lynne."

"Teagan's always been there for you. She's going through a stressful time. She's been so unhappy. Can't you let one little mistake slide? She seems to have a lot on her plate."

"I never knew she felt that way about me, that I've been such a *bother* to her all this time. She hurt me. She wasn't just any old friend. I trusted her."

"It was a mistake," Lynne says, concentrating on the road before her. "She was having a bad day and had to let off some steam. So she's not the 'perfect friend' every day of every week. Why does it matter? Who is?"

I tug a loose thread on my jeans. "How do I know she hasn't always felt that way about me? How do I know she hasn't been talking about me behind my back for years? And this time she happened to get caught? I can't get her words out of my head."

"You've never once gotten annoyed with her? You've never told anyone she did something that bothered you?"

"Well—"

"I thought so. The only difference is she put it in a quick message to me and you weren't supposed to see it. It's just like you telling someone about her and she isn't supposed to hear it. That's the problem with texts and emails," Lynne says.

"I'm trying," I say, being honest. *Besides, I do miss her.*

Lynne gives me a gentle nod. "Atta girl."

"Turn's coming up," I say. "Where do you want to go for lunch?"

"You decide. As long as it's not inside a mall."

•   •   •

"Just try and relax, Suellen," Dr. O'Connor says, patting my arm.

"I am relaxed," I say, thanks to Brahms and Valium. I close my eyes, allow myself to be transmitted to another place, far away from stark blue hospital gowns and cold stainless steel equipment and the metal table I'm lying on.

Adam and I are dressed in ski clothing after an exhilarating day on the slopes at the Mountain Creek Ski Resort on New Year's Eve. We're sitting in a chalet before a roaring fire, snow-white mountain views all around, sipping hot chocolate. Adam says something funny. I throw back my head and laugh, let my hair down under the ski cap, shaking it out. "Only a few more hours to go," he says, reaching for my hand. "It's going to be our year."

Except for a little tugging, I can't feel a thing since the area near the tumor was anesthetized. Right now the only things on my mind are: where Lynne and I should go for lunch and hoping the scar will be small.

"We're almost done here," Dr. O'Connor says to me.

"How will it look?" I say. "Will it leave a very big scar?"

"No. Just a small nick near the areola," Dr. O'Connor says. "It should heal nicely, barely noticeable."

"That's good," I say. In my mind, I've already left the hospital.

•   •   •

An hour later, I'm dressed and starting toward the waiting room to find Lynne. Dr. O'Connor stops me in the hallway. "Suellen," he says, "I need to talk to you."

"Everything okay?" I say.

"Come. Let's step inside this office," he says, pointing to the empty room.

Immediately, I'm alarmed. "Can I bring my friend with me?"

"Certainly," Dr. O'Connor says.

The mind is a funny thing. It can play all sorts of tricks when it needs to – imagine things that aren't there, refuse to let things in. Dr. O'Connor is talking, but his words overlap, getting all bunched up inside my head so that I have to force them apart with all my strength, separate them into types – the kind I want to hear, the kind I don't. These are the ones I don't – malignant, staging, metastases.

"Wait. Wait," I say, holding up the palm of my hand. "I don't understand. Are you telling me I have . . . that I might have cancer? Is that what I'm hearing?"

Dr. O'Connor half-sits, half-leans on the edge of the desk when he leans forward to put a hand on my shoulder. He looks straight into my eyes through thin wire-rimmed glasses. "Suellen, the frozen section showed some cancer cells."

"It has to be a mistake," I say. "I've had lumps before."

"This one's different." Dr. O'Connor says it with such finality, I recoil in distrust.

"Dad will be home tomorrow. No. What day is it today?" I look at Lynne for help. It's the first time I've looked at her since Dr. O'Connor ushered us into the room. Her head is cocked, her mouth open like a dazed sparrow, her eyes still registering shock. *Lynne, my rock.* "Lynne?"

"Friday," Lynne says, finding her voice. "It's Friday."

"Right," I say firmly. "Of course." I let out a strange laugh. "Dad's somewhere in the Bahamas or Turks and Caicos maybe. I forget. Anyway, he should be home in a couple of days," I say, looking back at Dr. O'Connor. "Sunday, I think. I want to go over this with him."

It's all too much for me to take in. I start to rise. "In the meantime, my friend and I have lunch plans."

Dr. O'Connor takes my hand in his and looks steadily into my eyes, the concentration so strong I'm unable to look away. "Suellen, you mustn't panic. There's no reason to. We're on top of this. Do you understand?"

Panic? Who's panicking? My friend and I are going to lunch.

"The treatment for cancer has improved tremendously in the past twenty years and the odds are better than ever. Early detection of breast cancer has a—"

"Cancer?" I mumble. I try to speak, but I have a feeling I can't trust my voice anymore. I will my voice to sound normal, and try to cover the quiver starting underneath. "I'm only twenty-eight."

Dr. O'Connor's face becomes softer, sympathy and kindness transforming it. "Suellen, call me if you have any questions." He scribbles something on a little white pad, rips off the page, and hands it to me. "Here's my cell phone number. You can call me if you need to. We'll need to do more tests, and I'll want to see you first thing Monday morning. We can talk some more then." Standing before Dr.

O'Connor, he wraps a fatherly arm around my shoulder. I find myself wishing he was greeting me at my dad's country club instead of consoling me as my doctor. "You're a strong, young woman. You're going to be fine."

"Of course. I know that," my alien voice says.

Lynne and I walk into the wide-open lobby. I can't suppress a strange laugh that startles Lynne. "You must want to kill me," I say.

"What?" Lynne says, puzzlement replacing the dazed look. "What are you talking about?"

"You took a personal day for this. I wouldn't blame you one bit for hating me."

Lynne stops in her tracks and turns toward me. "Stop it. You're my friend. I don't ever want to hear you talk like that. Do you hear me?" She pulls my cell phone from her purse and passes it to me. "Here. You should know this thing has been vibrating for the last hour."

"Oh! My mother. How do I tell her?"

My mind reels with the beginnings of what I will say to her. *'Mom, there were . . . there may be . . . the frozen section showed some . . . I have breast cancer.'* Thinking it through and saying it to myself, I realize my mind has found a way to let it in. "I can't call her," I tell Lynne in a voice that starts to waiver. "I can't."

Lynne puts an arm around me. "You don't have to right now if you don't want to."

"There has to be some mistake."

"Let's go over here." Lynne steers me toward a lounge area and draws me to the sofa.

"But I feel fine. I *am* fine. My horoscope said something. What was it? 'Your day will take an unusual turn today.' I never imagined anything like this."

"Do you want me to get you something? Some water?" Lynne says.

"No. Stay with me. Don't leave."

"I'm not going to leave you. I think you should come home with me today."

"No, that's okay. I don't want to—"

"I'm not going to leave you alone," Lynne says. "You're staying with me tonight, do you hear? No use arguing."

"Lucy. I need to feed Lucy."

"You left enough food and water out for her. She'll be fine."

"I still don't believe this is happening. I'm young and healthy. Why? Why me? It's because I deleted that stupid email chain letter I got and didn't pass it on. That's what this is."

"Look," Lynne says, shaking her head at me and taking my hand in hers. "Don't expend so much energy on *how* or *why* right now. Focus on *what* you do know. You found a lump. You stayed on top of it. You didn't ignore it. You took care of it. Those are the only absolutes here."

I nod, trying to appear sober, even to myself. I want to understand. I'm trying to understand.

My cell phone signals a new text message. "Adam." My voice sounds shrill in the small, cold lounge. "Poor Adam." Somehow I feel worse for him than I do for me. I read his text. It's the first time I feel like crying.

"Does Adam even know where you are?"

"No. I haven't said anything to him about this." I feel myself panic all of a sudden. I wonder how I'll tell him, running the scene through my mind. My head shakes no. A jolt of reality strikes me hard and fast, my racing heart slowing to overwhelming sadness. "I can't tell him," I drop my head in my hand.

"It's okay if you're not ready to yet."

"No. You don't understand. I can't tell him at all."

"I don't follow."

"It isn't fair to spring this on him. Our relationship is so new. I mean, how would I feel if it was the other way around? It isn't right."

"But Adam's different. You said so yourself. He's not like anyone you've ever dated before."

"That's just it. He'll feel sorry for me. That's how he's made. I don't want that from anybody. And I certainly don't want to put him in the position where he only stays with me because, well . . . what kind of man would he be if he left after a cancer diagnosis?"

"But, Suellen, he has a right to know. You shouldn't be making that decision for him."

"It's like I told you. Adam's a really nice guy. He'll do the decent thing. I won't do that to him."

Adam texts me another message.

Adam
I just want to say hi to my girlfriend.

"God, this sucks."

"What're you going to do?" Lynne says.

"I don't know yet. I can't deal with this right now. I may not know exactly what I'm facing, but I do know I don't want to put this on him. It just isn't fair."

"No, Suellen," Lynne says.

Feeling the need to move, I stand and look straight at Lynne. Her face is a mixture of complexity and disbelief.

"Don't you see?" I sway from side to side. "How will I ever know now if Adam's with me because he wants to be, because he's falling in love with me, or if it's just out of some kind of pity? I couldn't bear that."

Lynne looks up at me from the sofa and takes a deep breath, letting it out in one long sigh. "Right now isn't the time to be arguing with you about this. Just promise me one thing, will you? Don't make any rash decisions. Please. Take one step at a time. This will work itself out. You'll see. It's like the doctor said, there have been many improvements and breakthroughs in the treatment of breast cancer."

There's that operative word again. "But Lynne," I say, "cancer's cancer."

When my cell phone vibrates in my hand, my heart skips a beat. Mom's calling again.

Lynne doesn't take her eyes off me. She looks at me like a friend. Like a mother. I can't put it off anymore. "Guess I should take this call."

I woke up this morning and stepped into a new day and everything changed. I take in a deep breath, the effect of shock sifting through me, and walk away so I can talk privately. "Mom," I say into my phone. "Sorry. I had my phone on vibrate." I bite my lower lip. *Don't you dare cry.* I have to be strong. This isn't just about me anymore. It's about Mom and Dad and Simon and Adam, and all the people caught in the emotional tsunami of a cancer diagnosis.

"Mom, there's something I need to tell you."

CHAPTER 17

My cancer diagnosis hovers over me like an unsettling dream. It's strange when you're living on autopilot. My body moves and life carries on around me, but it's like I'm not in it. An onlooker in somebody else's life.

I clutch a sofa pillow to my chest, thinking about my phone conversation with Adam last Sunday night. He had just gotten back from his seminar. I told him something had come up and I wouldn't be able to get together with him on the following weekend, that I was spending it with Dad and Eve since they just returned from their cruise. He sounded disappointed but, in typical Adam fashion, said he understood. I might have been a little curt, but I don't know any other way to keep my diagnosis from him without hurting him. No matter how this goes down, he's going to get hurt, and it kills me.

"I'll call you again tomorrow," Adam said. Which he did. And I let it roll to voice mail. The message has been idling there for three days. I haven't listened to it, afraid of what hearing his voice will do to me.

Teagan's name appears when my phone rings. No doubt Lynne's talked to her. This call, I'll take. "Teagan."

"Thank god you're okay." She sounds rushed and breathless.

I flinch. "Teagan, I didn't even start treatments yet."

"No, I mean, I just saw Steve."

"Steve? Where?"

"Coming out of your complex."

"What? How?"

"I'm here right now. I wanted to call you first so you could tell the guard to let me through. That's when I saw him."

"Are you sure it was him?"

"Yeah. He was in a police car, but it was definitely him."

"Did he see you?"

"Don't think so. He barreled out of the parking lot really fast."

"All right. Hold on. I'm going to tell the guard to let you in."

I open my door a crack and see Teagan walking up my steps, a bottle wrapped in a brown paper bag clutched in her gloved hand. She hesitates on the top landing under the porch, and takes in a deep breath.

I open the door wider, and Teagan just stares at me, like she doesn't trust what her emotions might blurt out.

"Teagan, come inside already. You're freezing us both." A twenty-degree drop in temperature has turned the weather into true January. "You could have just called me."

She gives me an honest smile. "I didn't want to give you the chance to say 'No.' I came over as soon as I got off work. I had to see you in person."

"I told you in my text yesterday I'm not mad anymore," I say, trying to sound lighthearted. "All's forgiven."

"I want you to know you can talk to me. I'm here for you. Okay?"

"You mean I can go back to being a pain in the ass?"

"That was wrong of me. I'm such a jerk."

"Oh, stop. You've the patience of a saint, girl!" I throw my arms around her and hug her tight. "Thank you for coming. I really am glad you're here."

Tears spring to Teagan's eyes. "I've missed you."

I blink back the tears in my own eyes and scold myself for allowing it, as if I could stop them somehow. "I've missed you too."

I steer Teagan toward my living room. "Just throw your coat anywhere."

"For you," she says, holding out the bottle.

I pull it out of the bag. "For us," I say. "Thank you." I put the Chardonnay down on my coffee table, next to the life-size Persian cat sculpture.

"So, how on earth did Steve get past the guard?" Teagan says right off the bat.

"That's the million-dollar question."

"Seeing him come out of your complex panicked me. I'm not going to lie."

"You did sound a bit frantic."

"I didn't expect to see him."

"Okay, I know how your mind works. If it's anything like mine, what gruesome picture did you conjure up in your head? Was I stabbed or shot to death?"

Teagan scrunches her forehead. "Smothered, actually."

"Honestly?"

"Honestly. My heart was racing so much at the way he was rushing to drive away. I imagined you lying on your bed, smothered by your pillow."

I let out an uneasy laugh. "That's it? No blood or gore?"

"Your dead eyes were still open."

"Oh, that's a good one."

"It was awful, Suellen."

Teagan seems to do a fast survey of my tidy living room, the hardwood floor, plush gray area rug, white leather sectional, a scattering of colorful pillows and paintings and photos. No signs of any struggle or Steve.

The large flat-screen on the wall above my mantle flashes pictures but no sound.

Teagan looks up at it, so I answer the obvious question. "It's muted. I do that a lot. Gives me a sense of not being alone, but without the noise. I was just on the phone with my dad."

I take Teagan's coat from her and throw it over a chair while Lucy leaps onto the coffee table, inspecting the wine.

"Lucy," Teagan says, taking a seat on the couch and patting her. "She looks bigger than I remember."

"Fatter you mean." I bring over two wine glasses and sit diagonally across from her. After opening the bottle and pouring the wine, I lean back, putting my stocking feet up on the table. The sun stopped slanting across my living room floor an hour ago.

"Take your shoes off and make yourself comfortable," I say before taking a sip of wine.

"What are you going to do about Steve? I mean, he's still stalking you."

"He's pathetic. He needs to get a life. Besides, I have bigger things to worry about now."

Teagan slides over next to me, putting her hand over mine and waits until I'm ready to talk about the 'bigger things.'

"I plan on going into the office tomorrow and finishing out the week," I say, "but then I'll be taking a leave of absence."

"How long?" Teagan says.

"Not sure. The good news is it was small. The bad news is it's still cancer. I met with my doctor again, along with my dad. Mom hit Dad with the news the second his cruise ship docked. Then, he phoned Dr. O'Connor. They're colleagues. Anyway, there I was in a room with them while they consulted with an oncologist from Sloan Kettering in New York via speakerphone, listening like some outsider. It was weird; I felt so displaced. But it was me they were discussing. My life." I go on to explain. "My grandmother died of breast cancer. She was fifty-six, so they're recommending genetic testing."

"What does it all mean?" Teagan says.

"If my breast cancer is hereditary, it'll have an impact on my treatment decisions from hereon. It will mean a double mastectomy."

"Like Angelina Jolie."

"Yeah. Like her."

"Your mother . . . did she ever have breast cancer? I don't remember you saying—"

"No. And she had a mutation screening done quite a few years ago, but the results were indeterminate then. She's going to repeat the test. My grandmother died in 1996, when testing for it just began. The oncologist said they're seeing the breast cancer gene expressing itself earlier in younger generations. Lucky me." Tears eke out of my eyes and then Teagan's while I go on to explain all that I'm facing in the next few weeks, a spiral of appointments and tests. It still feels like I'm talking about someone else.

"I'm leaning toward a lumpectomy since it was small, but I could be looking at surgery for a double mastectomy if my blood test results come back positive for the BRCA gene mutation. That would mean breast reconstruction, too. And, chemotherapy, either way. Mom's planning to fly up in a few days to stay with me. We're going to meet with a genetic counselor together. My blood test results should be in by then. After surgery, Mom wants me to go back with her to Florida for my treatments and to convalesce. Dad wants me to stay here." I take another sip of wine. "It's beginning to sink in how much everything has changed."

My mind takes me back over a week ago, to the euphoria I felt while Adam made love to me. I squeeze a throw pillow against my chest as if it could quiet my breaking heart.

"Oh, Suellen, I'm here for you," says Teagan. "Whatever you need. I'm going to miss you at work. Tell me what I can do."

"It means a lot to me you're here. That's all. Speaking of work, tell me, what have I missed? I need a distraction from the whirlwind week I've been having."

"You already know Jeff's wife paid Lisa a visit last week."

"Yeah. I would have loved to have been a fly on that wall."

"The whole office is buzzing. Lisa's lying low, hiding in her office, mostly, with her door closed."

"Lying low. Now that's funny," I say. "I never thought I'd say this, but I'm going to miss work. I'd prefer a shot of happiness right now, but a little office gossip fits the bill." I glance over at my kitchen wall clock. "It's after seven. Are you hungry?"

"Mike will be closing the store in an hour," Teagan says. "By the time he gets home, we usually have dinner around eight or eight-thirty."

"I'm going to order something. Dad and Eve wanted to take me out to dinner but I simply can't do it. I just want to curl up right here on the couch with a good movie. Me, Lucy, and this bottle of wine. A dose of Ben Stiller is what I need right now." I pause, nibbling on my lower lip. "Is it possible? I mean, would you be able to stay? Have dinner with me?"

"I was hoping you'd ask," Teagan says. "Mike can heat the chicken parm I made last night. It's his favorite."

"It's no wonder. I've tasted your chicken parmesan."

"You have?"

"You brought it to lunch once. I was going to ask for your recipe when I was deciding what to make Adam for dinner a few weeks ago." I close my eyes for a split second. "Guess I won't need it anymore."

"Why not? You could still—"

"No, I won't," I say, my voice catching. "I'm not going to put Adam through all this."

"What're you saying?"

"I'm saying he doesn't have to know."

Teagan peers at me, confused.

I bound from the couch and head to the kitchen, opening up drawers. "I may not have a stocked refrigerator, but I have an impressive collection of take-out menus."

Teagan gets up from the couch and walks over to me. "Suellen, can we talk about this some more?"

"I'd rather not. I know. Shocking coming from me, but my mind's made up. I've been with Adam for less than eight weeks. I'm not going to dump this on him. He's much too good a person. He'll feel obligated to be with me. I couldn't stand that. I don't want to be a burden. I want to be his girlfriend. It'll be better if he thinks I don't want to see him anymore."

Teagan's face has the look of mistrust. "Better for whom?"

It's a rhetorical question that doesn't need an answer. I stare back down at the menus in my hand and flip through them. "Do you want to take a look at the menus?"

"You pick," Teagan says.

"You know what? I feel like a Margherita pizza. What do you say?"

"Sounds good."

"Sure Mike's not going to mind?"

"After he has something to eat, he'll wind up falling asleep on the couch anyway. He's working late all week because he's planning on taking next weekend off for his older sister's wedding. She's getting married again."

"The one whose husband left her?"

"That's the one. She's having it out in Pennsylvania with around fifty guests," Teagan says, picking up her wineglass again. "She's marrying a great guy. He's already been more of a father to her two kids than her ex. Good guys like him don't come around very often."

"No, they don't." The truth of her words crushes me. Teagan sees it on my face.

Whisking past her is-it-something-I-said expression, I pivot. "Do you have a dress for the wedding?"

"Yes and no. I'm still trying to decide between two that have been hanging in my closet."

"Come with me. I have just the dress. Actually, I have several in mind."

I take Teagan into my guest bedroom and open its walk-in closet. "Help yourself to anything while I order our pizza."

When I return to Teagan, her mouth is hanging open, her eyes trance-like. "If you don't see anything you like, we can also take a look in my master bedroom closet. It has even more than this one."

"I- . . . I'm speechless," Teagan says.

"Let me know if you need help finding anything."

"Suellen," Teagan says, finding her voice after a while, "you didn't tell me you had a boutique in your townhouse." Her gaze shifts to the tower of shoe boxes stacked along one wall, and then to the farthest corner of the closet where clothes hang with store tags still on them. On a few other shelves are designer handbags of every style. "Suellen, you could have a different purse for every day of the year." She looks at some of the price tags and gasps.

"See anything you like?" A wave of self-consciousness sweeps through me. Maybe this wasn't such a good idea.

"I don't know where to begin." Teagan reads off the names of designer labels as fast as she flips through them – Gucci, Prada, Armani, Chloe. "I mean, I knew you had a vast wardrobe, but this feels like I've ambled into a fashion house in Milan." She lingers admiringly, looking at all the clothes as if under a spell, then trips over a Bloomingdale's bag tossed on the floor.

I pick it up and move it out of the way. Then she spots another bag and another and another. Nordstrom, Saks, Neiman Marcus. It's the same with each. Shopping bags thrown aside with tags still on the clothes.

"I didn't get a chance to hang them up yet," I attempt to explain, but Teagan's awed expression has somehow changed.

She pulls a hanging receipt from one of the bags. "You bought this over two months ago," she says, looking shaken.

"I liked it at the time I purchased it." Teagan remains quiet and pensive. "Okay, so I have a weakness for clothes. And shoes. And handbags."

"I'll say. This is a massive collection." As she speaks, a sad look replaces the captivated one on her face.

"I know what you're thinking. And no, I don't have a shopping addiction. Shopping is more like a hobby to me. It makes me feel good. For a while." Even to my own ears, it sounds weak.

The closet walls are beginning to feel like they're closing in on me, an avalanche of designer clothes smothering me. I gulp down an urge to cry. My hands begin shaking, my lips trembling. I try to take in a deep breath, but my lungs refuse to fill. My short staccato breaths get shorter and shorter.

"Suellen?"

I bring my hand to my throat. "I- . . . I can't brea—"

Teagan rushes to me and wraps her arms around me. In between gasping for breath, I start to sob. *Not even Gucci or Fendi can take away the pain I feel.*

"Shhh," Teagan says. "Just breathe. I'm here."

Huddled in the depths of my walk-in, I cry over Teagan's shoulder, releasing a torrent of tears. She holds me tight, letting me cry out all the anger and pain and fear I've been repressing. Before my cancer diagnosis, going back as far as my childhood. I cry for all I'm facing, even though I don't know what that is. I cry for what I'm doing to Adam. For the horrible choices I have to make. For the bad ones I've already made. I cry for the thirteen-year-old me who never allowed herself to cry, the way Simon had. I cry for all I've lost, and for all I'm going to lose.

"Shhh. It's going to be okay," Teagan says, patting and rubbing my back. "Everything's going to be okay. You are the strongest person I know."

CHAPTER 18

It's the coldest day so far this winter. Icy precipitation obscures my windshield. I push up the heat and defroster, while the wiper blades swipe, leaving clear semi-circles.

It astonishes me how sensitive my head and ears are to the cold. I check out my new haircut in the visor mirror, a feathered pixie with long fringe bangs swept to the side. I might even like it if it didn't imply life change.

"With your oval-shaped face, you can wear any style short hair," my stylist reassured me while I flipped through hairstyle magazines. "But are you sure you want to take off so much? Might be too drastic, sweetie. Gradual would be easier."

"Gradual and chemotherapy aren't always in sync," I said, clinching it. "I'm just doing what has to be done."

"Oh. I'm sorry," the hairstylist said.

Eyes misting, I watched as thick locks of my hair fell to the floor, scissors snipping and cutting, the white floor soon covered in rich brown.

I swipe the page-boy knit hat I had thrown into my car earlier from the passenger seat, pull it down over my ears, and wrap a scarf twice around my neck. Somewhere, some young person who's lost their hair will benefit from the eighteen-inch ponytail I've donated to Locks of Love. At least that's something I can feel good about. I wish I could tell Adam but then I would have to tell him about the cancer. A quiet flash of a conversation we had several weeks ago comes to mind.

We were sipping wine at a candlelight dinner when I told him about the pressure of living up to my father's high standards. When I mentioned Dad had a research grant named in his honor from the American Heart Association, Adam said, "That's wonderful, Suellen. But what about you?"

"What about me?"

"You must have a passion of your own?"

"I'm keeping my options open for now." I didn't think being a shopaholic counted. "Haven't found a good fit yet, I guess. Why do you ask?"

"I want to know *you* . . . the real you," Adam said. "Not just the person you put out."

"*I* don't even know her," I said, hoping he believed I was being honest.

Then Adam said, "You will. Give her time." From his vast memory bank, he pulled out a quote by Pirkei Avot he says he keeps posted on the wall by his desk.

"If I am not for myself, who will be for me?

But, if I am only for myself, what am I?

And, if not now, when?"

"How do you do it?" I said. "Here I am, still stumbling through life, trying to learn who I am and what I want, and you seem to know yourself so well."

Adam shook his head and laughed. "And I look at you and think, 'how does she do it?' While I analyze and plan my life out, you take each day as it comes. You're spontaneous and exciting."

"You mean reckless, don't you?"

The light coming from the candle flickered in his eyes as a smile formed on his lips. "All anyone has to do is look at you to know you love life. You do what your heart tells you. It's what I love about you."

The memory of Adam's beautiful smile sparks love in my mind, making me miss him so much it hurts. My thoughts are all over the place, getting all screwed up. Here I am thinking about Adam, remembering snippets of our conversations, his laugh, wondering how

I'm going to survive losing him when I should be thinking how I'm going to survive cancer.

Right guy. Wrong timing.

Friday was my last day at work because I need time to prepare for surgery on the following Thursday. I even had lunch with the girls downstairs, and Catherine joined us, too. The five of us were huddled in the elevator going down, Teagan, Lynne, Carol, and Catherine encircling me. It was touching really, the way they kept close, as if to form a kind of protective shield around me. There's safety inside the fusion of friends.

I kept it together, trying to appear all right in front of them. "Too bad today's not Tuesday," I had said. "I hate missing burger days."

"When you get back, I'll buy you all the burgers you want," Lynne said.

"Yes, and do hurry. I'd much rather be working alongside you than with Lisa on the Rojas file," Catherine said.

We took turns making small talk, filling up dead air, each of us doing our best to pull off 'normal.' Whatever that is.

The road feels slippery as I drive back to my place. I read the text that comes in.

Adam

Is it something I said?

Why, why, why? I want to cry and yell and scream. It makes me so damn angry. I internalize it and punch the steering wheel instead.

A black SUV steals in front of me, and I have to slam on my brakes to avoid hitting it, causing me to skid. "That's right," I scream. "Cut me off, jerk." But my windows are up and no one hears me.

I right my car and look in the rearview mirror. Steve's in his police car right behind me. *Damn it.* If I wasn't feeling so angry, it would alarm me. But now, even Steve can't upset me anymore. Then he turns on his police light. *He's fucking pulling me over.*

"Driving a little reckless, are we?" he says, leaning into my window.

"Really, Steve? You saw that black SUV cut me off."

Steve's taunting grin makes me want to vomit, and I have to swallow the bile rising in my throat. "So you just happened to be in my area?" I say, letting my voice hang short of sarcasm. Any answer would incriminate him, so Steve says nothing. I never said Steve was stupid. "Actually, I'm glad I bumped into you, or rather, that you bumped into me." I turn a stone-cold smile and force it out. "I could use some company right now. Can you stop over?" Cancer has somehow emboldened me.

Steve either has lost his voice or thinks he's lost his mind. His expression is dumbfounded. I can imagine he's actually asking himself, 'Did I just hear her ask me to come over?' After a short pause, he clears his throat. "I have a little time. I can stop over."

Minutes later, Steve's car speeds up to the guard's gate just as I head toward my front door. I give the okay to let him pass. Sam's finally gotten the message. Steve pulls into my driveway, and I watch him walk toward me, his shoulders upright, hands deep inside his leather bomber jacket pockets, a this-is-turning-into-my-lucky-day look growing on his face.

"Hey," I say as he approaches me on my stairs' top landing.

Steve gives me a squint-eyed grin and leans into me as though he wants to plant one on my mouth. "This doesn't get you off from me writing you a ticket," he scoffs. "Just so you know."

I manage a smile. "Let's go inside. It's bitter cold out here."

As soon as I let us in, Steve says, "I knew you couldn't stay away for long. Admit it," he says, "You've missed me." The grin on Steve's face works half his mouth.

My stomach churns as I feel a stop-start anxiety coming on. I took a risk having him over. *What if I'm wrong? What if this doesn't go the way I think it will?*

I go over to the small table in the entryway, lay down my keys, and start to unbutton my coat. "I'm glad you stopped by," I say, my back toward Steve so he can't see my face. I can feel him come up behind me. He grabs the back of my head and turns it so I'm facing him. He kisses me on the lips while he leans into me. My body clashes with my mind as it remembers him.

I pull away to catch my breath and try to look like I'm enjoying this. Steve's wearing his I'm-so-sure-I'm-getting-laid-today smile, so all I can think about is the pleasure it will give me when I wipe that look off his face. I cheat and return the smile.

"My throat's dry," I say, unraveling my scarf. "Get us a drink, will you?"

Steve goes straight away to the kitchen.

"When's the last time you bought any food?" he yells. "There's nothing in this fridge except soy sauce and Perrier. And some green shit."

"Care for some wheatgrass juice?" Lucy rubs up against my leg.

"Some what?"

"Never mind. I'll take a Perrier."

A ping from my phone.

Adam

I'm coming over.

My fingers fly. I'm freaking out.

Me

No. You can't.

The phone rings and I know I have to answer it. I have to stop him somehow.

"We need to talk." Adam's voice jolts me to my senses. "I don't know what's going on with you, but something's changed."

"Adam, this is not a good time—"

"I have to see you," Adam says.

"No. Please. As I told you, I just need a breather." I move toward my bedroom.

"You can tell that to my face when I come to see you," Adam insists. I have to keep that from happening. I'll come apart as soon as I see him. "I won't take no for an answer."

I gasp. It will take him an hour to get here, less depending on whether he's already left. "No. You can't."

"Give me one good reason why I shouldn't."

"Because I'm—" I grip the phone tighter, my voice breaking. "I'm not alone."

I reach to close my bedroom door just as Steve's voice bellows from the living room. "I can't believe there isn't any beer."

"Who's that?" Adam says. "Who's there with you?"

Steve comes to the bedroom and pushes against the door, suspicion creeping out through a mask of coolness. "Here you go," he says, handing me the bottle.

I take it from him and say in a deliberate manner, "Thank you, Steve." I'm far and away the worst person that ever lived.

The abrupt silence from Adam's end makes me cringe. "Steve's there?" The hurt and confusion in his voice pierces through me like a knife. A flood of tears lies behind my eyes and I can't find my voice. *Don't you dare lose it.* Another heavy silence. Then Adam says, "Oh . . . fuck. So this is what you meant by a 'breather.'" He's never cursed in front of me before. "Why, Suellen? You told me it was over between you two. I trusted you. Why are you doing this? What's happened to you?"

I'm going to lose it.

For a moment, I forget Steve is standing there. Then he brings his face near mine, his mouth so close it's as if he's speaking into my phone, "Come on, babe. Hang up."

"I don't know who you are," Adam says before the phone goes dead.

Just like me inside.

I stare at my phone, not moving. I might as well be a mannequin.

Steve starts caressing my neck with his lips. "You going to tell me who that was on the phone?" he says, the heat of his breath matching the fire in his jeans.

I swallow the lump in my throat and take in a deep breath, forcing the coldness back. "No one important," I say, sounding hollow. Adopting Steve's own words to me makes it easier: *You and me, we're alike. Users.* It's easier when I convince myself I don't care.

Steve leans in harder, plants kisses up my neck, his five o'clock shadow scraping my cheek as he reaches my face. He pulls my hat off my head and starts running his fingers through my hair. "What the—" Steve jerks his head back and stares at me, confused and stunned.

Instinctively, I reach up to my neck, where my hair no longer is. "Had it a wee bit chopped off today," I say. "What do you think?"

"Hacked's more like it."

"Don't hold back now, Steve. I wouldn't want you to spare my feelings."

"Why the hell would you cut your hair?"

"That's what I wanted to talk to you about."

"You asked me here so I could see your new haircut?" Steve backs up, looking confused and off-kilter.

"Not exactly," I say. "I have cancer, Steve."

Steve cocks his head, looking stunned. Now there are two mannequins standing in my bedroom.

"It's breast cancer. I'm having surgery in a few days, and I'm going to be going through chemo. This is just the beginning. I'm going to lose all my hair soon."

Steve's reaction is like the after-effect of too much wine. Slow and untrusting. Then he gives it to me full. "Shit."

"Yeah, shit," I say, gulping down some water.

There's something in the way Steve raises his eyes, like he's brooding over his next play. What do you do when the script takes an unexpected turn? He fidgets with his jacket, his gray eyes staring at me. I'd like to say I find warmth in them, a tiny speck of empathy, but there's only shock and discomfort. The news has put him off his game.

But I'm not done yet. For good measure, I add, "I'm going to lose the girls, and I'm not opting for reconstruction." Steve stares at me, mouth agape. "Sucks for me, doesn't it?" I say, heading back to the living room. I put down the Perrier when my cell phone trembles in my hand. *Adam?*

Somehow, I'm surprised when I hear Dr. O'Connor's uncharacteristic and formal hello. I brace myself. "My test results all in?"

That my day could get any shittier than it already has did not seem plausible, but what it descends into staggers me. And I'm not easily staggered. Dr. O'Connor tells it to me plainly. My blood test results are conclusive for the BRCA1 gene mutation. Most likely passed down to me from my Jewish Ashkenazi ancestors. A consultation with a genetic counselor prepared me for this, but it still comes as a shock.

Minutes into my conversation with Dr. O'Connor, somewhere between the words "bilateral mastectomy" and "chemo," I observe Steve out the corner of my eye. I had almost forgotten he was still there. Looking ill at ease and bobbing from one foot to the other, he catches my eye, then runs a hand through his hair like he's trying to work up the nerve to say something. "I should go," he finally says.

The man who isn't afraid of anything looks disturbed. Beneath Steve's cool mask, I see a bungling little boy. Can it be I found the one thing that scares him? I would feel sorry for him but I haven't the room. With my phone still glued to my ear, I usher Steve to the front door and give him a semi-wave as he brushes past me to the outdoors.

Hunching his shoulders against the abrupt chilliness, Steve twists his head around and throws me a half nod. "Good luck," he says awkwardly. "Or whatever you say to people with cancer." And then, just like that, he's gone.

Have a nice life, Steve. I shut the door.

CHAPTER 19

When everything is surreal, from being confined to a hospital room three days in a row to the life I've been living the past couple of weeks, hearing the latest office gossip is a much-needed and welcome diversion. Happily, Teagan obliges.

"Let me see if I have this right," I say to her. "Lisa didn't make partner?" I try sitting up taller against the pillows Teagan has propped behind my back, feeling the unremitting constriction of bandages across my chest.

"Want me to get you another pillow?" Teagan says.

I shake my head. "No. This is good. I want to hear what's been happening."

"It's not hard to figure out why. Ever since Jeff's wife paid her a visit, things have cooled between Jeff and her. Lisa may have overplayed her hand."

"More like she underestimated the wife," I say. "The sad part is, she was more than qualified and would have been an influential partner. She's a hard worker and a go-getter."

Teagan looks inside the water pitcher on my nightstand. "I think you need more ice," she says.

"I still can't believe it." The ice can wait. Girl talk is what I need.

"Look. Jeff isn't crying the blues. He's already moved on," Teagan says, rolling her eyes.

"He doesn't miss a beat, does he? Who this time?"

Teagan shakes her head at me. "I can't. We should wait for Carol to come back. I don't want to take the fun of telling away from her."

"She had better hurry and get back here before my mother does." I look up at the clock on the wall. Carol's bringing me a Happy Meal from the McDonald's downstairs. While another nightgown is the last thing I need, I convinced Mom otherwise. She's due back from the mall soon. I haven't been able to eat "real" food since Mom arrived five days ago. Even though a low-fat, high-fiber diet is to become my new normal, it doesn't mean I can't indulge once in a while. Starving oneself before chemo treatments begin would be worse.

"You must be feeling better," Teagan says. "You're back to your usual hungry self."

"I'll feel much better when I can get these friggin' tubes out." On both sides of my chest, post-surgery fluid is draining pink. I run my fingers along one of them. "There's less drainage today I think. My doctor says I'll be going home soon."

"When do you think?"

"Could be tomorrow. If I had my way, I'd follow you out of here right now, but my father and my doctor are plotting against me, keeping me here against my will."

Teagan leans over a bouquet of yellow roses and pulls out the card. "Catherine sent you these? They're beautiful. And the plant is from Lynne?"

"Yes. She came by after work yesterday. I was having a bad day. Poor Lynne."

"You're entitled," Teagan says.

"I was very cranky. You're luckier than she was. I'm a lot better today."

Since my surgery, every day has had its own personality.

I remember little about the day after my operation, my mind floating in virtual reality from the painkillers and the anesthesia wearing off. The day passed in a blur, but one strange and troubling dream stands out. I was running barefoot through clouds, trying hard to reach Adam. "I'm sorry. I didn't mean to hurt you," I said, reaching toward him. "Can you forgive me?" The closer I got to him, the more his look changed, until I was face-to-face with Steve. My heart sank with my body, descending beneath sheets of white clouds.

At some point, I woke up to find my mother sitting in a chair beside my bed holding my hand. My father's tall figure stood at the end, staring at my monitors. Mom was saying something to him about taking me with her to Florida for my treatment regimen and to convalesce.

"Her doctors are here," Dad said.

My mother focused her eyes on my father but would not let go of my hand. "We have good doctors there, too," she said. "Dr. Rosenfeld's a well-respected oncologist who also happens to be on the Board of the Palm Beach Pops and is a good friend of mine. It would be best if she were near me."

Dad said, "Best for whom?"

Even though I was awake, I kept my eyes closed. I was ten years old again, humming one of my favorite songs. *Your Mama Don't Dance and Your Daddy Don't Rock n' Roll* erupted inside my head, shutting them out like in the days before they divorced. They didn't even notice I had pulled the sheet up over my face.

The second day was lost in a confusion of doctors conferring and nurses checking my vital signs. In my mind, I escaped to the clouds again, drifting toward freedom and allowing myself to think of Adam.

I had tried to call him back after I let him think I was back with Steve. I reconsidered telling him the truth. The need to explain plagued me, but he refused to pick up and never returned my call. I couldn't blame him. I couldn't put in a text or voice mail all I was going through, so I was brief in my text, saying only, *I can explain. Please call.*

He didn't.

By the third day, when I cared what day it was, I was beginning to take hold of myself again because I complained about everything from the pictures hanging on the wall to the constant disturbances by nurses during the night.

Today, Saturday, I would characterize as lonely. The twist my life has taken is sinking in amid gushing gloom. Suspension's not a delusion – it's become my reality. I feel Adam's absence stronger than ever and for the better part of the morning, I've been fighting tears. I may have gotten rid of Steve, but I lost Adam in the process.

I miss my old life, my friends, lunch hours. Teagan and Carol's visit draws me out, reviving me. "Maybe you can sneak me out with you, Teag. What do you say? We'll pull these things out and get out of here."

"Oh come on now," Teagan says, trying to lift my spirits. "You'll be home before you know it."

How can Teagan know that I feel like I'm living someone else's life? I would give anything to have my old life back, my old problems. Adam.

"What's important is you look terrific. I mean it. You're amazing."

"Yeah? Wait 'til you see the girls," I say, looking down at my bandaged chest. "They're going to be a whole size bigger than the originals when this is all done. I figured if I had to have them reconstructed, I might as well do them up."

"I love your attitude, girl."

"The tattoo nipples are going to take a little longer. Not until after the implants are put in." I fall back against the pillows and stare up for a moment at the ceiling. "So much to think about, so many decisions to make," I murmur. "I liked it better when my biggest worry was what restaurant to eat at. Yesterday, my oncologist talked to me about fertilization preservation, before I undergo chemo. He wanted to go over my options with me."

Teagan takes me in with her eyes, the expression in them larger than ever. I have struck a nerve.

"It's overwhelming. Besides surviving, I need to think about becoming a mother someday. As if my plate isn't full enough already. I'll be an aunt soon. Did I tell you my brother and his wife are having a girl? She's due at the end of May. Maybe by then, I'll be able to hold her."

Our twinship is an emotional and stressful factor in this heritable disease, putting my brother and mother on high alert now for precancerous mutations. My brother is also getting tested now. My diagnosis has shed a light and a darkness. I don't know why I feel so bad about this. As if I have any control over it. I tell myself that now that Pandora's Box has been opened, they can be armed, not bushwhacked like me. There's value in knowledge.

I recline a little on my pillow. "You know, Teagan, I didn't appreciate what it was like for you all these years, trying to have a baby. I didn't . . . I *couldn't* appreciate what you were going through."

Teagan puts her hand on mine. "It's no one's fault. We take so much for granted. We're all guilty of that. Look. When you're ready, you can ask me anything. Anytime. I've become rather an expert on the subjects of fertilization, and adoption."

I look into Teagan's eyes. "How's the adoption going by the way?"

"Coming along, though slower than I'd like."

"Is that normal?"

"Yes. You have to go through quite a process. Anyway, I look at it this way. It's giving me more time to put the necessary funds together."

"That's good, right?"

Teagan rolls her eyes. "At least now I have something to look forward to. Anyway, you don't want to hear about all this."

"Yes. I do," I say, coming out of myself.

"If we go the international route, China's adoption program is the most efficient. Our caseworker told me and Mike that she works with reputable adoption agencies and attorneys who handle private domestic adoptions as well. We're going through adoption counseling, exploring our options, trying to decide what would be a good fit for us. If we do this, we need to go in with our eyes wide open."

"Can they deny your application for any reason?"

"Yes, if they don't think we qualify."

"You and Mike would be amazing parents. Of course, you'll qualify."

"There are all kinds of requirements besides the usual ones. It goes on and on. But the one that gets me is 'must be in a stable marital relationship.'"

"Ha. Half the biological parents out there would get disqualified."

"It can be discouraging," Teagan says. "I don't want to bore you with all the details, and there are many."

"If I have to think about something, I'd rather it be about baby options. Thinking about death can be such a downer. I'd rather think about life. I wish I could put mine on fast forward. You know? Skip ahead to the good part again."

Carol enters my room.

"What took you so long?" I say.

"Long line. Every patient here must have sent someone down for food on their behalf. I noticed a few carts in the hallways with meal trays on them. It must be lunch time."

"C'mon, give it here," I say urgently, motioning for the McDonald's bag in her hand, the aroma of beef and fries and pickles evoking a sweet nostalgia.

I never tasted fries more delicious. "Now, give me the gossip," I say, starving for both.

Carol plants herself on the edge of my hospital bed. "You heard Lisa was passed over for partnership, right?"

"Yes, yes. Teagan told me. And that Jeff's already moved on from her. Not surprising." I unwrap the cheeseburger. "And that's the all-breaking news at Bender & Simpson?" I say, a little disappointed.

"That's only the half of it," Carol says, then cuts her eyes over to Teagan.

"Don't worry," Teagan says. "I didn't tell her. I saved the best part for you."

Carol looks back at me and says, "You'll never guess who Jeff's shacking up with now."

"You know you're going to have to work for it," Teagan says.

"Ok, so who this time?" I say, taking a huge bite out of my burger. I don't remember anything tasting this good before. "It has to be someone from the office, someone we all know." *Why else would Carol be so eager to tell me?* I start with our lunch group. "I can rule out Lynne, and Catherine," I say thinking aloud. "Ummm . . . Rachel?"

Carol whirls her head around to face Teagan.

"I didn't tell her. I swear," Teagan says, holding up both hands.

"It's Rachel?" I cough out.

"How did you know?" Carol says, deflated.

"I didn't."

"Can you believe it?" Teagan says.

"She stopped coming to lunch with us," Carol says.

"Been-there-done-that setting another record now is she." It isn't a question but Carol answers anyway.

"You bet she is. It's sickening the way she flirts with Jeff."

I take another bigger bite of my burger. I refuse to have my appetite spoiled.

In the hall outside my room, Mom's voice filters in.

"No need to bother delivering that tray of food there," she says to someone coming in my room. "I brought food in for her."

"Oh crap." In one fell swoop, I close up my half-eaten burger, toss it back into the bag with the fries and hurl it at Carol who catches it in her lap.

"Ma'am," a woman's voice says, "you can do whatever you want. I'm just doing my job, and that means delivering this tray of food to that room."

"Fine. I just thought I'd save you the trouble. But if you must, you must." Mom strides into the room, several shopping bags billowing around her. Her steps are quick and light, as though her feet don't even touch the ground. "Hello," she says to Teagan and Carol. "How nice to see you both again."

"Again?" I say.

"Your friends came by a couple of evenings ago. You were sleeping. We didn't want to wake you."

Carol and Teagan both nod.

"You should have woken me," I say.

While the hospital dietician drops off my lunch tray, Carol slides off my bed, my Happy Meal concealed behind her back.

Mom deposits an armful of shopping bags onto a chair across the room and comes over to me with a small bag. She rolls the tray table nearer my bed and moves the hospital's food onto an end table, then places the bag she brought in front of me, pouring out its contents. "Here you go," she says. "I found a wonderful little Korean place that serves tofu burgers and seaweed salad." She turns to Carol and Teagan. "If I'd known you were here, I would have brought back more tofu burgers."

Teagan and Carol respond more or less in unison. "Oh, no thank you. That's okay. We ate already."

"When we get you home," Mom says, "Clara will fix you some of Morris and my favorite meals."

Home. Now that's a strange word. *Where is my home? Certainly not with Dad and Eve. With Mom and Morris in Miami? I don't think so.*

Mom circles my bed while she removes her jacket. We all watch her, mesmerized. This petite woman who leaves no doubt in anyone's mind that she's in control. I love my mother, but as I gather the broken pieces of myself, I know what I have to do. Later, I'm going to tell her I'm not going back with her to Florida, where she has already arranged healing counsel, yoga, and transcendental meditation for me. I plan to stay in New Jersey. I need to have my friends around me. This is where I belong if I'm to become whole again. My work and my life are right here.

Still, I marvel at my mother's energy as she fusses over the room and me. She could run circles around all of us. With my hair short, I look like an enhanced print of my mother when she was younger, only with more meat on my bones. Now, my mother is rail thin with no hips at all. I tell myself that's me in twenty-five years. Not the first time I've thought this, but the first time it startles me. I want to live to see it. I want to live.

"It's awfully warm in here," Mom says. "Are you comfortable? Let me fix your pillows for you." She flits about my room like Peter Pan, laying out my dinner, adjusting my pillows, fixing my drain tubes, checking the thermostat.

"What's that smell?" Mom says suddenly, staring at me for a moment.

Carol shoots me a look, her eyes widening with panic.

"Today's Salisbury steak," I say, gesturing toward the hospital tray untouched on my nightstand.

Mom closes her eyes and shivers. "Thank goodness I got here in time."

Teagan, Carol and I exchange glances.

"I couldn't decide which nightgown to get so I bought all three," Mom says fussing with her new purchases. From the Nordstrom bag, she pulls out a floral lounge set. A pink cotton nightshirt comes from the Victoria's Secret bag. "What do you girls think?" she says. "I kind of like the floral one."

"They're both pretty," Carol says, inching nearer to Teagan.

Behind her back, Carol passes my Happy Meal to an unsuspecting Teagan who catches it before it falls.

Teagan mutters to her, "You fink."

"What was that?" Mom says.

"Pink. I like the pink one," Teagan stutters out, my Happy Meal bag now hidden behind her back.

Mom holds up a baby blue satin nightgown. "This one really caught my eye."

"Oh, I like that one," Carol says.

Teagan manages a closed-lipped smile. The moment Mom turns her back, she sticks her tongue out at Carol and I stifle a laugh.

"Suellen, you haven't even touched your tofu burger."

"Oh. Right," I say. "Guess I'm just not very hungry right now." I'm having too much fun watching Teagan and Carol play hot potato with my Happy Meal.

Somehow, Teagan manages to give it back to Carol and then moves away from her.

"I can return any of the nighties you don't want," Mom says to me. "Or you can keep them all."

Carol makes a rushed decision. Leaning up against the back wall, she lets go of my meal behind her. I hear the clunk before I realize what she's done. "In the garbage?!" The words spew from my mouth.

"Really, Suellen," Mom says. "I'll just return them if you feel that strongly about it."

CHAPTER 20

Mom sips her tea, concealed behind a bone china cup. "There are things in life we have no control over and can't do a thing about," I tell her. "But you can do something about this." Mom's test result for the defective BRCA1 gene is also positive. She sits forward on my sofa, the English teacup balanced over the saucer in her other hand. I bought two elegant china tea sets from Williams Sonoma a few years ago for when my mother visits. She drinks black tea like water. "Of course, not all people with BRCA mutations will get cancer," I say. "But the risk does increase with age. You just need to stay ahead of it." Reminds me of the game of Risk my brother and I used to play, an exercise in strategy and conquest. Only this is real life and death we're talking about.

Mom looks at me finally. She's been so helpful and caring these last couple of weeks. I admit I'm relishing having her home with me, all to myself. There were those quirky years when she wanted to be my girlfriend. But since my cancer diagnosis, she's been exactly what I need right now. My mother. She takes the last swallow of tea, the cup rattling as she sets it down on the coffee table.

Since the mutation doesn't skip generations, her positive test result didn't come as big a surprise to us, just disheartening proof. I had to have inherited it from one of my parents and my mother is of the Ashkenazi Jewish heritage, one of the ethnic groups more likely to carry it.

Mom's feeling all kinds of emotions, first guilt for not repeating the indeterminate test she had years ago and then sorrow for what I'm going through, shock that her risk of developing breast cancer has markedly increased because of it. "Knowledge can be empowering," I tell her. "If you let it. I wish I'd known before finding out the way I did."

My mother expends an audible breath and sags back on the couch.

"I'm sorry for the way that came out," I say. "Besides, would I have taken prophylactic measures in my twenties? I doubt it."

My brother took the test as soon as he learned about it since we were told there was a 50-50 chance he might have inherited it as well. It's no surprise he's concerned it could be passed on to his daughter. Mom's making it a point to notify relatives who may also be untested or undiagnosed.

"Thank heavens your brother's was negative," Mom sighs, expressing our relief, and then she's quick to reassure me. "You know BRCA mutations do just as well as the general population after treatment for breast cancer." She's been doing her own research. It's like we'd been hit with a tsunami, the newsbreak waves carrying surges of fear to all who might be affected. I'm still riding out the waves.

While Mom and I swap positive outlooks, each trying to make the other feel better, I realize the time has come for me to cut her loose. "This is nice. Your being here with me," I say. "But you need to get back to Morris soon – to your life in Miami."

"Oh, honey, I want to be here. I enjoy being with you and seeing Simon, and if you two don't come down to see me more often, I will just have to come up. Soon there will be three of my hearts in New Jersey."

"I'll be fine. I'm going to continue working from home through my computer, and I'll go into the office once in a while as soon as I'm allowed to drive again. I've got to keep myself busy."

My doorbell rings and I go to answer it. My neighbor, Gladys, stands at the threshold holding a casserole of some kind. "Hi, Gladys. Come on in."

"I just wanted to bring you over a chicken and rice dish I made. How are you doing, dear?" Gladys sees Mom over on the couch. "Hello."

"Hello, Gladys," Mom says. "Nice to see you again. What wonderful dish have you brought over now?" *Wonderful for thee, but not for me.*

"Oh it's just something I made for myself, but I had extra and wanted to bring it over."

I take the casserole dish from her and place it on my kitchen counter, chuckling inside. The weight of it tells me the portion size could feed up to four people. "You didn't have to—" I start, but the gratifying look on Gladys' face stops me. "Thank you for this. You're too kind. Please, take your coat off and join us."

"Sorry, but I can't stay," she says. "My son's picking me up to take me to an appointment. I just wanted to bring this over." Lucy wanders over to her and rubs against her leg. "Well, hello there, Lucy."

"Thank you again for taking such good care of her while I was gone."

"My pleasure. Anytime."

I see Gladys back out. Mom lifts her hand in a thank you wave. "You see," I say when my neighbor has left, "I have Gladys here too. I'm in good hands." Mom joins me in the kitchen while I go over to the chicken and rice dish and lift the lid. "Mmmm. Boneless too. And it still feels warm, like it just came out of the oven. Think I'll have some." I know Mom won't touch it so I take down one plate for myself. No sooner have I taken a serving spoon from the drawer than my phone rings.

"Hello, ma'am. Sam at the gatehouse. You have a visitor."

"Who is it, Sam?"

"Adam Isaacson."

I go into a spasmodic freeze as the serving spoon falls out of my hand. My heart pounds inside my chest and sweat bursts out behind my neck.

Mom sees it. "What's wrong? What is it?"

"I- . . . I have a visitor." *Has my mother ever heard me sound so timid before?*

"Who is it?" Mom says.

"Adam."

"Why, let him through of course. I should like to meet him."

"Fine," I tell Sam before racing to my bathroom. "Mom, will you please get the door for me?" I stare into the vanity mirror and look down at my chest, the post-reconstruction bra supporting my uncompleted augmentation. I exchange the blouse I'm wearing for a looser-fitting one, so nervous my fingers keep missing the buttonholes. I splash cold water onto my face and finger-comb my wispy bangs.

I can hear Adam and my mother in the living room talking. Mom's high-pitched voice is amplified by her enthusiasm at meeting him. Adam responds with consideration. *You can't cower in here forever.* I spread a pink gloss over my lips and walk out to face him.

When I enter the living room, Adam's sitting on the couch, half hidden behind a vase of tall flowers on the coffee table. He stands up quickly, our eyes lining up with laser beam precision, focused and penetrating. We stand in loud silence for long seconds, staring at one another, each waiting for the other to start.

"Look at the lovely flowers Adam brought over," Mom breaks the uncomfortable standoff. Adam's face is etched with pain. It hurts me to see it there. I reach up to the back of my neck, touching my bareness. Tears pool in my eyes and I force them to stay open as long as possible before they loosen.

"Thank you," I stammer, walking over to him, the whiff of roses and lilies hitting my nostrils. "The flowers are beautiful." We meet in a tentative embrace. Mom is saying something to him about a drink. Good thing one of us remembers how to be a gracious host. She places a glass of water onto a coaster on the end table closest to him.

"Are you sure I can't get you anything else?" The emotional discomfort in the room is so strong even my mother finds it hard to talk. Her Mom clairvoyance kicks in fast. She goes to my front hall, throws on her jacket, and pulls my car keys off the wall hook. "I'm going to leave you two. I have a few errands I need to run. It was nice to meet you, Adam."

"Same to you," Adam says, still looking at me.

The door closes behind her and I plop down into my sofa. Adam remains standing. "When did you find out?" I say finally, staring at Lucy as she checks out the floral arrangement.

"Yesterday."

"How?"

"Todd. Someone at your firm posted something on Facebook about prayers going out to Suellen for a complete recovery."

I wince. "Of course."

Adam does a short pace in front of me. "Why, Suellen? Why didn't you tell me? I would have been there for you."

I breathe out one long-held exhalation and dare myself to look at him. Tears stand in his eyes, my own eyes brimming. "I never doubted you would. I think I know you well enough to know you would have been all in. You would have also worried and put me before you. You would have wanted to help take care of me. You would have been all of that and more. I won't do that to you. We're just getting to know one another, we're not even . . . it's all too soon." A tear works its way loose from my eye. "I'm so sorry if I hurt you. Either way, you were going to get hurt. I chose the lesser of the two."

"Do you think so? Do you really think it didn't hurt me to feel like I had been lied to? That you were still seeing your ex behind my back? That kind of deception nearly killed me. I thought we were good together."

I wind myself back to that harrowing day almost three weeks ago. My phone conversation with Adam echoes in my ears, as does the sound of his anguish when he heard Steve's voice in the background. "My ex was stalking me. At first, I tried to deny it, but Steve kept showing up near here and a few times I caught him following me. I didn't want to worry you, so I kept it to myself."

Adam takes a seat on the couch next to me and waits for me to continue.

"That day – the day you phoned me and said you were coming right over to see me – I totally freaked out. I had invited Steve over after he pulled me over for some absurd driving violation. I wanted to let him know I had breast cancer."

Confusion spreads out over Adam's face. "Why would you do that? Why would you tell him and not me?"

"The same way I know you, I know Steve. I told you. He was not a nice person."

"Was?"

"After I told him I was going to be having surgery and treatments for my cancer, he bolted. I don't think I'll be hearing from him anymore."

Adam shakes his head. "What a shithead."

"He saw that I got my hair cut real short to prepare for what the chemo will do to me and when my doctor called after you did, hearing the details during my phone conversation scared him off."

"Oh, Suellen. I can't believe he would react like that. This doesn't excuse what you did to me though. Do you hear me? You didn't have to take this on yourself and leave me out of it. You had no right to decide this without . . ." Adam's voice begins to crack. "You had no right." He throws his arms around me and holds me against his shoulder. "I'm sorry I'm yelling at you. I'm sorry for all you've been through. I was devastated all these weeks thinking you went back to him."

We both fight back tears.

"I was devastated enough for the both of us." A tear skates down my cheek, rolls under my chin. "It's okay for you to be angry with me," I say, trying to regain my composure. "I understand. I didn't like the choice I had to make. The choice I made. I should have been truthful with you." Adam pulls back and looks away. He looks so sad that it makes me sad. I half hope he will come out with a quip from his vast repertoire of famous movie lines, but he stares down at the floor instead.

"You have to understand. It's been such a confusing and scary time for me. I handled it poorly. I know that now." I stand up from the couch then to deliver my best *Pretty Woman* impersonation. "'Big mistake. Big. Huge.'"

It must have worked because Adam emits a soft smile and the mood lightens a little. "Come back down here," he says, patting the couch next to him. "Talk to me. I want to know what you've been through, and what's ahead. And no holding back," Adam asserts. "You hear me?"

"It was small and localized, stage one. No lymph node involvement." I fill Adam in on what my last few weeks have been like. He lets me talk, asking a few pointed questions here and there. "I'm BRCA positive, so I went full removal to reduce the risk of recurrence. Oh, and full disclosure – I'm still under reconstruction." I look down at my boobs. "It'll take about six months to complete and I'll soon be starting chemo. It's my insurance policy." I look into his eyes, for the reaction in them, but all I see is unyielding sorrow. I shouldn't have unloaded all this on him in one fell swoop, but didn't he say not to hold back? Maybe he didn't mean it. Maybe he was just being thoughtful Adam. Is he feeling sorry for me? For us? A month ago, we were tearing each other's clothes off and throwing ourselves onto the bed, teasing one another and laughing. Adam's a creative foreplay guy. I loved how he would kiss and fondle my nipples. He won't be able to do that anymore. I'm already mourning the loss of my perky B cups. I feel a brief pang inside my chest as flashbacks of things I don't want to remember rush through me. I see Adam running his hands down my long hair, smiling with sensual mischief, his words and gestures exciting instead of commiserating. I miss the fun-loving man who could make me laugh like crazy, like a couple of kids just having fun before the seriousness of our professional lives recommences. Before life's bombshell blindsided us.

"I'm glad it's all out there now," I say to Adam. "The way I ended things has weighed heavily on me. I needed to conserve my energy for what I had to do, but I never wanted things with us to end the way it did or to hurt you. You didn't deserve that."

"I don't see it that way. Whether we're deserving or not, truth is truth. I forgive you, but it doesn't change the fact I'm still angry with you for not telling me," Adam says.

I acquiesce. If it were the other way around, I'd feel the same. I don't know why I never thought of it that way before. "You have every right."

Adam talks to me with the kindness and compassion of a friend, careful and attentive. A friend who is also hurting. We were flying high, discovering love, and bringing out the best in each other. There were butterflies and giddiness and magic. It was all there. Just on the cusp of something special. Adam gives me a soft kiss on my lips. As we cuddle together on the couch, I can't help wondering how long it will take for us to be happy like that again – to pick up where we left off and continue what we started. I'm depressed when I'm without him. Oddly, I feel depressed with him. I sense the shift, the change in us. It's like we're on pause now, our ephemeral happiness thwarted for a time. Time that now doesn't seem to be on our side.

"Have you had lunch?" I say going over to the kitchen and bringing down another plate, my shoulders feeling a little lighter. "We're having chicken and rice."

•   •   •

We all live with uncertainty in our lives. A cancer diagnosis makes it ubiquitous. Adam and I have been going through a time of readjustment. He's everything I knew he'd be. Thoughtful, considerate, patient. I'm moody – even more than usual – quick-tempered and on edge most of the time. I try to put myself in his shoes. My world turned upside down. His didn't have to. We'd only been together for two months.

While I adjust to my life after cancer, Adam placates and listens, our young relationship being tested in the harshest of ways. Working from home helps get my mind off the drawn-out, repetitive days – IV infusion treatments every three weeks, slogging through on the day after, perk-up days inevitably following. Repeat. We haven't had full sex since I started chemo. Adam's more anxious with that level of intimacy, touching me like I'm a fragile doll who will break easily. I get it. I'm not so desirable these days. I live in pajamas and go to bed early. I get depressed a lot. It's part of who I am now.

I rub my smooth head. It still seems unreal that I'm undergoing cancer treatments. I wonder how long it takes for a person's heart to catch up to their head which has long registered something bad has happened. The head is factual and aloof, but the heart wants what it wants. It defends and refutes.

Adam's dependable check-in phone call rouses me. "How're you doing today? I'll be by to see you on Saturday. Can I bring you anything?"

"I'm the same as I was yesterday, Adam, and the day before that one."

"Okay. Good," Adam says, because what else do you say to someone who's going through cancer treatments?

"Is it?" I say with derision. "Are you so sure it's good?" If he knew the thoughts going through my head he wouldn't think so.

"Look. We're going to get through this."

"We? No, Adam. *We* are not going to get through anything." *Why is he making this about him? He doesn't have to. He can walk away whenever he wants to.* It makes me feel guilty somehow. "I- . . . I'm schlepping through," I say. "That's the best I got."

"You know I'm here for you, Suellen." Adam is ever consistent and reliable. I can quote him verbatim as to what he's going to say even before he says it. *Let me help you. Talk to me. You don't have to do this alone.* "Tell me what I can do for you," he says. He's become so predictable and scripted. I miss his spontaneity. How can he possibly know how to act with me now? How can he know what I need or want when I don't even know what that is? I want to turn the clock back. This is my new normal, but it doesn't have to be his. He doesn't have to slog along with me. He didn't sign up for this. He signed up for a fun new relationship, traveling and discovering new places, new restaurants. Having lots of sex.

"You know what you can do for me?" I say curter than intended. "Give me space. I need space right now. Teagan's spending the day with me on Saturday, so you don't need to come over."

"Oh." Adam sounds disappointed. Or does he? I don't know what to think anymore. "The following weekend then," he says.

"We'll see. I'll let you know." I'm snappy with him. I want to give him an out.

"Suellen—," he says.

"Take a break, Adam. Go do something fun on the weekend. Go to a brewery. Go hiking or fishing or whatever else your heart desires. Just go."

The magnitude of what I said hits us both. My emotions are all over the place. I can't keep them at bay. I'm frustrated and angry, and I'm feeling sorry for myself. I don't want to have to keep putting on a happy face around him or feel remorseful for what this is doing to him. I feel myself falling back on what I do best whenever things get too tough for me. I start pulling away.

CHAPTER 21

Lucy and I rise out of bed. Teagan's coming over in a couple hours and I have some things I want to take care of before she gets here. Since my recent chemo infusion was over two weeks ago, I'm feeling energetic today. There are some projects I want to tackle before my next infusion tires me out again.

I head over to my closet and stare down at the bags of brand new unworn clothing and shoes, and designer handbags I'd forgotten about. I bring over the black plastic bags and boxes I purchased and start to assemble them. I've been spending more time with myself, assessing my life's choices and have become disgusted with my squandering habits. A new kind of energy surges through me. One of taking responsibility and giving and benevolence. I think about Edwina and Shaquana and how Edwina gives of herself to care for children who've either lost their parents or been taken from them; the extreme position Shaquana found herself in to save hers and her daughter's lives from further dangerous abuse or death; Adam, who donates his time and money to Habitat for Humanity, a charity that's close to his heart. They've all made sacrifices for the benefit of others, whether it's for survival or passion.

My shopping passion leaves me the way it starts. Unfulfilled and unsatisfied. I think about the triggers that send me to the stores – loneliness, boredom, unhappiness. Whatever it is I'm looking to fill, I never find it there. When life throws up a red flag, it makes you think about what matters, the meaningful things you've done so far, and how you'll be remembered. I can see my epitaph, *She had a treasure trove of things.* No! I can't let that happen.

Teagan looks flabbergasted as she navigates through the maze of boxes and bags in my front hall. "What's going on? I didn't see a moving van outside."

"I'm clearing out my closets. That's some things I'm donating."

"They're going to have to open up another branch for all this stuff."

"Come on in. Give me your raincoat. You can go through and take anything you want."

"I would if I was two sizes smaller."

"Your raincoat is soaked." I hang it on the coat tree to dry.

"The rain's not letting up."

"There are some handbags over in this box," I say, pointing to it.

"Those I might have a look at."

"We're having tacos. Hope you don't mind. I wanted to go out for lunch, but it's too dreary outside." I bring over some sodas and water, adding it to the table spread of tacos and fixings. "Mike working late today?"

"Saturday's are his busiest days."

"I didn't feel like putting on my wig. I don't when I'm home," I say, patting down the black textured head scarf I'm wearing.

Mom had insisted on taking me to a chic wig boutique in Brooklyn she'd heard about from an orthodox Jewish woman. When I saw the exorbitant price tags on the human hair wigs, I argued that a synthetic wig would hold the style better and that, after all, it was only temporary. But, Mom brushed away my rationale and I walked out with a luxurious wig that closely resembled my own hair, only better.

"Do whatever makes you comfortable. Are you planning on coming into the office more now?"

"Yeah. I miss being there. The camaraderie. The gossip." I laugh.

"You sure you're ready?"

"I think so. Mentally, I'm long past ready. One last infusion treatment and then I get my implants in a couple more months. I've expanded to near D cups now." I push out my chest. "How do they look? Good, right?"

"They look amazing," Teagan says.

"Yeah. I call them my Barbie boobs. I think they can stop inflating them now. Then onto the implants and nipple tattoos. It'll help cover the scars. Maybe I could ask them to tattoo butterflies."

"Is that even an option?"

"It ought to be."

"You went right back to working from home after your surgery at Suellen speed, and now you're taking on spring cleaning projects. How do you do it?"

"You know me. I never could sit still."

"You're my go-to for inspiration," Teagan says.

"Tell me what's going on with your adoption?" I lay out napkins and take a seat.

"My adoption dossier is thicker than the lawyer's diary. I'm trying not to focus on the length of the journey still ahead. Mike and I are working with a lawyer the agency recommended who handles private domestic adoptions."

"Wow. That's awesome. Let me know if I can help in any way. I just handled a foster-to-adoption pro bono case. I may be able to answer some of the questions that will arise."

"I'm afraid of getting too far ahead of myself. I've been disappointed before. Five failed in vitro attempts, fertility experts who said they could help us. I don't want to have to add adoption to the list of failures."

"Hey. This is going to happen. I have a really good feeling about this."

Teagan sighs. "I'm ensnared in yet another waiting game." She dribbles sauce on her tacos and gazes at the tower of boxes in my front hall. "What else is on your to-do list? You look like a woman on a mission."

"It's amazing the things that pop into your mind when there's so much downtime."

"Like taking on spring cleaning projects? Or bigger, bucket-list kind of stuff?"

"I haven't even tackled the bucket list stuff yet. But I guess I can add coming to grips with my shopping addiction to the 'things-that-make-me-happy' portion of the list."

"Your list has sections?"

"Sure. I've already done the crazier stuff, like going skinny dipping and singing bad karaoke."

"You went skinny dipping?"

"A few times, so I can check that one off. Then there were those riskier things, like when I took Dad's Porsche out pushing the speed on an open country road. He was away, obviously. Dad wanted me to check on his house while he and Eve were on vacation. I might have done a little more than just check on it. My brother almost had a heart attack when I told him. Then there are those even riskier ones. Like dating a psychopath."

"You must be talking about Steve."

"Check."

"Have you heard from him since you told him about your cancer?"

"Not a smidgen. It's like he fell off the face of the earth."

"Not such a bad thing," Teagan says. "Your bucket list is uniquely you." She grins.

"Oh, I'm just getting started. I keep adding to it. A checklist of feats I want to explore. I think I'm done with the crazier portion though."

Teagan opens up her phone and Google's bucket list items. "Okay. How about this one? Have you ever slept under the stars?"

"I went to sleepaway camp every summer until I was sixteen, so I can check that one off."

"Ever given blood? Made something from scratch?"

"Yes and yes. Meringue pie I made for Adam." I let out a long sigh. "Ohhh, Adam."

"What is it?" Teagan says.

"I wasn't very nice to him when he called me last. I told him I needed more space."

"Okay. Nothing wrong with that."

"I don't know how to explain it, but it's like having him around reminds me of what we were before cancer screwed us all up. No matter what we do or where we go, it's there with us. I see how he looks at me. Don't get me wrong. He's all I knew he'd be, but that's just it. He looks at me differently now, with sympathy and compassion, like a sufferer in need of a carer. I can't blame him. He sees me fatigued, my skin is pale, my head is bald. I look like someone who needs taking care of."

Teagan rests her hand on my arm. "You should try to connect with others who might be experiencing the same feelings as you are. You know, like a support group. People who know what you're going through and can shed some light."

I nod. Teagan's right. Adam and I are both in uncharted waters. I've never been so vulnerable before. He's never had to be a friend caregiver before. Since the rewind button isn't an option, the only way we can do this is to push forward. However we come out in the end.

•　　•　　•

"You're a really good person, Adam," I say, "and a truly good friend." I'm sure it was Adam's intention when we first met to be more than just a friend, but that's what it's turned into these last few months. If our relationship was nearing a ten before, it's been dialed back to a four or five. But that's okay. A best friend is the therapy I need most right now.

My last chemo cocktail wears me down. All I want to do is take a hot bath and nap. I have little appetite, but I don't want Adam to have to eat by himself. I nibble on a wing. "What did you wind up doing last weekend?" I say.

"I went out with a bunch of friends. Todd asked about you."

"How's he doing by the way?"

"Good. I met his new girlfriend."

"Sounds like he's doing more than good." Awkwardness hangs in the air between us as it often does. "Adam, I wish I could give you more of me. You deserve more. I'm so sorry for what this is doing to us."

"Suellen, you're my best friend. I'm here with you because I want to be. There's nowhere else I'd rather be." He cups my chin and looks into my eyes. "I don't want you to feel like you have to keep apologizing to me."

"Don't you miss . . . the way we were?" I look into his face and study his eyes. He can hide his feelings all he wants, but his eyes give him away. It hurts too much to look into them, see the sorrow there.

"Suellen, you need to stop this."

I turn away before he can reach me with his pity. "I tried to spare you all of this." I scrape back my chair and get up to go over to my bedroom. "I'm not very hungry. I need to go lie down." I slip under my bed covers. As I lower my head onto the pillow, my headwear slides off my bald head but I don't bother to put it back on.

Meeting when we did was unfortunate in its timing, allowing for a fleeting pleasurable couple's fling. Maybe we only get to have one short season. Or, I can look at it another way. Meeting Adam when I did was a blessing for what was to come. Although that doesn't seem fair to Adam. *I don't know what's happening. Why do I keep having these conversations with myself? Am I losing my mind?*

Adam is straightening up in the kitchen. I hear him moving about, talking to Lucy. *You are more than I deserve.* He comes over and lies down behind me. I roll over inside my blanket and close my eyes, and he spoons me into his body, massaging my shoulders and neck.

What do you do when the universe seems to be conspiring against you? When your world has thrown you a fast curveball? You do the unselfish thing. You do what's fair to the other person. You help them get out of its way. You respect their ability to make their own choice, not out a sense of obligation or with burden, but out of love. You let them go, no matter how hard it is. You hand it all over to fate, with its cruel sense of humor and equally astonishing grace.

My hazy mind fills with thoughts of Adam and what this is doing to him, and the one that comes to me like an epiphany before I drift off to sleep. *That is why I need to set him free.*

CHAPTER 22

The magnolia tree outside my bedroom window is in late bloom, a subtle yet poignant reminder of the time that's passed. There has been no change in the rainy weather lingering all week. No trace of summer since the beginning of May. I haven't seen Adam in the last couple of months. There was no argument, no fight, just a gentle resignation, an inevitable sense of ill-timing. It was subtle at first, winding down to a few short phone calls, then texts mostly. We both blamed it on work, but what it came down to was one thing. The pressure became too much for us. Letting him go was one of the most difficult things I've ever had to do. And the most courageous.

I'd hit a crucial turning point in my life and while my surgery and treatments have been successful, I know, in a deeper sense, I have more healing to do. I can come out stronger, take stock of my life's choices, go to a place I've never gone before. At least I hope I can.

As I take steady steps toward this new search-for-healing chapter of my life, one of the best things I've done was to return to the office. It helps keep my mind busy and my heart happy. I refuse to let cancer be my whole life. Little by little, I'm gearing myself up again to get back to the business of living, not just enduring. I'm more energized since I returned to work full-time, my mind filled with legal examinations, drafting pleadings, and lunch banter.

After doing legal research all morning in the firm's library, I return to my office and see my phone message light on. The message was left two hours ago, around the time I had retreated to the firm's library.

There's also a voicemail message left on my cell phone. Simon has been trying to reach me.

"Hello, Aunt Suellen." My brother's voice is high with emotion and happiness as he croons out the details of his daughter's birth on my recording. "Jeannie came into the world right on schedule weighing seven pounds three ounces and with an impressive pair of lungs I can tell you. She's really excited for you to meet her. She already has one tiny little gripe though. They can't seem to feed her fast enough." He chuckles. "Now who does that sound like?"

I put my head in my hand and smile tears of joy.

"Love you, sis."

"I'm an aunt, I'm an aunt," I squeal to no one but myself. I turn off my computer and inform the office manager I'm leaving early. I grab my purse from its drawer and race from the office so I can drive over to the hospital.

Teagan catches me flying down the hall. "Did you just scream?"

"I'm an aunt," I say. "I'm heading over to the hospital now."

There's a hint of despondency in her eyes but she rebounds, like someone who's had a lot of practice at hiding her private heartache. She gives me a hug. "Congratulations, auntie."

"I can't hold out until five o'clock. I'm way too excited."

"Don't let me hold you up. Go," Teagan hollers. "Just don't speed."

Going down in the elevator, I shoot off a quick text to the person I want to share this with.

Me

Adam, I'm an aunt.

Peering through the large window at swaddled newborns lined up in rows, I find her. Tiny features are scrunched on a pink face inside a snug, white blanket, her hair dark and silky, her eyes closed, and sleeping soundly. She's perfect.

My phone chimes.

Adam

Twice the love. Congratulations to all.

Simon walks over wearing his resident doctor's white coat, looking both tired and elated. We stare into the glass together. "I'm waiting for her to open her eyes," I say.

"Could be a while. She tired herself out crying," he says.

"My twin's a dad now," I say with humility and wonder. "You're going to be an amazing dad."

Simon slings an arm around my waist, and we nestle closer. "You're going to be an amazing aunt."

"How's Sarah feeling?"

"She's good. Taking a nap now."

Simon and I have always had a close relationship, partly because we're twins, but also because we became overprotective of each other during the worst of our parents' frequent skirmishes. When they would become intense, Simon would withdraw by crawling into his bedroom closet. I was the act-out one, angry and screaming to get their attention. I thought I could shut them out if I yelled louder, or that maybe it would make them stop bickering. I was old enough to understand my dad took care of sick people in his profession, but what my young brain couldn't understand was that he was a cardiologist, a healer of hearts, and yet he was breaking ours.

I grew up thinking all parents hollered and screamed at each other. I'm happy Simon has a caring, loving, and supportive wife in Sarah. Her close-knit family loves Simon, too, and treats him like a son. Simon pushed ahead, without compunction or resentment. Unlike me, still clinging to anger. When our parents split up, he allowed himself to cry. I never did. At least one of us has hope of changing the trajectory from all the collateral damage done.

Dad and Eve are coming down the hall, Dad flashing his brows over lowered eyeglasses, Eve managing a subtle smile. I may not be Eve's biggest supporter, but she is Dad's and that's what counts.

"So," I say to Simon before they reach us, "I think you should insist Jeannie call Eve 'Grandma' when she's old enough to talk. What say you?"

Simon snickers. "I love where your mind goes."

"That's why we're twins."

Simon and I do our best not to go negative when it comes to Eve, but a little lighthearted fun doesn't hurt. Dad gives me an affectionate hug and pats Simon on the back. Eve gives us each a proper embrace. "You're looking well," she murmurs in my ear as her cheek glides over mine. I wouldn't say we've grown closer, but things have been better between us, less rivalrous at least. Too bad it took a cancer diagnosis to get us there.

The next thing I know, an enormous pink Teddy bear and bronzed, bald man careen toward us. I recognize my mother's dressy flats below the stuffed bear she's carrying. "There they are." I'd know Morris' loud voice anywhere.

Handshakes and hugs are exchanged, and Mom pushes the overstuffed teddy into Simon's arms, its legs flopping to the floor. Now Simon vanishes behind it.

Morris' belly laugh resonates up and down the hall. It's odd not to see one of his expensive cigars dangling from his mouth – like he's missing a facial feature.

I know they didn't carry that huge plush toy with them on the plane ride from Palm Beach. It's the same one that took up the entire front window of the hospital's gift shop.

"Where is she?" Mom says, looking through the glass pane.

With his arms full of Teddy, Simon mumbles, "She's in the second—"

"No. Don't tell me. Let me find her. There she is. I see her. Oh, Simon, she's beautiful." Tears well in her eyes. "She looks like my kids. Yes, she does. She has the same chubby cheeks as Suellen did when she was born."

I scoot over to let the grandparents and adjuncts get a better view. Aromas of wood and spice and sweetness permeate the air from remnants of expensive cigars and flowery colognes, mingling with convivial chatter, a respite from their many disagreements and differences. Truth is my parents are much happier people with their new life partners. From their perspective, it was fundamental to their well-being. From Simon's and my perspective while in our teens, it meant a quieter house.

There are many versions of families. Ours may be less cohesive than some, but through all the upheaval and division, the good comes out despite it all. Hope has an equal. It's love.

Welcome to our crazy family sweet Jeannie. We already love you.

CHAPTER 23

I'm staying late at work to do some catching up. Now that my social life has been severely curbed, that includes Fridays. I continue searching inside the pantry room cabinet shelves where the snacks are when Lisa joins me. Our eyes meet and Lisa smiles in her inimitable way without creating a single crease in her cheeks, like one painted on a plastic doll. Like me, she's dressed in slacks for casual Friday, but she's anything but dressed down. Lisa's best version of casual wear is a smart black and white striped blazer over skinny black slacks with her hair clipped back to reveal dangle hoop earrings.

"I don't usually see you here this late on Fridays," Lisa says, her tone flippant. With her hair pulled away from her face, she's less able to hide her smugness. After losing her bid for partnership, she's added bitterness to her persona's repertoire. She takes a plastic cup from the cooler dispenser and fills it with water. When she turns around, she looks at me, cocking her head in that should-I-say-something way that tips me off.

"I've been meaning to tell you your hairpiece looks adorable. You wear it so well." It's Lisa's weak attempt at being amiable.

"You know, the thing I learned about wearing a wig is you never have a bad hair day," I say. "It's going to be hard for me to give it up."

Lisa looks up at the ceiling and purses her lips. "I wouldn't know. I've only done hair extensions."

"Here they are," I say, pulling a box of Tagalong Girl Scout cookies from the back shelf. "I knew they were in here somewhere."

Catrina strides over to the sink and puts a watering can under the faucet, filling it up.

"So this is the reason why the plants all look perky on Monday mornings," I say, pleased to see a friendlier face.

"I want *your* job," Lisa says to Catrina. "Maybe you get a little disappointed when a plant dies, but no one loses sleep over a dying plant." I can't believe Lisa's taking her frustrations out on the kind plant lady. "The only thing you have to worry about is whether or not the plants get the right amount of water." Lisa's not ready to quit. "Life doesn't get any less stressful than that." I cringe. Catrina turns off the faucet, unfazed.

In a smooth-over attempt I say, "The palm tree in my office has gotten really big. I brought a cut from it home. Do you have any suggestions you can give me? I haven't got a green thumb like you."

From her apron pocket, Catrina pulls out a packet of plant vitamins and sprinkles it into the watering can. "Kentia palms like fluorescent light which is why they make perfect office plants. Just don't put it in direct sunlight and I'm sure it'll do fine. Plants flourish in a cheerful environment." She smiles at me warmly.

Lisa pulls a face. "Humph. The palm in my office looks a bit drab these days. The sun is really strong in the mornings. Perhaps that explains it."

Catrina and I say nothing – only give Lisa a look.

Catherine joins us in the pantry room holding her eight-month-old son in her arms. Catherine had also been in the running for partnership but pulled her name out so she can focus on her twins.

"Is that Brian?" I say. "I can't believe how big he's gotten."

"My husband and daughter are waiting in the car outside for me," Catherine says, sounding rushed. "I had to come back because I forgot the cake I bought during my lunch hour. We're driving straight to my mother-in-law's house for her birthday party."

Brian sees the cookie in my hand. "Is it okay if I give him a cookie?" I say.

"Sure," Catherine says, bouncing Brian up and down in her arms.

Lisa leans her face down in front of Brian. "Aren't you a little cutie?" she says. Brian reaches for her gold hoop earring but Lisa flings her head back before he can grab it.

"Easy, Brian," Catherine says. "He's been known to rip people's earrings off."

Catherine grabs her cake box in one hand while still carrying Brian in her other.

"Have a nice weekend," Lisa says, looking past Catherine. Then I see what she's looking at. Jeff Simpson is headed our way, a navy blue jacket neatly folded over one arm, briefcase dangling from his other hand.

Trying to appear unaffected, Lisa looks away from him and gets right into Brian's face, tweaking his cheek and speaking directly to him. "So-long, little fellow. Come back and visit us again."

"There you are," Jeff says to Lisa, setting down his briefcase. "I'm glad I caught you. I just stopped in to grab a file. I'm catching a plane in a few hours."

"Oh?" Lisa says, unable to hide the surprise in her voice.

"I'm leaving for LA," he says.

"All business?"

"Rebecca's coming with me."

Ah, the wife.

Lisa's face registers astonishment. She bites down on her lower lip, her focus never leaving Jeff. She struggles to maintain her cool, but she looks out of sorts, like someone who's had the rug pulled out from under them, but hasn't acknowledged it yet. The attitude's still there, but the confidence has waned.

Catherine and I share a look.

"Who is this little guy?" Jeff sidebars.

Lisa answers him before Catherine can. "This is Brian." She's become his surrogate mother.

Brian kicks to be let down, his small fists pounding the air. Catherine puts the cake box down on the counter and lifts her son higher in her arms, shifting him to her other hip.

"Put a gavel in that little man's hand," Jeff says. "There could be a judgeship in his future." He turns to Lisa. "I want you to cover Thursday's motion for me in the Kleinman case."

"Sure," Lisa says, getting it out of the way to ask the next question. "How long will you be gone?"

"A week," Jeff says. He gives Brian a gentle tap on the head and then picks up his briefcase.

Brian starts to twitch again. "Well, I'm off," Catherine says, picking up her cake box. "Have a safe trip, Jeff."

There's a chocolate smear from Brian's fingers over Lisa's cheek and I start to tell her. "Lisa, you have some—" She waves me off with a bleak smile, anxious to be alone with Jeff. *Suit yourself.*

I dash down the hall after Catherine and Brian. Jeff's footsteps are not very far behind. "I'll call you when I'm out there," I hear him say to Lisa, his pace quickening.

I glance back at Lisa and see she's still where we left her, seething with fury. I wish she could see herself now, a disjointed version of her haughty persona.

The palm plant in her office is doomed.

CHAPTER 24

Teagan whips out a compact mirror from her purse and checks herself in it. "Arrgh! Sleepless in Livingston needs serious makeup magic."

"You look fine," I say. "It's only lunch."

"I can hide better in my office than in the firm's dining room. Just give me a sec and I'll walk down with you. I want to shoot off this email first." She snaps her compact shut.

I take a seat in the chair across from Teagan's desk and wait while she finishes composing her email, lifting the framed photo in its corner to look closely at it. Teagan and Mike are standing in front of a gigantic elm tree on an extended get-away weekend in Cape May. Teagan's blonde hair was long then, worn loose past her shoulders. The picture was taken several years ago, a trip she had timed during one of her so-called "fertile windows". The photograph depicts all the brightness and optimism that was theirs that day, a freeze-frame of hopefulness. You can see it on their faces.

Teagan pushes up from her chair.

"I always liked this photo of you two," I say, returning it to her desktop.

"I really should update that. We look like a couple of kids there. I love that tree. It's even bigger and more beautiful in person. The Inn referred to it as The Good Luck Tree, believed to bring good luck to all who touched it." She rolls her eyes at me.

The pre-cancer-diagnosis-me would have come back with some words of optimism for her. She could benefit from one of my dry-wit lines right now, but I can't seem to give it to her. Living with a cancer diagnosis for the past five months and spending hours in chat rooms where the women talk about what their diagnosis and treatments are doing to their families and relationships has used up whatever positivity I had in me. Their stories run the gamut from heart-wrenching to encouraging, but I'm still rebounding from life's blow. I give her a weak smile instead.

Teagan reaches her purse from the bottom desk drawer and closes the adoption folder still open on her desk. A quote written in her handwriting on the outside of it catches my eye.

When a child is born, there are two births:

The birth of the child and the birth of the mother.

"Ready?" she says, coming around to my side.

I rise up and we exit her office together in the direction of the elevators. "Didn't sleep well last night?"

"I don't think I even got four hours. Kept tossing and turning. Too much on my mind. My adoption case worker just gave us the breakdown of all the costs and expenses and Mike's getting all stressed out, which stresses me out." She hits the down button for the elevator. "Then I told him we need to start thinking about a baby's nursery. We've been using one of the spare bedrooms as a storage room and he needs to clean it out. Most of the stuff in there is his, but he keeps putting it off. Like he doesn't believe it's ever going to happen."

Lynne meets up with us by the elevator. "Have you two heard?"

Teagan and I look at one another. "We haven't seen Carol yet, if that's any indication," I say.

"Not even the gossip queen knows," Lynne says. "The news just broke."

The elevator doors open and we're relieved to be the only three people in it. As soon as the doors close Lynne says, "Lisa gave her resignation today. Says she's been offered a better position at Wright & Young in Manhattan."

"She didn't get what she wanted here, so I guess she wants to move onto greener pastures," Teagan says.

"Gee, I'm going to miss her," I say. Lynne and Teagan's faces turn simultaneously toward me. "It'll get boring around here. I mean, who else are we going to talk about?"

The elevator dings, the doors glide open, and the answer stares back at us. Rachel holds a cardboard lunch container in her hand.

"Eating with us today?" Lynne says. Rachel hasn't joined us for lunch in quite some time – not since rumors started circulating about her and Jeff.

"No. Leaving work early." Avoiding our eyes, Rachel swaps places with us and hits the button that will take the elevator back up to her floor.

"And you were worried we'd get bored," Lynne says, when the doors close.

·   ·   ·

I open my Styrofoam container, the heat from my eggplant parmesan hitting me smack in the face. Comfort food's what I need today.

I'm enjoying the exchanges with my lunch friends. I'm not in love with my life, so listening to them talk about theirs is a welcome diversion. Carol's wedding is at the end of fall, and she keeps us steeped in every phase of her planning, even the most minute of details. Today's topic is floral centerpieces and candles. Teagan's making plans to add a new baby to her marriage. And Lynne has been seeing someone, a widower named Lou whose son went to school with one of her daughters.

"I think our relationship has hit a crossroad," Lynne says, coming right out with it. She lifts the lid of her lunch container.

Carol looks up from her grilled cheese, her eyes so wide with curiosity that I think the proverbial saying doesn't only apply to cats. "What do you mean? Things were going so well. You said so yourself."

"They are," Lynne says. "So good he wants to marry me."

Eggplant gets stuck in my throat and I have to wash it down with water.

"Really?" we all puff out.

"Yesterday, Lou was acting melancholy most of the day," Lynne says. "I told you about the son he lost to addiction? Well, it was the second anniversary of his death. He started talking about the people he's lost in his life and how he doesn't want to lose me. I told him I didn't plan on going anywhere and then he took my hand in his and said, 'Let's get married.'"

Now I can feel my eyes widening. "And?"

"What did you say?" Carol says.

"I said, 'There's no need for us to do that.'"

Carol looks disappointed.

"I was trying humor," Lynne says. "I didn't think he was serious."

"Did it work?" I say.

"No. Lou became even glummer. I think his feelings were hurt. The rest of the afternoon I managed to steer him from the topic of marriage, but I don't know how long that will last."

"Why don't you know how long it will last?" Teagan says, looking puzzled.

"Because I'm not sure I ever want to be married again." Lynne scoops tuna onto her fork. "The talk of a merger scares the hell out of me. I can't lie. I've gotten used to being alone. I like things just the way they are."

"That, coming from you? A few months ago you told me how I should do everything in my power to save my marriage," Teagan says.

"That's different. You already have a stake in it. You and Mike have just been going through a rough patch. Marriages go through that."

"Thanks to you and Suellen, Mike and I have been working on each other again, for the sake of a new baby. And for us."

"It's what *you* wanted. We just coaxed you a little."

I nod in agreement.

"Do you love him?" Teagan asks Lynne. Her question heartens me as a wave of emotion shoots through me.

"I'm not sure when I knew exactly," Lynne says, leaning back in her chair. "But I remember a morning a few days ago after my girls went back to school and Lou slept over. He'd made me a wonderful omelet oozing with cheese and garnishes of parsley and hot sauce. I thought I was waking up in the Marriott. I took my first bite and said, 'You're amazing. I love you.'"

I chuckle, but Teagan shakes her head. "It doesn't count when you're speaking from your stomach."

"Another hopeless romantic," Lynne says with a sigh.

I remember when she had accused me of the same thing months ago. I almost lived up to it. I could have with Adam. It pains me to think of it.

"Okay. If you must know, I told Lou I loved him, speaking from my heart."

I feel my face flush and look at the beaming faces around me. There's a little hopeless romantic in all of us.

"I also think Lou's getting nervous that my girls will be home for summer break soon. The logistics will be harder. Do we get together at my place? His place? A hotel? Lou's car?"

"Ha," Teagan says. "I haven't made out in a car since . . . well, since before Mike and I got married. Might be fun to do that again."

"It is," Lynne says.

We dissolve into giggles.

"Lynne, you're my idol," I say.

Lynne closes the lid on her lunch container, signaling she is through. "One mortifying experience was enough for a lifetime," she murmurs while shaking her head.

Carol's hyper-zoom adeptness kicks in fast. "What was so mortifying?"

"Oh. It's too embarrassing. I can't even believe it happened."

Now we all zoom in. "You're not going to leave us hanging," I say.

Lynne leans back in her chair and relinquishes a sigh. "Lou and I had just left Rockefeller Plaza after seeing the Christmas tree. Oh, and what a sight."

We stare at her with eagerness. "Yeah, yeah. Beautiful tree," I say, hurrying her along.

"That can't be the mortifying thing that happened," Carol whines.

Lynne chuckles. "After the swarm of people, we were anxious to get out of there, to be alone together. We hurried toward Lou's car in the parking garage and were finally heading back to New Jersey, but the traffic coming out of the City barely moved. The congestion of holiday traffic continued even after we exited the Lincoln Tunnel." Lynne glances around the table at us, her captivated audience, feeling the need to present an explanation. "You have to understand, I haven't been with anyone in several years—"

"We get it." I grin.

"Go on," Teagan says, her green eyes animated with anticipation.

"It took all the restraint I had to keep from touching him while he drove. His square stubble chin, those brown Bogart eyes. When Lou turned off the busy highway, I realized I didn't just think it, I asked him to turn off at the next exit. His car came to a rest along some tall, wild hedges adjacent to a vacant lot, a this-is-good-enough assessment of the area made in an instant. He turned off the engine and we started kissing. The next thing I knew, I had wriggled out of my coat and he'd unbuttoned and removed my blouse. My bra was flung over the rearview mirror. We were still kissing when I thought I heard a tapping sound, but my brain pushed it away. The second time was louder." Lynne puts her forehead in her hand. "I can still see it. Lou's head came up slowly and turned all the way around, like in the Exorcist movie."

A squeal comes from Carol's direction but we don't look away.

"Under a light beam a young-looking face under a policeman's hat stared back at us. With my arms crisscrossed over me, I screamed. 'My blouse! Where's my blouse?' Lou twisted around to search the back where he threw it, his elbow knocking into the side of my head. I swear his fingers must have turned to all thumbs. I could have shopped for a new one and gotten it home faster than it took for him to give it to me."

We're all laughing now, tears running down our cheeks. Lynne is in full storytelling mode. Even she is crying with laughter. "He hurled my blouse at me so fast it smacked me in the face. When I pulled it from my eyes, Lou's hair was sticking out on his head. The Bogartian look had turned Laurelesque."

I'm clutching my stomach, trying to squelch the shriek of laughter.

"While Lou rolled the window down, I was still struggling to get inside my blouse. I'd managed to slip both arms in, but my fingers were inept when it came to the buttons. Then I heard the officer say, 'license, insurance, registration.' Lou lunged for the glove compartment, cursing under his breath while he delved inside it. The policeman asked him if his car was disabled. Then he told him to put the inside light on. His poker face was in our window, looking inside, his eyes bounding from Lou to my dangling bra and then falling on me. I was cringing and clutching my blouse closed where I couldn't seem to button it. I wanted to die."

"What happened next?" Carol says.

"He sent us on our way. But not before he gave us the name of a nearby hotel."

"I can't believe you've been keeping this story from us," I say.

"Anyway, I still don't think logistics for being alone together should be grounds for marrying," Lynne says. "We'll just have to figure it out. Of course, Lou says he'd marry me tomorrow but he's got to know I may never be ready for that."

We all get up to throw out our lunch containers and head over to the elevator to return to our floor. As I begin to come down from Lynne's hilarious story, remorse and regret creep into my mind. I wonder how Adam's doing. It's been a while since he last sent me a friendly text. He says he's been busy on cases at work. I'm tempted to drop him a text, check on him. But what would I say? *Hey. It's me. The girl who broke your heart. Just want to say Hi.*

God, I miss him.

CHAPTER 25

It's the wrap-up of another Friday, the beginning of looking forward to a weekend of being alone with myself. My Saturdays and Sundays are now measured in hours reading Kindle books or watching movies on Netflix and sleeping longer hours. The only social aspect is when I connect with other breast cancer survivors and high-risk women contemplating preventive surgery on a BRCA blog platform. In my old life, I would have been gone by now, ready to jumpstart the weekend. Now I linger at the office, telling myself there's more work I can accomplish, more that could be done, while outside my office, computers shut down, the hallway growing quieter. Fridays just aren't what they used to be. I'm still waiting for my real life to begin again.

I went to my early morning oncology appointment before coming to work today. I always take the earliest one I can. All indications that my breast cancer is behind me encourage me forward. Even my hair's beginning to come in. The cap of my head's smoothness is now coated with dark peach fuzz. I still wear my bob-style wig to work. I've gotten rather attached to it. Hopefully, with the weather edging toward summer, I won't need to wear it anymore. My color has come back, and my doctor's visits are more spread out, although I'll need to be followed up for five years before I can be fully discharged.

When I walked out of my doctor's office after the first appointment, the waiting room was filled with patients – young, old, men, women, all coping with varying stages of disease and treatment and prognosis. An elderly man who once sat next to me while I was waiting to undergo a chemo treatment said to me, "It's a good day when you wake up and can see the sun shining." There's always a place for hope. I learned that from some of the most resilient people I've ever met.

I step out into the hall and head toward the pantry room, wondering if I'll find any more of those Girl Scout cookies among the office's snacks stash. The only lights left on are in the hallways. Individual offices have gone dark and quiet as has the buzz of tapping keys and ringing phones and chattering.

When I reach the pantry room, I notice one of the office lights down the hall is still on. It's Jeff Simpson's office. I hear talking.

"You know I wish you the best," I overhear Jeff say in a cavalier voice.

Then another, higher, distressed-sounding voice. "'Didn't I mean anything to you?'" It's Lisa's.

I scurry into the pantry room, trying to make as little noise as possible. I don't want to be seen. Today is Lisa's last day. No one threw her a party or suggested an after-hours get-together to wish her well. She didn't make many friends at the firm, except for Jeff. But then that depends on one's description of a friend.

Before I can make a surreptitious move back out into the hall, Jeff walks past, his gaze straight ahead, attaché swinging alongside him with the energy of a pendulum. He would have seen me if he had glanced to the side, but he didn't. He exits through the door that will take him to the elevators, determined to be out of here.

I sigh and step out into the hall now that the coast is clear, no longer craving cookies. But the coast isn't clear. Lisa stumbles out of Jeff's office, her distraught face streaked with tears as she treks along the hall. I recognize brokenness when I see it. I've been there a few times myself. Evidently, her purposeful veneer isn't bulletproof. She's as startled to see me as I am to see her.

"You're still here?" she says, sounding curt and swiping at her wet eyes.

"I could say the same to you."

"I'm finishing up packing and then I'll be out of here for good."

My instinct is to give her a parting hug, but I'm not sure how Lisa will receive it. Her usual flawlessness, as she leans against the wall, looks tattered and as abstract as the modern teal and gray painting above her head. I can barely make out facets of her puffed-up personality. "Good luck with everything."

"Same to you," she says.

I assume she's referring to my cancer. "Oh. I'm doing good." I gaze at the abstract art, and then back at her again. "Wright and Young's a great firm. I know you'll do well." I mean it. Lisa's lurch at a casual sexual relationship with Jeff may have ended badly, but Lisa is driven and smart, with a personality to be reckoned with.

Lisa lets out a short sigh. "Yes, well, sometimes plans get thwarted," she says in a salvage attempt. "That's just the way it is."

I see a trace of regret, but then she lifts her chin in classic Lisa fashion and looks me straight in the eye. "I should be a Manhattanite before the year is out. I'll be getting an apartment there."

"That'll be exciting," I say as we start back down the hall together.

"At least now I'll be able to put my membership in the New York Bar to use."

Andrew, a guy from our mailroom, appears outside her office doorway. "Are the boxes all ready to go?" he says.

Lisa goes over to him. "Yes." I hear her say. "If there isn't enough room in my car's trunk, you can just put them in the back seat."

I turn off to go into my office.

"Wait," Lisa says from her office doorway. "I want to give you something before I go. Can you stop in my office for a sec?" Andrew is stacking boxes on a folding hand truck. "Those all have to go too," Lisa says pointing to more taped boxes on the back wall.

All at once, my eyes fall on the distinctive framed diploma lying on her desk, waiting to be packed up. Inscribed in Latin except for her name and the year, Lisa's diploma is almost identical to mine – Columbia Law School, Magna Cum Laude, Doctor of the Science of Law, 2007. Ten years before me.

"I'll have to make another trip," Andrew says, carting off some of the boxes.

Lisa tosses him her car key and then focuses her attention on a succulent garden terrarium on the credenza. "Would you like to have this for your office? It will be too much of a bother for me to take it."

"Are you sure? It's so pretty," I say.

"I'm sure." She lifts it with both hands and passes it to me.

"Thank you," I say, turning to leave. "I'll let you finish here."

"Have a great summer," she says.

I do a turnabout and face her again. "Say, I was wondering . . . by any chance would you be free to have dinner?"

"I- I . . . was planning on just heading home," Lisa says. She looks at me quizzically, like someone who's come to distrust sincerity.

"How about it? Let's you and me get out of here," I say. "You choose the place." I get the feeling neither of us wants to be alone tonight. I can have dinner with her, without pretension or judgment. Just two women, making our way, plowing through.

"It has to be someplace that serves liquor," Lisa says.

"Absolutely."

Lisa's face softens, warming to a kinder version of the person she puts out. "I guess I could. Yeah. That'd be nice."

Sometimes we have to bring our own sunshine.

•　　•　　•

I was dispirited and broken after the cancer, but the steps I'm taking to rebuild myself are getting easier, my visions for myself are clearer. Emptiness is filling with resolve, and my life's next phase is starting on more purposeful ground. On this breezy, warm Monday morning as I drive myself to work, I think about some things I can get involved with – charities and fundraisers, worthy causes where I can make a difference. While the pro bono case I worked on was one of the most heart-wrenching, it was also the most impactful and meaningful.

Dad's efforts are with the American Heart Association, Mom's are in the arts. Like them, I can do more. I *should* do more. I have the means and the time and have been asking myself, where do my passions lie? Adam's voice is inside my head. What are my core values? What moves and fulfills me? Maybe some of Adam has leaked into me. I can't deny that it has. Adam has infused me with his altruism. The person I was is not the person I want to be anymore.

I never gave much thought to my relationship with money. It was just always there. My careless, reckless approach toward it overflowed into my life on so many levels. I wonder why I never saw it before, the meaninglessness of my life's choices, the hurtful patterns, the pathology of self-perpetuating harmfulness, voids ever widening, never filling. It was all so foolish. The direct deposits go in, but I don't pay attention to them. I think about that, none too proudly, as I recall a time when Teagan told me she was waiting for her paycheck to clear so she could put it toward a riding lawn mower she wanted to get Mike for his birthday. Whenever she spoke of planning or budgeting, it was so unfamiliar to me, and I never felt more wealth-shamed.

Dad gifted me my car and he owns the townhouse I live in, which is paid for. He pays the property taxes on it and the income from the interest on my trust takes care of the rest. I get quarterly trust account statements, but I'm embarrassed to admit I rarely look at them. I just file them away, sometimes still in their unopened envelopes. And if that weren't enough, Morris set up a never-ending expense account for Mom that she uses for herself, and she gifts me and Simon from it generously.

I'm not working for a paycheck. I work to feel productive, and to be challenged. There's nothing more satisfying than problem-solving, or taking on a research project that catalyzes a successful lawsuit. I also work for the social and camaraderie aspect. Mostly, I work for self-preservation. I may never have to worry about money, but my relationship with it is an unhealthy one that needs to change. I have a responsibility and a moral obligation to give back.

I pull into a space in the firm's large parking lot. It's early, so I get a spot close to the entrance, just behind the row of reserved spaces. Bright yellow daylilies sway along the walkway leading to the building's entrance. I want to have time to use the exercise room on the lower level, where the dining area is. I've allowed an hour for it. That's another thing I've made a conscious decision to work on. I want to build my strength back up again. Yoga and meditation helped me during the treatments, but now I'm adding more cardio to my regimen. I take out my key card and swipe it to get inside the workout room. A couple of male lawyers are already in there doing some weightlifting. I don't know them well, just in passing.

"Good morning," I say, going straight over to the NordicTrack. They nod their hellos.

I start my drill. Riding, resistance, rowing. A wall-mounted television is on in the upper corner of the room, the volume down low. I consider putting in my music earbuds but I listen to the news on the television instead. The Breaking News ticker appears on the screen in bold letters, followed by a group of men in suits gathered in front of the cameras. I read the news bar scrolling under the picture frame. *Over a dozen people charged in New Jersey massive health care fraud scheme involving durable medical equipment.*

"Hey, isn't that Todd from our office standing next to the Attorney General?" one of the attorneys in the room says.

I step off the elliptical machine and hurry over to look up at the television screen. My eyes follow each of the men lined up behind the one who's speaking at the microphone. "That *is* Todd," I say, recognizing him. I have to squint my eyes to be sure who I'm seeing standing right next to Todd, my heart arguing with my head. The familiar face, wavy dark hair sliding across his forehead, stalwart stance. It's Adam. My heart squeezes as I hold my breath. If a two-dimensional picture of myriad tiny pixels on a flat-screen television can take my breath away like this, what would seeing him in person again do to me?

"Where's the remote?" I say. "Can we make this any louder?"

"Largest health care fraud scheme in New Jersey history investigated by the Attorney General's Office and State Police…"

I catch bits and pieces, my eyes never leaving Adam. He's standing with his arms behind his back, feet apart, looking relaxed and confident. "Hey, Adam," I say softly. "Hope you're doing okay. You look well." Tears begin to blur my vision.

The picture breaks into a Toyota commercial and just like that, Adam's gone, zapped from the screen, but not from my mind. I may have let him go, but I still struggle with my emotions. My feelings for him linger in my heart and my soul. For a few moments, I remain frozen in place, unable to move, while a memory of him making love to me plays for a moment. I was falling in love before my focus shifted. Before my world turned upside down.

CHAPTER 26

"You might as well go on without me," Teagan says with the phone cradled in her shoulder. "My adoption caseworker has me on hold."

I'm enthused by the hint of summer in the air, flowers all in bloom, a brilliant blue sky. I wonder if we can eat our lunch out on the picnic tables, but it doesn't look like Teagan's able to focus on anything other than her call.

"Something's come up. I can feel it." Teagan bites down on her lower lip, her nervous tell. "Oh god, Suellen. What could it be? My caseworker usually sounds cheerful, but she sounded so serious before she put me on hold."

"Do you want me to stay?"

"No. I'm probably just being paranoid." She covers the mouthpiece with her palm. "Go on ahead. I'll see you down there just as soon as I'm done with this call."

Lynne and Carol are already there when I exit the elevator on the lunchroom floor.

"Catherine may be joining us today too," Lynne says.

"Oh, good. She hasn't had lunch with us in a while."

Cream of mushroom soup is on the menu today. My favorite. I pay for the soup and grab a pack of crackers to go with it and a large chocolate chip cookie, my weakness. We settle around the table, each of us opening and spreading our lunches out in front of us.

"How's your mom doing?" I say. Catherine's mom, who'd been her grandchildren's primary caregiver, had a mild heart attack.

"Mom's doing much better. I've been looking at daycares, but I may have found someone to take Mom's place. Someone who will watch them at my house. Keeping my fingers crossed."

"Sounds like it's a lot to juggle." I often wonder how women balance career and family. I only have to worry about myself and that can seem daunting enough.

"I may cut back on some of my hours too, until they're older. At least that's what I'm thinking. These years will go by quickly. I don't want to miss them."

I look up to see Teagan walking over to our table. It's already 12:35. Lunch hour is half over. Sitting at the far end, I've saved her a seat. "Where's your lunch?"

"We thought you weren't coming down," Lynne says.

"My caseworker phoned me right before noon. You know, from my adoption agency." Teagan takes the empty seat next to me.

"Everything okay?" Lynne says.

"More than okay."

Carol cocks her head to one side. "What's going on?"

"I'm still trying to process it all." Teagan takes a breath before she begins. "It appears the agency received a very generous donation. Because of someone's kindness, my lawyer fees and expenses will be subsidized."

"Seriously?" Lynne says.

"I wasn't sure I heard her right either, but she said there's no mistake about it. The donor requested the funds go toward helping defray the cost of adoption for adoptive families and I was on top of the list. My social worker told me they have a family fund set up for that."

"That's incredible, Teagan. Does Mike know yet?" Carol says.

"No. I just found out. I haven't been able to get him on the phone yet. He must be with a customer. I'm still in shock."

I lean my head back against the wall behind me, a pair of long silver earrings dangling past my bob wig, and fiddle with the collar of my blouse.

"I'm still trying to wrap myself around this," Teagan says. "My caseworker wouldn't tell me anything about my benefactor. Only that it was a woman who preferred anonymity."

Catherine's eyebrows shoot up. "Are you saying someone's paid your entire bill?"

"Yes, that's what I'm saying. Except for travel and hotel stay, and incidental spending of course. We're going to need to go wherever the baby is when it happens. We might have to stay a week or two, enough time to check out the child's physical health and have a chance to bond. And meet the mother. As most domestic adoptions are open now, the mother will continue to be in touch with us." Teagan's hands go up to her cheeks and she lets out a scream. "I was like, 'let me get this straight, are you telling me I could be bringing a baby home and all that's left for me to do is put together some spending money?' I must have asked her that three times."

"You should eat something," Lynne says. "You have to keep up your strength."

"Here," Carol says, pushing her plate over to Teagan. "Have the other half of my turkey club. I didn't even touch it."

"I couldn't possibly eat a thing right now. I'm still shaking. Now all Mike and I have to do is wait to be matched. It's like being on call."

"At least now your financial concerns are out of the way," I say.

"Yes. I'm—" Teagan looks over at me. "What did you say?"

"I said, at least your financial worries—"

Teagan holds my gaze long enough that it makes me uncomfortable, her spinning eyes expressive and dramatic, as if she's piecing together the coincidences of everything. When a light goes on inside her head, I recognize it in her eyes. She releases a little gasp, and her eyes fill with tears. "Oh my god."

I busy myself with my empty soup container but can't stop the smile that animates my eyes, also glistening with moisture.

"This is all so wonderful," Carol says. "We may not realize it, but I believe there are angels among us."

Looking at me Teagan says, "You have no idea."

Lynne eyes the both of us with suspicion but says nothing.

Teagan lip-syncs so only I can see it. "Thank you." She blots a tear with her finger.

I clear my throat. "All right, all right. Not to change the subject, but I hate to see a good turkey sandwich go to waste. Someone going to eat that?"

Carol sighs heavily. "Leave it to you to think about food at a time like this, Suellen."

My mouth curls slightly. I break off a piece of my chocolate chip cookie and pass the rest around to share with everyone.

Carol diverts her attention toward the doorway. "Take a look at who just walked in," she swoons.

Lynne twists her head around to look. "Who is he?"

"New hire?" Catherine says.

"No, I would have heard," Lynne says.

"He's a looker." Carol blinks several times. "Wait a sec. I know him. Isn't that—?"

I'm unable to move. My eyes are telling me what my mind won't believe. The piece of cookie drops from my hand.

"It's *him,*" Carol whisper shouts to everyone at our table.

Adam's gaze finds me and he walks over to our table.

"Adam," I say in a way that makes it sound like an apology.

We hold a stare between us. I stroke my wig, and try to register that Adam is standing in front of me, in the firm's dining room, and not an optical illusion. And then he says something very Adam-ish. "Nobody puts Baby in the corner."

Someone gasps. Carol exclaims, *"Dirty Dancing."* Teagan elbows her in the side.

I continue to gaze at Adam. I may have also stopped breathing.

•   •   •

Little white petals blanketing the base of a nearby dogwood tree symbolize the end of spring. I stare down at the ground because it's easier than looking into Adam's eyes, and wrap my arms around myself. It's been three months since we last saw each other. The bench alongside the tree offers us a private retreat where we can talk on the firm's expansive landscaped grounds.

"I saw you and Todd on television the other day. Big bust, huh?" I say finally, looking him in the eye.

Adam nods. "Tell me, how have you been? Are you doing okay?"

"I'm good. Really good."

"I knew you would be," Adam says. His positivity and confidence touch me.

"I appreciate that." I lower my eyes again.

"It's the truth." Adam's dose of honesty is like a warm puff of air. "Todd and I are only here 'til tomorrow afternoon. We're staying at the Marriott not far from here. We're investigating a restaurant chain for violation of executive liquor license orders." Explains why he's here.

"So Todd decided to stop over and say hello to not-so-old friends?" I say.

"Yeah. And I hoped I'd be able to see you too," Adam admits. He turns to me in full force. "It really is good to see you. You look great."

I lift up my face. "So do you."

"I've missed you," he says, wrapping his arms around me in a hug. We stay like that, me leaning against his shoulder, holding back tears, and silently breathing. I can't believe how good it feels after the months of separation. The flutter in my stomach tells me I still have feelings for him. They weren't lost despite everything that's happened. I want to kiss his face. I want to tell him all that he means to me, how much of him I have taken with me, but a sense of cautiousness stops me.

After a brief, wordless interlude, Adam says, "What else have you been up to, besides working a lot like me?"

I smile because it's Adam. Asking questions, genuinely interested in the answers. "Rebuilding myself mostly."

"Why do I get the sense you're not just speaking physically?" Adam says.

"You always were a deep soul," I say with a grin. "This healing journey can get pretty heavy."

"I think about you a lot," Adam says.

And there's that flutter again. "I think about you too." I push a flyaway strand of wig hair that's blown into my eye.

Now Adam looks at the dogwood's shower of petals, lost in thought. I sense he wants to say something, but he holds back.

We rise from the bench and stroll over the green grassy hills toward the office building. Our conversation is casual. It's as though there was no lapse in our seeing one another. I can see Mr. Bender's all-glass corner office, the tall cane floor plant in the center of the window.

"Can you join Todd and me for dinner this evening?" Adam says.

My heart picks up speed. "I'd like that."

"You choose. You know this area best."

"I know just the place."

Adam laughs with ease. "Somehow, I knew you would."

We walk through the building's main entrance and grab an elevator to take up to my floor. "Suellen," Adam says, allowing pause. There's something about the way he says my name that makes me think he's trying to prepare me for what's coming next. "I should tell you I just started seeing someone." The ride to the third floor upsurges at the exact same time my heart drops. I'm unable to speak for a few moments.

"I met Diane a month ago."

I can be strong. Cancer showed me what I'm capable of.

"I wouldn't think you'd be alone these months, Adam. Diane's lucky to have you." I hope he can't see what my smile is hiding. "I want you to be happy."

"We can continue to be friends though, right?"

My thudding heart misses a beat. I feel like I just got back on the Kingda Ka roller coaster ride of emotions. "Of course. Friends." Staying in the friend zone might be easier. It's the lie I settle on.

"Your friendship means a lot to me. I mean it, Suellen."

I can respect that. "I feel the same about you." I tuck it away and tell myself to just be happy with that. "Come on. I'll show you my office."

Keeping Adam as a friend is too important to me, I realize. I don't want to lose touch with him again.

Adam steps inside my office. Across the hall Teagan glances with curiosity around her desk through the open doorway. Her Cheshire cat grin makes me want to laugh and cry at the same time.

Adam leans into the photo on my desk. "Is this your niece?"

"Oh, yes. Simon's daughter. Her name's Jeannie. I absolutely love her." I sink into my chair. "Grab a seat." I have to force down the scream searing inside me. *Adam's sitting across from me in my office. It's great but tough now that I know he's seeing someone else.*

"Do you know who Todd's visiting with?" I say.

"No. I'll text him."

"You can wait here until he shows up. I have some work to finish up before I can leave and meet you both for dinner. I'm looking forward to it."

"Sounds good. I just texted him. I'm guessing he knows where your office is."

"My office hasn't changed."

"It's a nice office with a great window view."

A file on my desk gets my attention. "Say, do you remember me telling you about a pro bono I handled where a foster parent wished to adopt a child whose mother was imprisoned for murdering her husband? It was several months ago, so you may have forgotten."

"The woman's husband was a violent abuser. I do remember," Adam says.

I should have expected that answer. Adam always took an interest in everything I told him. "Well, the adoption's going through. I just received a letter from the State and from the girl's foster mother thanking me for my endorsement."

"That must be a good feeling for you." Adam's realness impresses me. He gives me a sanguine smile that ignites so many reminiscences of him.

Todd's voice is coming down the hall greeting everyone.

"How does it feel being back here?" I say, getting up to welcome him into my office.

"Like I've been gone forever and like I never left. Does that make sense?"

I chuckle. "Yeah, somehow it does."

"How are you doing?" Todd asks me.

"As I was telling Adam, I'm doing good, thank you. I appreciate your bringing him by. It's so good seeing you both."

Adam rises from the chair. "Suellen's going to meet us for dinner tonight. Seven good?"

"Perfect," I say.

"Where to?" Todd says.

"I was thinking of the Greek place on Route 10. You must know it."

"Sure. I love that place."

"Picking up where you left off I see," Adam says. He answers Todd's questioning look. "Suellen's foodie bucket list."

"I'll make the reservations. You're going to love it too," I tell Adam, smiling. "Trust me."

When they are gone – and only when they're gone – I close my eyes from the sting of tears starting to burn behind my lids. I lean my head back in my chair and sit in my thoughts for several minutes. Adam's honest disclaimer about having a new girlfriend feels like a train wreck in my heart, but it's one I put into motion. I let him go, to do and be whatever he wanted. I trusted the bigger plan and gave it up to fate. I never expected he would take part of my soul with him.

I'm truly happy for Adam and I feel good about that. He deserves to be happy. And someday, I can feel that way again too. It just can't be with Adam.

My outlook on life changed the second I heard the dreaded C-word. I've learned to appreciate the positives. The course my life took has helped me focus on the good things that come my way, like a good prognosis and clear tests and having Adam back in the picture. And in less than five hours, sharing dinner with good friends.

CHAPTER 27

My head fairly glistens with new hair growth. I run my fingers through the front pieces to see if I can create some bangs, but they're still not long enough. Four, maybe five more weeks I convince myself. When the hairs come halfway down my forehead – the marker I've set for myself – then I'm ditching the wig.

I secure the wig cap on my head and then take the wig from its stand and place it over the cap. It's a chic, straight-hair chin-length wig the color of dark chocolate. I look like a sixties woman in the blue, metallic-flecked shift dress I have on. Three-quarter sleeves cover my thin arms, so the weight I've lost during chemo isn't as noticeable. I'd be a rail if it weren't for my enhanced fake breasts, the transformation of my body in harmony with my new outlook of finding the good in every situation. I feel confident in my new breasts. My plastic surgeon has become my new best friend.

My phone rings and I answer it. Adam and Todd have arrived at the gatehouse. Since the restaurant is close to my townhouse, Adam, ever thoughtful, phoned to say they'd pick me up so we could all go together.

I open my front door, still in my bare feet, and welcome them inside.

"Nice digs you've got here," Todd says, coming into the living room.

Adam gazes around in a sentimental sweep as memories seem to flash before him. I'm wondering if it's those where I dragged my weary body around and dozed a lot or my favorite one, a trail of our clothes leading to my bedroom where he made love to me all night long. The emotional clarity hits me hard. My heart thumps inside my chest, and, in a lingering, psychic moment, our eyes meet and it's as if we're the only two people in the room. He's remembering that too.

Lucy appears out of nowhere and rubs up against Adam's leg. "Hey, Lucy," he says, bending down to stroke her fur. I'm touched he never forgets her name.

Todd looks at me with a discerning eye, like these last few minutes are telling him everything he didn't fully know. I'm not sure how much Adam has told Todd about us, but from the look on Todd's face, I'd say he knows it all now.

"I put some cheese and crackers out on the kitchen island," I say. "Please help yourselves while I put on my sandals."

As soon as I'm inside my closet, I cover my face in my hands and instruct myself to breathe. Our new casual-relationship pact is going to be harder than I imagined, but I have to comply with it. Since I'm learning how to be my own best friend, I can be his best friend. I slip on gold slingbacks and grab my shoulder bag. At the doorway, I pause and take in a deep breath before returning to Adam and Todd.

"I didn't offer you guys a drink," I say, joining them in the kitchen.

"We'll get a drink at the restaurant," Todd says. "If we leave now, we'll be right on time."

Walking to Todd's car, I realize my neighbor is watching through her window, a wide smile breaking out on her face. I give Gladys a hearty wave and she waves back.

Glancing out the rear window as Todd drives us to the Greek restaurant I spot Steve's jeep going in the opposite direction. He can't see me and doesn't know Todd's car. A woman is with him wearing dark sunglasses and there's a flash of blonde hair. She slings it back, laughing. I lean my head back on the seat with a glad sigh.

•　　•　　•

"*Airplane*," Todd says. "That one still has to be the funniest movie of all time."

"That was a good one, but I have to go with '*There's Something About Mary*,'" Adam says. "I must have seen it over a dozen times, and it gets funnier every time I watch it."

"Oh my god, yes. Ben Stiller," I say. "The scene with Mary's dog was hilarious." I bite into a pizza slice appetizer of feta and Greek yogurt, hoping to reduce the heady side effects of the ouzo. Todd is drinking the aperitif with me, but Adam takes a pass.

"I've got one," I say. "'*Mrs. Doubtfire*' with Robin Williams."

"That one's a strong contender," Adam agrees.

"Although I must say, I was rooting for Pierce Brosnan's character," I say.

"That's because you couldn't separate him from his James Bond persona," Adam says.

"I could. I did. He's just so hot. I mean, he's the male equivalent of Angelina Jolie or Nicole Kidman or whoever it is you guys find sexy."

I laugh, and for a few fleeting moments, I'm happy. I push the appetizer platter closer to Adam. "Come on. You didn't even try the stuffed grape leaves."

"No, but I had the bruschetta."

"I can see your culinary tastes haven't been upgraded."

"Diane's family owns a steakhouse in Lawrenceville," Todd says. "It's a match made in heaven."

The joyful moment shatters. Adam gives me an uncomfortable smile and I shift in my seat before casting my eyes to the floor, afraid what they'll give away.

I realize this calls for a follow-up. "So how did you two meet?" I say, keeping my voice cheerful.

"Todd's fiancé introduced us," Adam says.

"Wait. What?" I turn to face Todd. "Fiancé? Todd, when were you going to tell me you're engaged?"

"I met her on an online dating site six months ago. She lives in Princeton Junction, not far from where Adam and I live in Lawrenceville."

"Wow. Those match sites are that good, are they?"

"We just hit it off. I knew I wanted to marry her after our first date. I know. It's crazy, right?"

"No. Not crazy. It's inspiring. So the phrase 'you just know' isn't just a cliché?"

"I guess not," Todd says.

The waiter removes our cleaned appetizer platter and sets our dinners out in front of us. A Mediterranean orzo salad, lemon chicken soup, and gyros.

"What about you? Are you seeing anyone?" Todd says.

"Me? Oh no," I say, with a barely concealed eye roll. "I don't think I'm ready to dip my toe into the dating pool just yet."

Adam has gone quiet.

"I'm going to have a glass of white wine with my dinner," I say. I'm rationing my alcohol intake since my cancer diagnosis to no more than three drinks per week, so I'm still within the recommended quota. "How about you two?"

Todd and Adam opt for a beer.

"You'll come to my wedding, won't you?" Todd says.

"Of course. When is it?"

"October 22, in Princeton."

"That's four months away," I say, raising my voice and sounding surprised.

"I know. Her dad's one of the senior members at his country club, so the ceremony and reception will all be there. There'll be lots of singles attending."

"Oh, then I'll definitely be there," I say with mock gusto. "You know Carol's wedding is the following month."

"Those two are finally tying the knot?" Todd says. "They were together for forever it seems."

I shrug my shoulders. "Some people just need to do more work to be ready. Not everyone's so eager to take the plunge." I give him a gentle smile.

"Like me you mean. I know. Getting married is momentous. But I didn't expect to fall in love when I did. I used to tell my mother all the time that I wasn't going to get married until I was at least thirty-five. And that was a hard maybe. I was going to sow my wild oats long before anything like that ever happened." Todd laughs at himself before he drinks his beer. "I can't explain it. I only know it became clear to me she was the one, and the next thing I knew everything I thought I wanted for myself went completely off the rails and I was shopping for diamond rings, and that's when I realized everything had changed."

I swallow a lump of remorse in my throat, my eyes filling with tears. As soon as I blink, they spill down my cheeks.

"I'm sorry. I didn't mean to make you cry," Todd says with a half-smile.

I put up my hand and reach for my napkin to wipe my eyes. "It's just that you explained it so beautifully." I can feel Adam's eyes on me, but I can't look at him. I'm afraid to look at him. I don't want him to see the pang of self-reproach in my eyes. I take a large sip of wine. "I'm a crier. I was wrecked watching '*Good Will Hunting.*'"

"It was *Forrest Gump* for me," Todd says.

"Jenny," we cry in unison.

And just like that, we're back to movies again.

Todd and I turn to Adam who has become quiet. I dare myself to look at him and he trusts himself to look back. "*Romeo and Juliet,*" he says just above a whisper.

"Wow," Todd says. "Nothing like bringing out the big guns."

"When it seems like the whole universe is colluding against you, yeah. It doesn't get bigger than that." Adam's heartrending reflection nearly undoes me. He looks at me with an intimate gaze and then, in one swift move, pushes off from the table and excuses himself to go to the men's room.

Todd clears his throat. "Umm, am I sensing something here?"

"It's a lot," I say, heartache thrumming through my body. "I hurt him."

Todd chugs his beer and then sets it down. "It really messed him up for a while what you were going through. He felt helpless and lost most of the time. I know it's none of my business but, why did you two end it?"

"It was my doing. I pushed him away. I sabotaged us. Me and cancer. I didn't want him to feel like he needed to take care of me. That helpless feeling he had? I felt it, too."

"I can't imagine what it was like for you or Adam," Todd says. "And I'm not even going to try. This is way too heavy. But for what it's worth, I don't think he's gotten over you."

"I'm not going to get in the way of a new relationship for him. I've hurt him enough. I'm just glad we can be friends."

Todd gives me an incredulous look but lets it go as soon as Adam returns to our table. I take a nervous gulp of wine while inside my chest my heart cracks just a little more. I can't let it show though, or I may never see him again. I may have survived cancer, but I swear this let's be friends thing is going to be the death of me.

CHAPTER 28

How the topic of craziest-place-you-ever-had-sex got underway I couldn't say, but it's the same as it is with many of our lunch banters. It starts innocently enough, and then it turns into something more outrageous. That's how we keep it fresh and exciting. Besides, everyone's in an upbeat mood and for good reason. It's September, post-vacations and shore getaways.

I scrapped the wig several weeks ago in a private ceremonious ritual in front of my bathroom mirror one morning before leaving for work. For one thing, it was too hot to wear outside. When I palmed the new hairs on my head and rubbed the baby softness, I decided it was time. I call my new pixie style *freedom* hair, its low maintenance being the obvious reason, but also because it's the last vestige of my cancer treatments.

When I had first walked into the office, I got lots of double takes, and then praises and good gasps followed by phrases like, "I wish I could wear my hair that short," or "I love your dramatic new look," and my favorite one, "I never realized short hair could look just as sexy as long hair." It's okay. I got that they were all trying to overcompensate for the reason behind it. In another week I'll be getting my nipples tattooed on.

Mom's visiting from Palm Beach for Rosh Hashanah, staying with me at my place, and spending time seeing her new granddaughter.

I'm actually enjoying her company. She's a lot less resistant and a lot more amenable since she became a grandmother, and since her daughter had cancer. I'm even thinking I can coax her into tasting tonight's savory brisket. Sarah's mother is making it and I've had hers before. She makes it with onion soup mix and some other seasoning zings. It's delicious.

As different as I often saw my mother and me, we do share one thing in common – the cancer risk marker. Coupled with her holistic philosophy approach, Mom's elected to get mammogram screenings every six months for now, but she'll be turning fifty-two, and her mother died of breast cancer at fifty-six. Mom may never get breast cancer, but there's no crystal ball, no way to ever know. It's like waiting for something that may not happen. But if it does, it wreaks havoc.

Morris stayed back in Palm Beach, all tangled up in his production company's newest concert. *A Love Affair with Sinatra.* No offense to Ol' Blue Eyes, whose music I happen to enjoy, but it's the audience of aging millionaire Sinatramaniacs that I don't fit in with. So it's listening to Sinatra on my iPod while taking a shower for me.

Carol's talking about wedding cake tastings when a text comes in on my phone. It's from Adam, and my heart palpitates, almost making me scream with enthusiasm. I have to force it back and swallow it down, hoping no one notices. The last few texts we exchanged were back in the beginning of summer, after we'd dined with Todd, and when I told him how much his friendship means to me. There have been few texts since. And now, here he is, dropping me a line again.

I want to take my phone into a private room and read his message to me alone, but I chide myself on how silly I'm being. It's not like his text will be so provocative as to warrant that kind of secrecy. It amazes me how he still occupies much of my brain. I tap on his message and try to keep my face calm.

Adam

How's it going?

Not so provocative.

Me

Great. Really great! You?

Adam

I'm good. Heard you'll be at Todd's wedding. It'll be good to see you again, catch up.

He wants to see me again. I am giddy. I keep my lips sealed, afraid the squeal roiling inside me will come spurting out of my mouth any second.

Me

Yes. I'd just responded. I'm looking forward to it. And to seeing you again.

Too much?

Carol's voice seems to come from a far-off place. "Are you still with us Suellen?"

"What? Oh. I was just reading a text that came in from Adam. He says he's looking forward to seeing us at Todd's wedding." Carol and Joe have also been invited and are attending.

Teagan gives me a hopeful look. She knows how I still feel about Adam.

"I can't believe Todd's beating me to the punch," Carol says. "Who'd a thunk it? I mean, this is Todd we're talking about, the guy who loved his singlehood more than anything else."

"Seems he's had a change of heart."

"A change of heart is trading in your old car for a newer one," Carol says. "A nuptial is a bit more dramatic, don't you think?"

"I'll say." I don't feel like disagreeing with her. Besides, I'm too distracted and ever more anxious to keep on texting Adam. I wonder if he's still seeing Diane. But, why wouldn't he be? Still, I have to know. But I can't just come out and ask him.

I gather up my lunch waste and throw it in the trash can. "I'm going to head back to my office. I'm leaving early today." As soon as the elevator doors close, I resume texting Adam.

Me

Todd's wedding weekend is loaded with activities. Should be lots of fun.

Adam

It's going to be busy.

Me

Especially for you. You're in the wedding, aren't you?

Adam

Yep. We both are.

There it is. The answer I was looking for. Yay. My heart sinks.

Wait. It still doesn't mean they're together-together. Adam had said Diane was a friend of Todd's fiancé, so of course she would still be included. There's a pathetic part of me I'm not too proud of right now.

Me

Excited to meet your girlfriend.

That was big of me.

I step off the elevator onto my floor and walk toward my office, waiting for a response, but it doesn't come. Reaching my office, I shut the door behind me. Still nothing. I clutch the phone to my chest and close my eyes. *Should I text him again? How long should I wait before I do so? Does my last comment even warrant a response?* And then those three lovely little dots appear again. He's texting.

Adam

Who's your plus-one?

He's wondering if I'm bringing a guest.

Me

Going stag. It'll just be little ol' me. 

There's another hesitation pause. *Ugh.* Silences can mean so many things in text messaging.

Adam

Still can't believe Todd's tying the knot. Didn't take him very long to go from determined bachelor to bridegroom. 

Me

He sure fell hard. Happens to the best of 'em.

Adam

Guess so.

Another text break.

Adam

Happy Rosh Hashanah.

I lean my forehead against the door. It only took one tiny word in a text message to bring me down from a hopeful high. How in the world am I going to be able to handle seeing them together? I realize I've never been in this situation before, loving someone you can't have. Someone I gave up. It hurts like hell.

There's a tap on my door and Teagan opens it to a crack to peek inside. "Hey. Can I come in?"

I wipe a tear from the corner of my eye and open the door wider to let her through. She takes one look at me and her sigh comes out in one long puff. "Come here," she says, wrapping her arms around me, her hug carrying with it all the weight of a sympathetic friend.

"Honestly," I say, "I don't know if my heart can take much more."

•   •   •

The candle is lit before sundown. The table is spread with raisin challah bread, matzo ball soup, mouthwatering brisket, honey-glazed carrots, and a couscous salad for Mom. Simon and Sarah live twenty minutes from me in the same town, a custom-built center hall with five bedrooms they hope to fill with their offspring. Jeannie's just the first of more to come. Sarah's mother, Esther, tries to get Mom to taste some of her brisket, and Mom does something I never thought I'd see. With noble aplomb, she puts some on her plate and takes a bite of it. "Esther," she exclaims, "this is delightful." But when Esther tries to put more on Mom's plate, Mom says with politeness, "Oh no, no, I couldn't. I haven't eaten meat in years. Small steps, Esther. Small steps."

Esther says, "Oy Vey." Simon and I laugh.

"I'll take it," I say with exuberance. "I love your brisket." Esther is every bit the nurturing Jewish mother, coddling and feeding you as a means of expressing affection. *Adopt me, Esther. Adopt me.* I look down at my full plate. My appetite has returned with a vengeance.

"Don't forget to save some room for dessert," Sarah says. "Chocolate rugelach."

I enjoy being with Sarah's parents, her warm mother, her mensch father. Spending time with them always leaves me feeling content.

Jeannie fusses from her baby swing and Sarah starts to get up. "Let me," Simon says, going over to pick her up. I watch him as he cradles her to him, kissing her forehead, and rocking her up and down. He has the dorkiest smile on his face and speaks to her in a language I've never heard. The scene is far and away the sweetest thing I've ever set eyes on. In a flutter of emotions, seeing my twin, the love in his eyes for his daughter, fills me with vicarious happiness.

•   •   •

"I was wondering what happened to – what was his name? Adam. Whatever became of him?" Mom sits across from me at my kitchen table on the following evening, forking her arugula and kale salad.

"Nothing. We're friends. That's all," I say, not looking up.

"Seemed like it might have been a lot more than that."

"It was, and then it wasn't." I poke a strip of steak too hard and the fork slips from my hand onto my plate. I push off from the table. "Will you have a glass of wine with me?"

Mom and I are having dinner together at my place this evening. Just the two of us. I already had the Salads House take-out menu pulled out since it was the only legitimate vegan place I could think of within twenty miles. I'm tempted to have Mom try some of my skirt steak, but then that could backfire on me. She might like it and the next thing I know, she'll be telling me I should move to Miami so we can enjoy eating skirt steak together. She still hasn't given up on my moving down there. I think she'd do almost anything to get me to move closer to her, including eating meat and poultry.

"I remember you made me a perfect Bloody Mary when I stayed over a year ago."

"I could make you one if you'd like. I'm reducing my alcohol intake, so I'll make myself a virgin."

"No. White wine will go better. Well, Adam let a wonderful girl go," Mom says.

"Actually, I'm the one who did the letting go." That's all I say. I have no intention of telling her more. I pour her a glass of wine and change the subject to something she'll enjoy hearing. "Do you know Jeannie gives me a big smile now when she sees my face? I think she recognizes me."

"She's too precious." Mom twirls her fork with a piece of acorn squash on the end of it and then points it at me. In the same way an animal can sense a natural disaster, I know what's coming. "Tell me, Honey, are you putting yourself out there again?"

It's her third day here, and it amazes me it's just now coming up. Jeannie has been a good distraction. My mother is ever interested in my love life, and if she had her way there'd be no set boundaries for the intimate details either. When she used to go off about her and Morris and their mutual libido, I had to remind her I was her daughter and not her friend. "I didn't just hear that," I said, covering my ears and humming over her loudly. The visuals were a lot harder to erase.

"I hope you're meeting guys. You ought to, you know." I don't think she notices she's shaking her fork at me now. "You're beautiful, in a Mia Farrow way with your short hair," she muses. "It's coming in thicker. And your svelte figure, except for those enhanced boobs of yours." She gives me an appreciative smirk. "Those long legs."

"Not so long," I say, staring at her still-uneaten piece of squash.

"You could be a model."

"Maybe if I was five inches taller," I say, playing along.

"Okay. A petite model." Mom finally puts the squash into her mouth.

I understand this is Mom's way of cheering me forward, encouraging me to let go of any anxieties I may harbor since my breast cancer diagnosis eight months ago, but I have one question for her. "*Who's* Mia Farrow?"

"She was the actress in *Rosemary's Baby.* You'll know her when you see her picture. She was married to Frank Sinatra for a short while." Mom pulls up a photo of her on her phone.

"I don't look anything like her," I say, laughing.

"No. You're prettier."

"Says my mother."

"From the moment you were born, your grandma used to call you *Shayna Punim.* Yiddish for *pretty face.* Do you remember that?"

I shake my head. "Not really. I wish I'd gotten to know Grandma Ellen better."

Mom lets out a silent sigh. "You have her eyes." She takes a sip from her glass and lets the wine sit in her mouth for a moment. "So," she deflects, "what are you going to wear to the wedding next month? I saw the invitation on your refrigerator," Mom says, answering my puzzled look.

"Oh. Right. I'm sure there's something in my closet I can wear. Something I've forgotten is there."

"Not getting anything new?" You'd think I just told my mother I was going in something I'd gotten from a thrift shop.

"Most things in my closet *are* new," I say.

"We're going shopping before I leave here," Mom says as if she hadn't heard me. She picks up her glass of wine and swirls it. "And then we can look at earrings to wear with the new dress. I'm thinking dangle earrings with your shorter hair. Something dramatic." She reaches over to touch my hair, sliding her hand over it and down my neck. "Or maybe hoops."

"Usually don't wear dangly earrings," I say. "Hoops, yes."

"That's because you always had long hair. Maybe we can also book a makeup appointment at MAC."

I watch my mother as she takes a sip of her wine, her face lit with such enthusiasm, a myriad of deck-my-daughter-out ideas filling her head. For a few seconds I see my six-year-old self, walking with her and Simon into the synagogue wearing a white lace dress during Shabbat. I'm tugging at the sleeves and pulling on my collar in irritation, my inner tomboy resisting and wanting to yank it off. The image makes me laugh.

Mom's in her element, and I can't deny that her happiness rubs off on me a little. "We'll get an early start on Saturday," she says. "We want to be able to check out a few shops and have lunch." It's classic Mom.

I haven't gone shopping in months, keeping to my new resolution. I realize I'll be doing this more for her than for me, but it's our thing. It's always been our thing. *Shopping, lunch, more shopping.*

"Since this is a black-tie affair, you'll do a full length."

"There's also a pre-wedding cocktail hour," I say. "And a brunch after the wedding." Might as well band together.

Mom claps her hands. "Fabulous. Then you'll need dresses for those, too. A chic cocktail dress. Something glamorous and sexy. Of course, we wouldn't want to upstage the bride now, would we?" She giggles. Maybe we aren't so night-and-day after all.

"Sure you don't want to try some of this strip steak?" I say. "It's good."

"You know, maybe I will have some," Mom says, to my complete surprise again.

I lean back in my chair, relishing Mom's enjoyment. Eating steak. Planning a day of shopping with me. Unlike when I was six, the contagion of happiness doesn't escape me.

Way to let Mom be Mom.

CHAPTER 29

The saying, 'you can't choose your family' is a sound one, but we do get to choose who we want to bring into it. Simon chose Sarah for his wife, the latest addition to our family before Jeannie came into the world. Sarah has one older brother who lives in Manhattan, so neither one of us experienced having a sister. By far, Sarah is the best gift my brother ever gave me. My unbiological sister. And now, mother to my adorable niece.

Having finished feeding Jeannie, Sarah lowers her into her crib while I stand back and watch, mesmerized. While Sarah was breastfeeding, an unexpected pang of sadness hit me. I won't be able to experience that. Maybe I wouldn't have minded, if only I could have been the one to decide it.

Content from being nursed, Jeannie's fallen asleep. Snug inside a bunny-patterned blanket, her four-month-old face peers out like a pink-cheeked bisque doll with closed lids, her fringe of lashes slightly darker than her downy reddish hair. I could stare at her for hours.

Back downstairs, Sarah pours us each a tall glass of decaffeinated iced peach tea and passes mine over to me. "I'm constantly thirsty," she says. "I know it's normal when you breastfeed, but I must drink a gallon of water a day." She sees my awed expression and adds, "That might be a bit of an exaggeration. Come on. Let's go sit in the family room."

Simon and Sarah's great room is the largest room in the house, an open-concept room of various neutral blends, dark wood, and huge bare windows that look out onto a wraparound deck and meticulously manicured lawn stretching as far back as you can see. Once a heavily wooded area, a smattering of newly planted trees now dot the landscape. Many of the large trees were taken down to make room for the neighborhood's new high-priced houses, most on a one acre-minimum of property.

"How long will she sleep for?" I say.

"She'll be up around two in the morning to feed again, and then around seven. Sometimes she still takes three naps a day. Thank you again for the pumpkin onesie. It's the cutest." Wearing no makeup, her auburn hair clipped in a messy bun, Sarah could pass for eighteen. They met through a friend, and Simon was smitten with Sarah from their first date. Up until she had Jeannie, she was teaching second grade. She loves kids and since she's turned thirty now, I have a feeling Sarah will be 'barefoot and pregnant' for the better part of the next five years. She's the quintessential mother, unruffled and flexible. We never know what kind of parent we'll be until we are one, I guess. But some of us, like Sarah, seem to be born with a mother's natural instinct, while others have to grow into it. With the exception of early-childhood nannies, guess you could say I was essentially motherless most of my young life. My own mother was the best-friend mother, or at least she tried to be. Now that I'm older, it suits us better.

"When does Simon get home?" I say.

"Not sure. He's on call this whole weekend. I'm glad you could have dinner with me. We don't get to do this often enough." Sarah looks down at her blouse. "I didn't realize my sagging breast was still exposed." She finishes buttoning up her blouse. "Did Mom get back home in time to make Morris' Sinatra production?"

"Yes. She'd have hated to miss that."

"Tell me, how are you doing?" Sarah says. "You look terrific by the way. I love your trendy hairstyle."

"Who knew textured fringe would be a thing?" I take a sip of iced tea and set my glass down on the table. "I'm working a lot and, well, working a lot," I say honestly. "I can't believe in January it'll be a year.

A life-changing one. Soon, I'll have to think about whether or not I want to continue paying the annual storage fee for my frozen eggs."

"Of course you must," Sarah says. "You don't know how you'll feel about it in years to come."

"I know. I've been researching my options, should I want to have a child. Surrogacy's one option, but since my cancer wasn't estrogen receptor positive, IVF pregnancy is not out for me. Still, I'd worry about passing on the BRCA gene mutation." I stare outside the window at a wild rabbit grazing on the grass. "I could do egg donation so as not to use my own genetic material, but then the baby wouldn't be mine in the DNA sense. You wouldn't believe how strict the criteria for egg donation are. Donors are fully vetted, and only three or four percent from a large number of applicants end up in a pool. They have to go through a psych evaluation and be medically qualified, of course. Non-smokers, and absolutely no one over twenty-nine is considered, though twenty-one-year-olds are preferred."

"That disqualifies me," Sarah says.

"And me," I say. We both laugh.

"You have to have at least some college education. They want to know your SAT scores. And here's the best one on the list: be attractive and good-looking."

"The donor must get paid a lot to do this. How much do they get?"

"About $10,000 in New York, plus all expenses paid." The brown rabbit skitters off in the dusky half-light, and I think how, in a few more months Jeannie will be able to appreciate a wonderful nature scene right from the enormous window.

"Wow," Sarah says. "It's amazing when you think about it. Women who might not have been able to have children many years ago now can."

"There's the cost factor certainly," I say. "My friend Teagan opted to do a domestic open adoption. She's had five unsuccessful attempts at in vitro."

"Oh, dear. I can't even begin to imagine going through that. What it must do to you emotionally and financially."

"It does take a toll."

"There's also the preimplantation genetic diagnosis method. That's where researchers are able to identify embryos without the BRCA mutation before they implant it in you."

"More reason why you need to keep your eggs in storage," Sarah says.

"Anyway, soon after child-bearing, were it to happen, I have to think about having my ovaries removed. It's a lot to think about."

"Okay, so choose not to think about it. Put the yearly storage fee bill on autopay. That way you don't *have* to think about it." An unseeable approach to minimizing stress. Sarah's got a whole kit of calming strategies she's put to work on her seven-year-olds.

"Hungry yet? I'm going to order our pizza," she says. "Simon will no doubt wind up eating at the hospital tonight."

As Sarah starts to put in our pizza order, her phone goes off. "Speaking of Simon, that's him calling. Suellen and I were just talking about you," she says into her phone. "What? Not coming home? You're sleeping at the hospital? Oh. Okay, hold on." Sarah looks over at me. "Simon wants me to put him on speaker phone. He thinks you should hear this too."

"Me? Whatever for?"

"Suellen?" Simon says. "Hey. What're you up to?"

"Umm, about to have dinner with your better half." Why does it sound like Simon's hit the pause button on what he really needs to tell me?

"A forty-six year old man was brought into the trauma center last night. He'd been struck while at the crosswalk by a vehicle making a right on red. Apparently, we're learning after he was hit, the vehicle veered into a telephone pole. The driver was drunk." Simon pauses for a breath. "Suellen . . . " My adrenaline surges. Somehow, I know what he's going to say even before he says it. "The driver of the vehicle was Steve."

I cup my face in my hands to calm my breathing. "Oh no."

"He was off-duty in his own car. A female passenger was with him at the time. They were not wearing seatbelts and were pummeled by the air bags when they hit the pole but not seriously injured. The pedestrian he hit had to have emergency spine surgery late last night. Looks like he's going to pull through, but he may be paralyzed."

"Oh dear god," Sarah and I say in unison.

"We just have to wait and see. It's all over the local news," Simon says at the same time as I pull it up on my phone.

A drug-recognition officer was called to the scene and determined that thirty-year-old Steven Holt smelled of alcohol, had watery, bloodshot eyes, and slurred speech. Charges identify Holt as an off-duty patrol officer. Toxicology results are pending on a blood sample taken from him. A red light camera showed that Holt never applied his breaks before he entered the intersection. Officer Holt is accused of driving while drunk and has also been charged with reckless driving while causing serious bodily injury. As a result of his arrest, Holt has been suspended without pay.

"Oh my god. He could lose his job over this," I say.

Simon is less concerned about Steve's future. "I'd say you dodged a bullet."

Seems I've been dodging all kinds of bullets. I don't know why I'm shocked. I shouldn't be. "Yeah," I say, "Guess I have." *Only by the skin of my teeth.*

CHAPTER 30

Carol, Joe, and I have checked into the hotel where we're staying for Todd's wedding weekend activities. This evening's welcome cocktail party is the first event in a three-day celebration. The historic hotel is secluded inside a forested area so guests can forget they're in the lively college town of Princeton. I wish the serenity being fostered here would carry over to me, but I'm feeling anything but relaxed. I convince myself that seeing Adam with Diane may just be the closure I need.

I stand back from the wall mirror to inspect how I look with a critical eye. My mother's voice is still in my head. "How adorable and flirty you look in that one!" Adorable and flirty in a backless electric blue skater dress wasn't exactly the look I was going for, but here it is. No more of those compression bras I had to wear post-surgery, no more bras period. Going braless has never been easier.

Carol texts me she and Joe are ready to go to the welcome gathering party whenever I am. I'm grateful they're here with me because I don't know anyone else besides Todd and Adam. I give my hair a quick shake. That's the thing about short, layered hair – the scruffier the edgier.

Joe's a sweetheart. Ever more conscious that I'm without a partner, he insists on taking my arm in his while Carol holds onto his other. I think he's enjoying the optics of being caught between two women.

The elevator doors open to the expansive lobby where a sea of wedding guests dressed in cocktail dresses and suits surround a bubbly overflowing champagne tower. "Are you guys ready to do this next month?" I say to Carol and Joe.

"I think so," Carol says feebly.

"I think I need a drink," Joe says.

I've never seen Carol look more daunted than she does right now. For the first time that evening, I catch myself laughing.

There's no sign of Adam or Todd. We're told the bridal party is engaged in a private activity. I feel better already. Plus, the champagne's beginning to do its job.

Carol whispers in my ear. "That guy over there's hitting on you."

A guy with a short beard standing to the side watches me. I catch his smile and give him one in return, the universal signal for "Yes, I'm single and available." It's been awhile, but I think I'm getting my groove back. Or maybe it's the dress.

"Hey, looks like Adam just walked in," Carol says.

My heart does a complete flip, and the drink I'm holding trembles in my hand. Were it not for the fact that I'd drunk half of it already, it would have splashed me, I'm shaking so much. I swig more champagne, working up the strength to turn around and look at him. Does alcohol-strength even count?

Someone intercepts him midway. Adam gives him a pat on the shoulder and glances over in my direction. There are over a hundred people in the hotel lobby and yet somehow my eyes telephoto him. He locks onto my eyes and smiles. My thrill at seeing him rises with the champagne bubbles. In his sleek navy suit and necktie, his good-looking, clean-shaven face sends shivers down my spine. I try to return his smile, but unlike with the guy in the beard, the muscles in my face won't do what I tell them to.

"Looks like he's working his way over," Carol says, throwing him a little wave.

The pain of seeing him again rushes me, and, just as I'm thinking it was a bad idea even coming to this wedding, Adam walks over.

"Suellen. You look amazing." He eyes me up and down, and my insides go all haywire. Then he gives me a wholehearted hug. "It's really good to see you again."

"You too," I say, willing the tears not to come.

Adam pulls back to look at me again. "I like your hair like that."

A cursory swipe of my bangs to remind myself of my new hairstyle. His smile buoys my spirits and I can smile back now, slowly but surely. Adam's genuine warmth and affection is winning me over again. Like I've been saying: it's just Adam. Kind, loving, adorable Adam.

"You're looking pretty good yourself," I say. I don't remember his pupils looking so big. I steer him over to Carol and Joe. "You remember Carol from my firm, and this is her fiancé, Joe. Next month, it'll be their turn to tie the knot."

"Congratulations," Adam says.

"Where's Todd and the rest of them?" What I really want to know is, where's Diane? My curiosity's goading me.

"They're still getting their pictures taken."

A waiter holds a tray of appetizers in front of us. "Think I will," I say, feeling the effects of too much champagne.

"I might need some help here," Adam says. "What exactly is that?"

I laugh. "I forgot you don't trust anything that isn't meat or potatoes."

"Whatever it is, it's good," Joe says, reaching for another before the waiter walks away with it.

I take a bite. "So, this is a date stuffed with goat cheese and wrapped in prosciutto."

"It's delicious," Carol says. "I wonder if we can add these to our cocktail hour, Joe."

Another waiter passes by us with a different tray of canapes – watermelon bites with feta cheese and mint. Adam takes one but passes it to me.

"Not going to try it?"

He grins and shakes his head.

"They're so pretty," Carol says. "Aren't you the slightest bit curious to taste one?"

"And just when I thought I'd made good progress expanding your palate," I say. The little pink, juicy cube fits perfectly in my mouth, and as I slide the toothpick out, I realize Adam's watching me. A shadow passes over his large pupils, his chocolate eyes are wistful, and a flash image of us eating Indian cuisine together grips me all at once. I wonder if he's thinking the same thing. His eyes close briefly and when he opens them, his gaze is more intense.

"There you are." A woman with long blonde hair and even blonder highlights wraps her arm around Adam and jolts us from our shared memory.

Adam's eyes drop down. He passes a hand across his dark textured hair and then introduces Diane to us with the preamble that she's his girlfriend. *She's beautiful. But, what did I expect?* My upbeat mood sinks a little.

"It's so nice to meet friends of Adam and Todd," Diane says in a natural tone that reveals nothing. She's dressed in a pink, pleated midi dress, her loose curls cascading over slim shoulders. Next to my playful backless swirl of a dress, she looks classic preppy. But then, I don't know why I'm comparing the two of us. My thoughts go back to something Adam had said at dinner with me and Todd a few months back. We were talking about Hollywood stars we found attractive, and he mentioned Gwyneth Paltrow. Then it dawns on me that I could be looking at Gwyneth's double. Diane's super-model body has that girl-next-door look, projecting classiness and suburbia. And then there's me. Darker hair and features, feisty to a fault.

We continue making small talk. "How long have you and Adam been friends?" Diane asks me.

I flinch from the regret still trapped in my chest as Adam's gaze falls on me. "Not too long." *We met around the age of ten, but there's no need to go there.* "Todd's a mutual friend of ours." One thing I pick up on is how nice she seems. But then, this is Adam's new girlfriend I'm talking about, the guy who makes good choices. Except when it came to me. He didn't deserve someone like me. But even Adam can experience a temporary lapse in judgment.

The guy with the beard is still watching me with an assessing gaze. I wish I could tell him it's a lost cause while Adam's here. I can't think about anyone else besides him, no matter how hard I try.

"What are these cute little things?" Diane says, looking at a tray of little boat-shaped tasters.

"Caviar with cucumber," the waiter tells her. She places one on a cocktail napkin for herself.

Another waiter behind him carries a tray with something that looks like beef strips on crostini. "Adam," I say with a little too much enthusiasm, "here comes something you'll like." As soon as I say it – hearing the way it sounds, all too familiar and knowing – I wish I hadn't.

Diane looks at me askance. "I know how much he likes steak," I say, overcorrecting with too much clarification, sinking me further. *Shut up, Suellen. Just shut up.*

Adam takes one and his eyes spring open. "Yes. Now this is more like it."

"Good call," Diane says to me. She stops the waiter. "We'll take another, please."

I'm certainly not as nice as she is.

•   •   •

The shuttle bus taking the discreetly eager wedding guests to the country club is fully occupied, a plethora of silks and satins and chiffons embellished with sequins and rhinestones and lace, the enclosed air infused with opulent scents of jasmine and vanilla and musk. When an orange whiff reaches my nostrils, the potpourri of various fragrances is almost too much, making me lightheaded.

"Wasn't that a nice touch last night when we were treated to cookies and warm milk in our hotel rooms?" Carol says.

The thought of warm milk right now makes me want to gag, and I have to force down a swallow. But for the sake of positivity, I nod.

We step off the bus into mild evening air that's still warm from the strong afternoon sun. The Tudor-style country club is aglow in the dusky atmosphere. All the women assembled in front are checking out each other's gowns, and the men are scoping out the women wearing them.

An off-the-shoulder, gold-metallic ball gown with a side slit is my look for today, a glamorous and dramatic contrast to yesterday's party dress. Carol's evening gown is a short-sleeved sheath the color of merlot.

"Stand right there," Joe says, holding up his phone camera and taking our picture.

"Okay, now you two," I say.

Carol rebukes Joe when he drapes a heavy arm over her shoulder. "Not like that," she says. "More elegant-like, hand behind my back." Joe's low grumble sparks an exasperated huff from Carol, but he complies by placing his hand on the small of her back.

I love these two. Their relationship is more on par with that of a seasoned married couple.

I spot Adam talking with the other groomsmen, drawing a slight gasp from me. I watch him while he's distracted, looking handsome in an Italian black silk wool tuxedo and bowtie, an orchid flower boutonniere the color of fuchsia sprouting over his breast pocket. I die another thousand deaths inside.

An unmindful sigh escapes my throat that doesn't get past Carol. "You okay?"

"I will be after I get a drink in me." It's the quickest way I know to allow myself not to feel.

"You still care for him, don't you?" Carol gives me a sympathetic smile.

"I just wish he didn't look so damn hot."

Carol puts her hand on my shoulder. "Suellen, you look absolutely beautiful. You are red carpet stunning in that gown. And that cleavage!"

"I *am* a bit bustier, aren't I? And no push-up bra either."

"You know you can have any one of the single guys here if you want."

"But I don't want," I say softly.

"Whatever happened between you two anyway?" Carol looks at me, trying to understand. "I mean, he may have a girlfriend, but I saw the way you two looked at each other. Things don't look too settled."

"He's moved on. That's as close to settled as it gets."

The guests are being moved to a terrace for the ceremony. One by one, the women are ushered to a seat. One of the groomsmen takes my arm. Chin up, shoulders back, he escorts me up the aisle at the same moment Adam looks up and sees me there. I want to pretend I don't catch his long glance. I want to pretend eyes can lie. It's easier when I don't know what's real or pretend anymore.

The picture of Todd and his alluring bride in front of a waterfall backdrop is breathtaking. Cobblestone paths pave the way to the sweeping golf course just beyond. Todd looks so happy standing before the woman he's about to marry, a beautiful slender blonde wearing her hair in a chignon bun speckled with hairpin pearls and dressed in a sleek, modern mermaid gown of satin. I realize I'm becoming emotional. I'm not alone. Carol and Joe look at one another and I overhear Carol tell him he can hang his arm over her shoulder any time he feels like it and the three of us chuckle gently.

After my first cosmopolitan, I'm feeling chipper in a mellow kind of way. Then, I discover I'm not sitting at the same table as Carol and Joe in the dining hall, and it sets me back again. Two tables are designated for those of us who aren't coupled up.

"Table eighteen's right next to nineteen," Carol says. "We're not so far apart."

Pulling out a chair that faces the dance floor at my reserved table, I scatter smiles around it as it fills up. We introduce ourselves to one another. Six men and four women. A gender ratio not unlike in the state of Alaska. The guy with the beard from the hotel cocktail reception has snatched the seat on my right. He goes by the name of Chris. He was a college friend of Todd's. The guy on my left is Tim. I can't remember if he said he was a friend of the groom or the bride.

While couples sway together on the dance floor to Ed Sheeran's "Thinking Out Loud," the unattached of us congregate by the bar.

Among the dancing couples, I see Carol and Joe and Adam with Diane. He holds her by the waist while she hooks her arms around his neck, her blonde hair splayed over his shoulder and the drink in my glass disappears down my throat. "Can I get you another?" Chris says. Or is it Tim? Or someone else entirely. I should try to engage more. Or, I could just drink myself into a stupor.

Mindful of my drinking quota, I opt for a club soda.

After the song ends, Adam and Diane work their way over to the bar together. I'm unable to tear my eyes away from them. I'm an expert in self-torture.

Diane grips his arm, and then she drapes it over her shoulder. Everything about the way she touches him – and she's always touching him – is proprietary. It looks needy. Or is it insecurity? I can't tell which.

Adam gets them drinks. No one's seen the bride in a while. The band has a special song they want to play for her at Todd's request. One of the bridesmaids tells us she's in the ladies' room having a tear in her wedding gown sewn. Todd is among us all of a sudden, shaking his head and rolling his eyes. Someone passes him a drink.

"How long does it take to mend a rip?" Todd says, looking frustrated.

Adam pats Todd on the back. "What is she doing back there? I never know what she's doing."

I burst out laughing. I think I'm the only one who does. Diane gives me an odd look so I unriddle it for her. "'*Wedding Crashers.*'"

She shrugs and emits a humorless laugh.

Adam shoots me an appreciative smile.

Diane reaches up to the back of Adam's neck and runs her possessive fingers through his hair. Maybe I'm reading more into it than I should. I shove my impression away.

The music changes, and Diane tugs at Adam's arm. "I love this song. Come on. Let's dance." Adam follows her to the dance floor, and I watch them until they become lost in the crowd.

Before I know it I, too, am on the dance floor, carried along by mass momentum. One fast song flows into the next so there's no beginning and no end. Soon, the dance space turns into an overflowing bedlam of under-forty-year-olds dancing the night away, Todd and his bride at the center of it all. A bevy of fuchsia bridesmaid dresses intermixed with a horde of tuxedoed men take up most of the floor. It's anyone's guess which of them will shut down the dance floor.

As evening progresses into late nighttime, the swarm of warm, flushed faces sweating out alcohol is all around us. I leave to go to the restroom, climbing a marble staircase until I reach a beautiful lounge with French country loveseats and elegant wall mirrors. Diane's in there talking with another bridesmaid, fixing her makeup in one of the vanity mirrors. I slip past her unnoticed.

"I feel like I'm losing him. He's vague and removed, like he's pulling away." Diane's speaking. At least I think it's her. I glance at her in one of the mirrors.

"I'm sure you're wrong about him," her bridesmaid friend reassures.

Diane notices me then and she hushes her friend. "Let's go," she says, her voice trailing as they exit the powder room.

I'm slightly buzzed, but I'd swear they were talking about Adam. *Did I just tipsy over to hallucinatory?* I can't still be experiencing brain fog, can I?

The dining room is pulsating with dancing when I return. There's no sign of the party slowing down. The music's all fast now, clearing the less zealous dancers from the floor.

"Where'd you go?" Carol tugs at my arm. "Come on. Dance with me. Joe's taking a break."

I'm dancing and laughing and singing to the lyrics of Whitney Houston's "I Wanna Dance with Somebody," but my heart is the biggest betrayer. I can look like I'm having a great time, fool Carol and everyone else, but I can't fool *it*. I find myself looking around for Adam, but I don't see him anywhere.

Joe joins me and Carol on the dance floor for the next number, and then Tim stumbles in front of me. He's drunk and falling all over himself. I close my eyes so he can't see how turned off I am. When I open them, it's Chris, and whoever else happens to come into my small cosmos. My wispy bangs fall into my eyes, and as I brush them away, Adam suddenly appears in my space. He is right smack in front of me, and I have to blink a few times to bring him into believable focus. His eyes flicker across my figure, my face, until they meet mine. Our bodies continue moving to the endless stream of music, but our eyes hold still, saying all the things we're afraid to say. Can he feel what I'm feeling?

Dancing bodies surround and squeeze us, but I see only him now. His eyes are transfixing, but a tinge of anguish burns behind them, and it hurts me to see it there. I didn't notice it before. It's as though we are seeing each other's thoughts. "I'm so sorry," I mouth to him, feeling the need to say it.

My brain cells are blasting off in the fast lane, my heart racing to keep up. When did the music get too loud?

The dance floor seems to shrink as the guests close in on me, blaring music rivaling the buzz of alcohol and noise going on inside my head, and then it's strange how I can't hear it anymore. There's no sound. I can hardly breathe.

Adam's eyeing me with a look of concern on his face.

I can't keep doing this. I have to get out of here. I need to be anywhere but here.

I break his gaze and run from the room, through the grand foyer, and out through French doors leading to a balcony and fresh, open air.

CHAPTER 31

I breathe in cool air, the quiet night steadying my breathing and calming my nerves. Bringing my hand to my chest, I lean against the railing, filling my lungs one small breath at a time. The doors swing open and Adam walks toward me.

For the longest moment, we just stand there, looking at one another wordlessly. I'm glad he can't see the tears forming in my eyes in the dark night.

"Are you all right?" he says.

"It just got to be too much for me in there." I fold my arms tight across my chest and turn away from him, looking out over the railing onto the expansive grounds.

"Can I get you some water?"

Adam's voice is closer. "No. I just needed to get air." I keep staring out. It's too hard to look at him. I'm in new territory. Self-preservation has to take over.

"Suellen," Adam starts. "How do I explain the enigma of my situation? Where do I even begin?"

"Can we just skip to the end, please?"

"Hypothetically speaking, if you knew your feelings weren't on par with someone you were seeing, would you tell them the truth? Or would you go on ignoring those feelings?"

I can feel the heat from his body close behind me. It's excruciating. I turn around to face him, my truth. "Me? I know me. I'd want to get the pain over with. One day, it will stop and then that person can be with someone who feels about them the same way they do."

Adam puts a hand on my cheek, wet with tears. "That's what I think too. It especially isn't fair or right for someone to be with a person when they're in love with someone else."

I cock my head and my true Suellen takes over. "Just to be clear, are we still talking hypothetical here?"

Adam grins. That beautiful, mischievous grin I always loved. "I've missed you," he says. He takes me by my shoulders. The touch of his hands on my skin thrills me and I close my eyes. When I open them, he's still staring. "I might have lied when I told you I hated you when I thought you were still seeing your ex. I needed to tell myself that to ease the pain. Even then, I think I knew I was falling in love with you. I've never stopped."

I release a small gasp and my head falls onto his shoulder. He smells so good, he feels even better. I graze his neck with my lips until it reaches his ear, and I whisper, "I might have lied, too, when I said I was excited to meet your girlfriend."

Adam throws his head back and laughs. He sees me rub my naked arms from the chill in the air and takes off his jacket, placing it over my shoulders. He leans over then and tilts my chin so he can kiss me, his lips parting mine gently. I swirl in a turbulence of emotions I can't tell apart. Hypotheticals and pretending aside, I tell myself, Adam is here, right now, kissing me, loving me. His lips feel exquisite and familiar, my brain shooting off sparks as it remembers. When his kiss changes, full of desire and craving, I respond with just as much longing, my mind grasping what is happening.

When we force ourselves apart, breaths heaving, I look into Adam's eyes. "I should never have come here," I say, my emotions piling up. "I'm sorry for everything that's happened. For all I've put you through. Put *us* through. I'm sorry for all the hurt I've caused you. But most of all, I'm sorry I ever let you go."

"Shhh," Adam says softly, kissing me on the forehead. "I'm glad you came. I had to see you again, to know if my feelings for you were true and not just in my imagination. I never stop thinking about you. The truth is, I've been in a relationship malaise for some time. The honesty of my relationship with Diane has been troubling me. She senses it. I know she does, even if she's in denial."

That would explain her hovering. "She seems nice."

"She's not you." Adam sighs. "She doesn't get me the way you do. I could never get you off my mind like you wanted me to. No matter how hard I tried. And I tried. I did." He tugs me into his chest and squeezes me tight, our bodies burning to how badly we've missed each other.

We stay like that, holding onto one another, hugging in a way that resembles clinging. I never, ever want to let him go again. I glance up at him. It's my Adam. "I've missed you so much. I didn't know it then. I've never been in love before. But, I had fallen in love with you too."

His eyes are on my mouth, and he's about to lean in to kiss me, but I pull back. I don't want it to be here. Not like this. On a balcony of a hall where Diane probably already has formed a search party for him. The way she hung on him wherever he went, she must be frantic by now. "No, Adam. We can't hide out here forever," I say. "They're apt to find us, and sooner rather than later. You need to go back inside. Diane has to be looking for you right now."

Adam runs his fingers through his side-swept hair and then drops his forehead to mine. "I'm going to tell her the truth."

"Tonight? At Todd's wedding?"

"I'm going to get the pain over with."

"Maybe it could wait a little. I mean, I want the idea of us to start as soon as possible, but could it maybe wait until after the reception?"

Adam shakes his head. "I want forever to start now. I can't bear the lie anymore. Truth is truth, Suellen."

"Adam, you can't be serious." I want him badly, but what's a couple more hours in the scheme of things?

Adam laughs softly. "I wasn't serious. Although I wish I was."

My chest rises and falls with my sigh. "You'll never change." I chuckle and then add, "Don't ever change."

"One more hour to go. I suppose I can hang in there." Adam kisses me on the lips again before he turns to go back inside.

I stare up at the sky and thank the proverbial lucky stars for an unbelievable dream come true when I realize I'm still wearing Adam's jacket. "Adam, wait. Your jacket." I try to catch up to him, flinging his jacket over my arm. When I come through the French doors, Adam turns around just as Diane and another woman wearing the same fuchsia-colored gown step between us. I seize up in the so-much-for-letting-her-down-easy kind of way, my eyes darting back and forth between Adam and Diane. Diane looks angry, her face heated red. Her bridesmaid girlfriend is equally blonde and equally angry. She could be the prototype for a millennial Barbie doll. She takes one look at Adam's jacket draped across my arm and her hands go to her hips as she glares at me. I'm still frozen in place.

Diane makes a sound like an animal that's been wounded, right before she gives Adam a not-so-nice slap across his face. "How could you?" she shrieks. I don't fault her. I might have reacted the same way. I wonder if she knows about our history, but I guess it doesn't matter either way. Truth can be painful.

I watch her with something like empathy, and I have to remind myself that Adam was mine before he was hers. Her screams attract some others, and a crowd of spectators hurry over. When Diane brings her arm up to swing at him again, Adam isn't having it. He grabs her wrist firmly. "Stop it, Diane. You need to calm down." Adam looks around at the rapt attention they're getting. "Come on. Let's go somewhere we can talk."

She's too far gone though. She continues ranting and crying and I start to back away when Carol and Joe burst through the crowd and rush over to me. Carol looks at me with eyes that are saying, "What the hell?"

Diane's high-pitched screams are going right through me. If I wasn't wincing, I might have seen, out of the corner of my eye, Bridesmaid Barbie charge me in an alcohol-induced rage. Before I can register what's happening, her fist makes an impact with my chin, the spectacle of a crazed woman under the influence. I don't hit back. I make a conscious decision to take it on the chin. Literally.

"Oh . . . hell, no." Carol shoves Bridesmaid Barbie so hard she tumbles back on her rear end.

A tux guy comes over to help her up, her arms flailing as she shouts, "You bitch!" She shrieks again, managing to wobble away from him. In a wild frenzy, she grabs a chunk of Carol's hair. In a flash, I grab a handful of Barbie's locks, pulling her head back as Adam's jacket falls unceremoniously to the floor. "Get your fucking hands off me," she hollers.

"Then get yours off her," I say. I love the way girls fight. It's all about the hair. Thank god mine's short right now. Finally letting go of Carol, Barbie spins around so fast I don't see the claws coming for my face. Just in the nick of time, two guys jump in and hold her back. One of them is Adam.

"Thanks," Adam says, nodding to the other guy, who'd managed to get there first.

"Yeah, thanks, Chris," I say.

"It's Tim," he says, restraining Barbie.

The guy who helped Barbie up from the floor clocks Tim right in his teeth. The two of them tumble to the floor fighting. Barbie's heel catches on Adam's tuxedo jacket that's being trampled in the melée, and she slips and falls onto her back. Now there's a heap of three bodies on the floor.

Cell phones are out, videotaping, and Diane hurries over to help Barbie up, tugging at her arm. She's a little less inebriated than Barbie who winds up pulling Diane down on top of her, boobs and legs and hair spilling all over. Between all the screaming and flowery expletives, the two of them succeed in getting all tangled up, littering the floor with rippling fuschia, crushed orchid petals, and loose rhinestones. Adam helps Diane off Barbie but as she stumbles back up, Barbie grabs hold of Adam's ankle.

"Don't you dare touch me," Diane cries, thrashing Adam with her fists and worse – long nails. *Hell hath no fury like a woman scorned.*

While Diane swings her arms at Adam, Barbie threatens to bite his ankle.

Yeah. That's not going to happen. The thing about evening gowns with a slit in them is you have a free leg. I stick it out and shove Barbie away before she bites down, freeing Adam's ankle. No one's helping her off the floor. I think everyone agrees she needs to stay down there a while longer.

Adam tells Joe to get us out of there and go back to the hotel. When Joe puts his hand on my arm to steer me away from the mayhem, I realize I'd been shielding my new boobs with my hands, the need to protect them still instinctual.

The band has stopped playing music. They can't compete with the uproar of the guests who are louder than they are. The hall's earlier subdued and formal vibe has turned frenetic, intensified by alcohol and adrenaline.

"We gotta bolt," Joe says, tugging at me and Carol, pulling us away from the jumbled scene of arms and fists and frayed satin, the earlier discretion and classiness a distant memory. Carol and I swipe our purses from our tables as I glance over at the commotion. The picture's all wrong. It looks like a full-out western brawl scene that got erroneously spliced into a Disney princess movie. And somehow they mixed up the wardrobe too.

I don't want to leave Adam. But he has more friends here than I do. Or did. I turn back to look as I'm walking away. Adam's pulling Diane up, easing her away from the chaos. She goes willingly, leaning into him, weeping. He holds her close and rubs her arm. It touches me, and I can't tear my eyes away.

"Keep moving," Joe coaxes until we reach the main entrance. When we're finally outside, he breathes out a heavy sigh. "You two okay?"

I pull away the blonde strands of hair that are still caught between my fingers.

"We could've taken them," Carol swears.

I shake my head. "Maybe the two of 'em, but not when the bridesmaids start emptying from the dugout."

Joe chuckles. "But seriously, the crowd was getting too hostile. It was time for us to go." A shuttle bus makes its way over to us.

"So does this mean we aren't going to the post-wedding brunch tomorrow?" Carol says.

I look at her. Unruly hair, eyes still ablaze. I burst into emotional tears, a strange mixture of laughing and crying at once.

The shuttle pulls up. Carol goes first, Joe reaching back to pull me along, onto the vehicle that takes us away.

CHAPTER 32

I'd been tossing and turning, unable to sleep, when Adam's text came in sometime after midnight.

Adam

I need a place to sleep tonight.

When I hear the knock, I leap out of bed and take a quick look through the peephole. He's leaning on the door frame, a suitcase in the other hand, his tattered tux jacket thrown across his shoulder.

"Oh, Adam." I throw the door open wide to let him through. "Look at you."

"I'd rather not."

Adam's white dress shirt is wrinkled and missing a top button, his tousled hair falls in waves over his forehead, and there are some scratches over his face.

"You okay?" I say.

He nods. "As okay as I can be after having just come from trying to calm a hysterical woman."

I wince. "I'm so sorry. I told you I shouldn't have come."

Adam's eyes bore into mine. "Stop it, Suellen." His stern voice startles me and I suck in a breath. "I don't ever want to hear those words from you again. Do you hear me?" His eyes are brimming with tears. He grabs me by my shoulders and pulls me into him, wrapping his arms around me in a tight squeeze. For a while we stay like that, holding each other in the middle of the room. My face is pressed into his chest, his breath in my hair. Tears course down my cheeks.

"Not how I wanted it to go, but it's over now." Adam sighs. "It's done."

My mind is still whirring from all that's transpired in the last few hours. I could sit Adam down, ask him the slew of questions running through my mind, talk it all through, but instead, I run my fingers through his hair, glide my lips over his neck, his chin, his lips. Adam's body responds to mine with ease and readiness. I want to please him. I want to make up for all the hurt I've put him through. I trace my fingers down the buttons of his shirt, unbuttoning each as I go, and slide his shirt off him. I reach up to hold his broad shoulders in both my hands. His hands come out to hold mine and slide their way down over my breasts. My heart stops and I take a few steps back.

Adam sees the distress in my eyes, the sadness I know is there. "I have no feeling in them anymore," I say. "They're just, as best I can describe them, numb."

His eyes close over in sadness, but there's longing there too. He comes over to me and kisses the top of my head, my wet eyelids, the bridge of my nose. He raises my arms and lifts my nightshirt over my head until I'm standing vulnerable in front of him in only my thong panties. I cross my arms over my implanted breasts with tattooed nipples, his eyes staring into mine. "You're beautiful," he says, moving closer. His lips graze my neck, gliding down with light kisses in the hollow of my throat. He trails circles in my cleavage, dragging his lips down to my navel, teasing me with the tip of his tongue. "Can you feel this?" he says.

He drops to his knees, his lips, mouth, and tongue sliding further down, to my thighs. He scrapes his teeth over the crotch of my panties before he shimmies them down my legs, lifting each and then placing one over his strong, sturdy shoulder. He grips my buttocks while his tongue traces and flickers between my legs. "And this? Can you feel this?"

My eyes close, my back arches and my head falls back. A sob escapes my throat. *Yes . . . yes.*

I hold his head between my hands, and it takes all my strength and willpower to move him off me. I clutch his undershirt in my fist to pull it off him, moving down to his belt buckle as he stands. "Do you have a condom?" I say.

He grins, removes his slacks, and pulls a billfold from its pocket. Then he lifts me and lays me across the bed. He crawls naked over me and stretches my arms up over my head, alternating his kisses with licks over my inner arms and wrists, encircling each of my palms and sucking my fingers. On his knees above me, I feel the swell of his genitals moving over my skin, but not inside me, torturing my senses. I lust for him. "Adam," I cry out, my eyes pleading.

I hear the tear of a condom wrapper. My heartbeat keeps pounding.

He straddles me, and I spread my thighs as he slides into me, my legs crossing over his back. The connection is unlike anything I've ever known, giving me everything. His body, his mind, his heart. His truth.

Tears are falling, my heart exploding. "I love you," I moan over and over again in between soft sobs, "I love you," and then he takes me to a full-body orgasm, right before his own.

Truth is so much better than hiding.

•　•　•

"Just do me a favor," I say to Carol, "Make sure when you tell our group at the office about all this you let them know how controlled I was. They'll never believe it." I rub the soreness in my jaw. "Barbie sure packs a punch."

Carol and Joe are sitting across from Adam and me in a diner booth downtown. I can just see the lunch group tomorrow. It will be the pinnacle of Carol's newsmonger status, and she won't even need to exaggerate. This has all the elements of a great tale – jealousy, deception, passion, fury. And let's not forget love. But I can append her narrative with that part on Tuesday when I go back to work. Or maybe Wednesday. Who knows when?

Adam leans in and brings his arm around me on the bench seat, gripping my shoulder. He sees me working out my jaw. "Does it hurt a lot?"

"Nah. I've had worse," I say.

"You'd a thought that Barbie was the one being cheated on," Carol says. "She was a crazy, mad woman last night."

"Who also happened to be pretty drunk," I say. I turn to Adam. "By the way, what's Barbie's real name?"

"Avery," Adam says.

"Avery. No. I'm still going with Barbie."

Adam gives a little laugh.

"I think the two of you would have stayed to the bitter end if I hadn't gotten you out of there," Joe says.

"You'd better believe it," Carol says. "The fun was just getting started."

She catches me glancing over at Adam. "Sorry," she says. "I'm sure this wasn't fun for you at all."

"No, it wasn't. I might have been able to take Diane aside and calm her down, but then Avery . . . Barbie had to go and escalate the whole damn thing." Adam shakes his head. "I had a good talk with Diane. She's still seething a bit, but hopefully, in time, she'll be less angry. Anyway, it's over now. That's all." There's a tinge of remorse in Adam's eyes. I feel it too. Neither of us wanted this to happen like it did. Caught in a swirl of fate beyond our control. But there are some things I *can* control. I can text Diane when things calm down, talk to her if she'll let me, attempt to explain. How could she know she'd come between two forces separated by misfortune, swept apart in a riptide of confusion and sorrow, waiting for the current to ease? It's not going to make her feel better, but at least I can try.

"I feel bad this happened at Todd's wedding. We didn't mean for it to," I say. "Not there. It wasn't planned."

"I texted Todd too," Adam says.

"Oh, no. Is he mad? Does he hate me . . . or you?" I say.

"Nah. They had already left to start their honeymoon. He says the hype going around is that it was the most fun anyone's ever had at a wedding. No one's going to forget it, that's for sure."

"I still think I need to send him an apology note," I say.

"Well, you'll have to wait until they get back from Machu Picchu in two weeks."

"Wow. Really? How awesome," I say.

I look at Carol and Joe. "I forgot if you told me where you two are going for your honeymoon."

"Hawaii," Joe says, finishing his last bite of chocolate pancake. "Never been there before."

"Kauai, Oahu. I cannot wait," Carol says.

"You're going to love those places," I say. "I was there a few years ago with my mother and Morris. They were secretly trying to fix me up with one of Morris' nephews." I shake my head. "But that's another story."

"Hmmm," Adam says. "I might be interested to hear about it sometime."

"It's not too exciting," I say. "Although it is if you consider the hilarity of it."

"Oh, now I'm curious," Adam says, kissing me on the lips.

We might have kissed for longer than a moment or two because when I look back at Carol and Joe, they're grinning at us. *Why does it feel like we're on our honeymoon?* Then Adam begins sliding his hand between my thighs under the table. When a sigh seeps out of me, I have to still his hand before going cross-eyed and losing it.

"Something tells me the two of you will be having your own honeymoon in the not-too-distant future," Carol says. "Where would you like to go?"

"Oh, I don't know," I say. "I never really gave it much thought. Tuscany, Fiji, Bali maybe."

Adam's hand is back on my thigh, edging toward the inside.

"Ah . . . malfi Coast," I stutter to cover the sigh that's escaped. I'm going to lose my mind. Adam's enjoying himself.

I lower my hand onto his lap then and begin to stroke and fondle him. "Are we done here?" he says, breaking out in a sweat.

Joe picks the check up from the table, and Adam swipes it from his hand with a little too much vigor. "Let me get it."

Carol and Joe have started to slide out of the booth, when Adam stands, his eyes darting to the crotch of his pants. "Give me your jacket," he says, holding it in front of his bulge.

"What's so funny?" Carol says as we head over to the front entrance.

I smile a secret smile. "I was just thinking how crazy this weekend's turned out."

"Yeah. No one's going to believe me when I tell them."

"You do have a reputation for embellishing," I remind her.

Adam pays the check and turns to us. "They'll believe you when they see this." He holds out his phone and frowns. Someone posted a video of Diane and Barbie falling all over each other on the floor. One of Barbie's boobs has nearly fallen out of her gown, and Diane's dress is scrunched up to her waist.

"No." I wince. They'd captioned it "Best entertainment of the night."

"So, there it is," Adam says. "Your proof."

"This is definitely going to give credibility to your standing in the news world now," I say to Carol. "It could open up a whole new career for you."

Joe has a good laugh. Adam chuckles and I turn to him and smile. I'm somewhat overdressed for a diner in a red crochet knee length dress with halter top I'd packed for the after-wedding brunch. It was either that or the clothes I wore when I arrived, which will need to be cleaned. Adam assists me with putting on my knit jacket before we head outdoors. He beams a smile.

I look over at him. "What?"

"Sorry. Was I staring again?"

"Yes, you were." *But I really like it.*

We walk behind Carol and Joe through the parking lot to our cars. "How is it you make me feel funny, smart, and beautiful whenever I'm with you?"

"That's easy," Adam says. "Because you're all of those things." He wraps his arm around me. "Ask me a tougher question next time."

"I wonder what else is going to turn up," Carol says when we reach our cars. "I hope someone took a video of me knocking Barbie on her ass. Now that would be something."

"I'll vouch for you," I say. "I will make a convincing witness."

"She had it coming to her, don't you think?"

"Truth is truth, Carol," I say, stealing Adam's line. My brain has already established there will be no more secrets between Adam and me. No more hiding or protecting. From here on in, only truth is permitted in our relationship.

We say our goodbyes and part. "See you back at the office," Carol says to me. "Whenever that is."

When we are inside Adam's car, he turns to me. "We don't get to choose who we fall in love with or who will love us back, do we?"

The heart wants what it wants. Emily Dickinson sure nailed it. "No," I say honestly. "Hence the word 'fall.' Someone always gets hurt. Love is designed that way. Otherwise, it wouldn't be worth all the hurt that goes with it." I look into Adam's eyes and see the empathy in them for the way things ended with him and Diane. The way it all came down is not Adam's way. "You're a good person, Adam. Don't ever forget that."

"I never imagined someone like you in my life. You're my perfect."

I realize true love doesn't choose perfect. What makes it perfect is how love chooses us. "I never imagined ever wanting someone in my life . . . until you."

"Have they left?" Adam says, his eyes bright.

"Carol and Joe? Yeah. They just pulled away."

Adam starts the car and drives it around to the back of the lot and parks it under a tree.

"What are you doing?"

"We're checked out of the hotel and we still have over an hour's drive to your place. I always like to finish what I start." Adam slides his hand over my knees, pushing up my dress. Considerate, pleasing Adam. "I may need some help with your panties."

"Who says I'm wearing one?"

Adam grins. "Says the lady in red."

Oh yes, truth feels so good. I'll thank my brain later.

•   •   •

I was asleep when I felt him glide over the length of my spine with his lips, the dimple in my back, the groove of my buttocks, stirring me awake. Adam and I haven't left my townhouse in three days. I don't know if it rained, if the sun came out, or if the world's still going on outside. I only know I finally have a home. Adam is my home. He's love and comfort and safety. I never knew how empty I was, until he filled me.

We've been ordering food in, watching movies, cuddling on the couch, curling up with Lucy, and well . . . you know.

I do not need to open my eyes to prove I'm not dreaming. For all the bad and all the hurt and fear in my life, I'd have to say it served a purpose. I know how good I have it now. I know how right it feels. The scales may not always be in balance, but I can try.

My body warms to Adam's kisses and caresses, tingling and surging with sexual arousal. That man really knows how to tip the scales.

Then he flips me over and stimulates me into a frenzied burn.

And we make love for the third time that day.

CHAPTER 33

Four months later

"Adam, I only got you a card," I say as we stroll along the promenade toward the seaside restaurant, a wavy, white divider separating the walkway from the sand. "What's all of that you're holding in your hand?"

"I couldn't decide on just one card," Adam says, squeezing my hand with his free one. "So I got you five."

"Am I that complicated?" I say. This makes him laugh, and I'm not sure if it's because he believes it to be true or not.

Adam brings my hand to his lips. "You're that charismatic." He kisses my fingers.

We'd visited with Mom and Morris in Palm Beach for a couple of days then continued on to Ft. Lauderdale for a couples retreat. Today is Valentine's Day. It's a beautiful warm evening, mid-seventies, pleasant. I'm dressed in a lace-up pink maxi dress, a paisley shawl draped over my bare shoulders. Adam looks sharp in lightweight, charcoal-gray dress slacks, a crisp button-down white shirt, and a navy jacket. It's a short walk to the waterfront restaurant from our hotel.

We nestle ourselves in a plush booth that overlooks a view of the ocean. Three red flameless candles of different heights flicker on the table between us.

"Happy Valentine's Day," I say, pushing my card toward him.

"Do you want me to open it now?" he says.

"Yes. Before the sun sets."

On the front of my card is a heart drawn in the sand; on the inside, a single word. *You.* "I'll have you know that's a customized card. Everything I came up with came back to that one simple word."

The waitress brings our drinks, and we order little appetizers of crab and cream cheese crescent rolls. Adam passes the first of his stack of cards to me.

"So, are the cards in any special order?" I say.

"Might be," Adam says.

And so begins Adam's sequence of love cards in different genres. There's a classic romantic one, a mushy-funny one, a pretty pop-up floral bouquet, and a musical one that plays "You Are So Beautiful" by Joe Cocker when I open it. The last one is the smallest card, an unadorned picture of a small desk on the front. I open it and read, 'Someday you're going to find this card in a drawer and we'll still be in love.' I cross my hands over my chest and heave a sigh, my eyes tearing up. "Okay. This one really got me."

The waitress sets two bowls of clam bisque in front of us and I have to smile when Adam takes his third spoonful. Maybe I've been a good food influence after all. And then, because I'm complicated in spite of the fact that I love the heady stage we're in – hormones flowing, moment-to-moment living – I have to ask him the question that's been rumbling inside me, the one that's akin to finding the card in a drawer someday. The future us. "How many children do you want?" I don't waste my question on whether or not he wants children, because why wouldn't he? This is Adam. Selfless, giving, playful Adam.

Although my question comes out of nowhere, Adam doesn't react. He doesn't even look at me. Accustomed by now to my outpourings, he takes another slow sip of his soup. "This is good," he says.

The silent moment turns into two, then three. I look steadily into his eyes. "I can't seem to shock you anymore, can I?"

He gives me a gentle smile. "How many children do *you* want?"

"I asked you first," I say. I should have known the way I posed the question was too specific and confining for Adam's analytical mind. I try another way. "Do you want kids?"

Adam looks into my eyes and holds my gaze. "Your question is out of sequence," he says. "What you should be asking is, 'Do you want to spend the rest of your life with me?' That should be your first question. Once that one is answered, the rest can follow."

We lay down our spoons and stare out the window to watch the sun descend below the horizon, a fitting allegory to the mystery of life. When I turn back to look at Adam, night has fallen. He's watching me, waiting for me to ask the question. The first in a sequence.

I can't seem to do it.

"Go on," he urges softly. "Ask me if I want to spend the rest of my life with you."

I look into the candlelight, then back into his eyes, my heart heavy. "It's too much to ask."

"Why do you think that?"

"Because it's all-encompassing. It's everything."

"Exactly."

"It's just that I'd want you to be happy," I say. "There are so many unknowns since, well, since my diagnosis. It's asking a lot of you."

Our waitress brings our entrées, and Adam and I lean back in our seats while she sets the plates in front of us. I hadn't meant to get all serious on him. I should have kept it playful and romantic. But I went there. It's too late now.

"That's an interesting word," Adam says, lifting up his fork and knife.

"Which?"

"Unknown." He cuts into his filet mignon and I watch him with curiosity. *Where is his mind taking him? What is he thinking?* He is an enigma of fascination.

"What if you and I never met? What if we never crossed paths? Where would we be right now? Would we be in love? Would we still be searching?" Adam gives me just enough time to flash through all the what-if scenarios. They are void of happiness without him. "Those are the unknowns I don't want to face," he says. "Because there's one thing

I do know. I want to go through the unknowns with you." Adam interlaces his fingers with mine.

How does he do it? Make my heart melt. I never knew love before him. I look down at my salmon croquettes. Suddenly, I'm not hungry anymore. My eyes fill with tears. I want to go back to the hotel. I want to make love to him. I don't want to think about what the future may or may not hold. I want to live in this very moment.

When our server asks if we would like dessert, Adam surprises me by saying yes.

"I really couldn't," I say.

Adam says, "We'll share it."

"Okay," I acquiesce, when all I really want to do is climb into bed with him. I gaze out over the dark ocean under a crescent moon while Adam excuses himself to use the men's room.

Shortly after he returns, the waitress places a plate of dessert between us, and I am instantly awestruck. A small round lemon cheesecake decorated with sugar seashells on a bed of sugary sand. "Oh my goodness! How incredibly creative. Are the shells all edible?" I say to the waitress, but she's already gone.

I pull out my phone. "I have to take a picture of this." Adam watches in silence. "I can't get over how real all the shells look. Clamshells and cockles, oysters, and sand dollars are scattered over a beach-themed plate. One of them catches my eye. A pretty pink conch. "Look at this one." I pick it up, turning it over in my hand. "Why, this one's real."

The bright twinkle of a three-carat diamond ring tucked inside startles me. I suck in a breath and hold it. Adam's no longer across from me. He's right next to me, down on one knee. "Marry me," he says. "There's no blueprint for the future, but there is one thing I'm sure of. I promise to love you for as long as forever."

He stands himself up, and I crumple into his waiting arms, my tears flowing.

Rubbing my quaking back, Adam says, "So is that a yes?"

"Yes, yes," I say to a clattering of applause throughout the restaurant. "Yes, I'll marry you."

•   •   •

The short walk to our hotel has somehow grown longer, every step a marathon. I might not have been completely truthful when I told Adam I only got him a card. The plunging lacy red corset under my sundress is itching to come off. Not swiftly. Slowly and deliberately. One delicate strap, one tiny hook at a time.

Yeah. The future can wait.

EPILOGUE

Eight months later: Breast Cancer Awareness Month

It's a quarter to seven when we leave our car with the valet at the New Jersey Performing Arts Center in downtown Newark, a few blocks from Rutgers Law School.

Adam and I enter the expansive lobby of Prudential Hall and head toward double doors beneath a white-and-pink banner that says, "Go for the Cure/North Jersey Fundraising Gala."

Holding Adam's hand, I lead us through a flock of cocktail dresses and black ties, waiters circulating, guests gathering, my eyes seeking a familiar face among them. Lynne spots me first, waving her hand in the air. She and Lou are talking with Carol and Joe near the bar in the back of the Hall when Adam and I approach.

"Suellen, you look stunning," Lynne says. She's dressed in a classic black, puff-sleeve dress with sequins sprinkled on the bodice. We greet each other with a brush of cheeks. When we pull back, she glides her fingertips over the fabric of my dress. "I love this."

I glance down at my dress, silvery flickers catching my eye. I'd debated whether I should try to blend in or stand out a little, but then I thought it made more sense to wear something that makes a statement, something that says, "I'm taking back control since my breast cancer." In a room dominated by black attire, my silver metallic halter dress sparkles, revealing bare shoulders and lots of leg. Mom will unequivocally approve when she sees me.

"And you look fabulous," I say to Lynne, looking over at Lou whose vigorous nod tells me he agrees one hundred percent. When we are used to seeing one another in business suits and office attire, formalwear is a striking change.

Carol looks flirty in a black crinkled chiffon dress with her burgundy hair gelled up in curls. Joe asks if he can get us a drink. Instinctively, I glance at the cocktails in everyone's hand.

"White wine," Lynne answers my look.

I turn to Carol. "Brandy, rum, and Cointreau with a little lemon. We fell in love with it on our honeymoon."

"Sounds dangerous. What's it called?"

"Between the Sheets," Carol says, chuckling.

"Figures," I say. "Think I'll have a Diet Coke instead." I brush my chin-length hair from my cheek and smile. "Is Teagan here yet?"

"Teagan phoned to say she'll be a little late."

Adam walks over to the bar with Joe while I scan the room, looking for my family since I haven't seen them yet.

"Thank you," I say when Adam and Joe return with drinks. I take a sip. I didn't realize how thirsty I was. "So, Lou," I say turning toward him, "Lynne tells me you're quite the chef."

Lou looks at Lynne who raises her shoulders in a giveaway sign. He laughs a little. "I have a very limited menu – steak. Anyone can grill a steak. Oh, and eggs. Omelets are my specialty."

"How about your Italian sauce?" Lynne says. "Don't forget about that." Lou nods modestly. Lynne wraps her free arm around his waist. "This guy knows how to season."

I keep glancing toward the entrance, for anyone from my family to appear, and am surprised when Simon and Sarah come up behind me. I spin around.

"Hey, sis," Simon says, kissing my cheek.

"I didn't see you two coming. How's my niece?"

"Getting a head start on the terrible two's," Sarah smirks. "Other days she's an angel."

"I can't get over how much you look like your sister," Carol says to Simon. "Although one of you is probably sassier than the other."

"Three guesses as to which one that is," Simon says. He and Adam look toward me and share a laugh.

"Mom and Morris were right behind us," Sarah says. "Mom just had to stop in the ladies' room first."

I spot Dad and Eve and wave them over. I kiss Dad and brush cheeks with the never-ruffled, impeccable Eve. She's flawless in a champagne silk suit, her hair pulled back in a sleek bun. There are some people in this world who you can't imagine ever doing anything other than posturing. That's Eve. Ever in control, ever unaffected.

And then the antithesis of Eve walks over. My mother. Morris is right alongside her.

"I could see you sparkling from a mile away." Mom gives me a warm hug in a form-fitting, black-crepe cocktail dress. She looks pluckier than ever. After careful consideration, Mom had a prophylactic mastectomy with reconstruction nine months ago. "I can only hope to emulate half your bravery," she had told me when she decided to go through with it. She gives Adam a hug, her eyes dancing between us. "You two look so good together." She goes over to Eve and I overhear her saying, "How does it feel being a grandma? Ain't it great?"

Thirty-eight-year-old Eve recoils and I have to suppress a snicker.

"Hey," Morris says, shaking Adam's hand. "Not long before your and Suellen's big day."

In my mind, I remove myself from the cluster of friends and family, all chatting and drinking and socializing. I can feel my heart swell. One of these people is more different than the next, but there's one thing they all have in common. Me. They are all here for me. Because of me. Adam notices the wistful look waxing across my face. He's my heartbeat, my sensitive half. He knows me better than I know myself.

"Hey," he whispers, giving my arm a squeeze. "I love you."

•   •   •

When we're ushered to our seats in the auditorium, I glance at the two empty ones reserved for Teagan and Mike, giving one last look toward the entrance for any sign of them. "I hope everything's okay."

Sitting several seats away, Carol leans forward and holds up her cell phone. "Teagan texted they just arrived." Then she turns hers off along with the rest of us.

Teagan and Mike are escorted down the aisle to their seats as Teagan mouths "sorry" to me before settling in. When I'm signaled to come up on stage, I realize I'm holding fast to Adam's hand. Rising, I pat his gently as I extricate my own.

As I stand at the podium looking out at a packed audience – my family, my friends – I think how far I've come. Not just in my wellness journey, but in my outlook on life. I see my dad, the man who was my first hero, not just the man who often squabbled with my mother. I can see clearly now the one who used to swing me and Simon in the air and took us for root beer floats against Mom's wishes. Who climbed a tall oak tree in his dress pants and patent leathers to rescue Simon. It's like everything good's coming into better focus, sprouting over a compost of bad. I see my mom, the unwavering woman who's living her best life with ostentatious-but-mostly-benevolent Morris, where she's free to be herself.

I start my speech by laying out the plain facts, that if you have breasts you can get breast cancer. Young women, men even, can and do get breast cancer. "I've always been an optimist," I say. "Winston Churchill once said, 'It's not much use being anything else.' Today, with the overall breast cancer death rate in American women decreasing, we can all be optimistic. But it doesn't mean we should stop our efforts to raise awareness."

I thank my family for the important role they played in my recovery, and for their unending support and love. "Like everyone, I too had my downtime. How did I get through it?" I look over where my friends are sitting. "I'll tell you in a few words: Teagan, Lynne, and Carol." I swore I wasn't going to get emotional, but Adam was right. I'm speaking from my heart. "I love our lunch hours. Not only did they make me laugh and forget, they helped me heal. A daily dose of friends. It's the best medicine in the world. I feel lucky to have them in my life." *And, as Adam confided to me, 'It's going to be a very long life.'*

Teagan is crying and Lynne is passing tissues to anyone who needs one. I have to look away. I'm not through yet. Now comes the hardest part. My lower lip begins to tremble.

"And to a very special person in my life. A person with an extraordinary sense of timing and an incredible sense of humor. Adam, you are one of the most stubborn people I know. Thank you for never giving up on me. Thank you for all the laughs, but mostly, thank you for coming into my life and showing me how good 'good' can feel."

From his seat, Adam nods up to me, his lips forming the words, "'I love you.'"

Three more speakers later and halfway through a performance by the New Jersey Symphony Orchestra, Teagan excuses herself to make a phone call. It isn't until the performance is over that I glance over and realize she hasn't returned. I look at Lynne who sends me a confused look. Rising, Mike says, "I'll go find her," and before anyone can say anything, he starts up the aisle ahead of us.

We've just begun to settle around a table in the dining area. I've been to numerous philanthropy-themed dinners with Mom and Dad over the years, both in New Jersey and Florida, but this time it's different. I helped with organizing this one, and I plan to get even more involved with breast cancer survivor charities and foundations. Adam and I are sitting at my family's table, but my friends' table is right next to it.

A couple of Dad's colleagues are also sitting with us, including Dr. O'Connor. I'm up and down and back and forth between tables so often Mom says I should put my chair in between the tables. As a waiter brings over our first course – mushroom strudel with Boursin cheese – Adam looks over at me. "Yes," I say. "You will like this." That's all it takes for him to try it.

Back home after Adam had proposed to me in Florida, I knew I needed to broach a thorny subject with him, but I didn't know how to start. One early morning, replete with pleasure from lovemaking, it seemed as good a time as any to bring it up. I scanned the bedroom ceiling to avoid looking into his eyes. "You know becoming your wife is the best thing that could ever happen to me." I rolled onto my side and ran my fingers over his bare chest. "Dad's a prenup guy. It's going to come up."

Adam kissed my forehead. "It already has."

"What? When?" I bolted upright in the bed. "You never mentioned it."

"Didn't have to. It doesn't change anything. It only strengthens us."

"How's that exactly?"

"I'm a forever guy. I'll do whatever needs to be done to ensure our union. It's the responsible thing for us to do."

"How is it that you make everything sound so easy?"

"Because it is. I work hard and invest wisely. By my own definition, I'm doing okay. That doesn't mean I'll ever become as wealthy as your family is, but I'm just getting started. I don't want there to be any other motives getting in the way of how I feel about you."

"Then I would have to insist on one thing. We do the prenup together. From here on out we're a team. A responsible one."

Adam grinned. "Sure. Teammates."

"Nah," I said. "Lovers."

For entrées, we have a choice of prime rib, chicken Marsala, and grilled salmon. Adam grins from ear to ear as he chooses the prime rib. Later, between courses, Adam and I get up and go over to my friends' table. "What's going on?" I whisper into Teagan's ear. "You seem distracted."

"Oh, Suellen. I'm so nervous." She pauses to take a breath. "We got the call today that Mike and I have been matched." Teagan clasps her hands over her mouth to quell a scream.

"That's wonderful."

Teagan drops her shaky hands. "I can't believe after all this time it's finally going to happen. The baby's birth mother lives in Georgia – a fifteen-year-old girl who's due to deliver in five months. It's a boy." She starts tearing up. "I feel like an expectant mother, minus the hormones."

"Are you sure about the hormones part?" I say.

"It's all so unbelievable." Teagan brushes away a tear. "Mike and I are going to need to take a trip to Macon when this thing happens." She flies her hands to her cheeks and trembles.

I lean down to wrap my arms around her. "Okay, then. This is what you've been waiting for, right? You've got this."

"The nursery is not close to finished, I'll need baby boy's clothes, and I'm pretty sure I'm forgetting some other things."

"You just need to come up with a theme," I say. "I can help with the rest."

Teagan shakes her head. "You've done so much already. Mike and I are overwhelmed by how generous you've been and more grateful than we could ever tell you. You've made this so much easier by your generosity. We can never thank you enough."

"You have," I say. Teagan sighs a smile. "Now let's get ready to bring home my godson."

Everyone at the table is tuned into us, so Teagan answers it for them. "It's a boy."

Mike wraps his arm around Teagan with a big smile. "Yeah. I'm going to have a son."

"Yay," Lynne shouts from across the table.

Carol looks over at Teagan. "Don't cry. You're making me cry."

The band's playing "The Way You Look Tonight." Lou turns to Lynne. "Shall we?"

Mike persuades Teagan to join them on the dance floor. Carol watches Joe fork his last morsel of strudel and then says, "Well?"

"Oh. Wanna dance?" Joe says.

"I thought you'd never ask."

"They all love you," I say to Adam while we sway together on the dance floor. "My family, my friends. You're quite popular."

Adam kisses the top of my head. "That's nice, but I'm mostly interested in how one person feels about me."

At the end of the dance, we wander back to our table. When the band starts the next song – Kenny Rogers' "Through the Years" Dad pushes away from the table and stands. I glance at an expectant Eve, but he walks around the table and comes to me instead. He holds out his hand, palm up. "I want to dance with my daughter." I'm more shocked than Eve looks.

"I've never seen you look happier," Dad says, looking into my eyes as we move together on the dance floor. "I couldn't be prouder of you."

I've spent years, if not my entire life, waiting to hear him say those words. I don't know what I should feel – or if I should feel anything at all. I think about all the missed opportunities, the father-daughter dances he was too busy to attend, the scheduled weekends with us he relinquished without even a fight, the generic birthday cards Eve no doubt selected for him. Our father-daughter relationship was not perfect and became less so after my parents divorced, but I learned to accept it for what it was.

Being the recipient of my dad's compliment is a rare gift, and I want him to know how much it means for his rebel daughter to hear him say those words. "I love you, Dad," I say, and kiss him on the cheek. I can let go of the past now since I'm in a new story.

"I always knew you were capable of anything," Dad says. "Your inner resolve and strength never cease to amaze me."

"That's because I never forget whose daughter I am," I say with a smile.

Mom and Morris are near us on the dance floor. Morris is saying something that makes Mom laugh. I feel Eve watching from the table, her disconsolate eyes never leaving us, then I see Adam go over and ask her to dance. When they join us on the floor, I can't help thinking Adam is one of the cleverest and most intuitive people I have ever known. Before the song ends, he and Dad switch partners and Adam says to me, "The look on Mike's face when he announced he was going to have a son – that was priceless. I can't stop thinking about it."

"Yeah, it was, wasn't it? Mike wasn't too eager in the beginning. It took him a while to come around to the idea of adopting. I'm so happy for them."

"I know we've talked about this," Adam says, "I want you to know that whatever you decide, I'm okay with it."

"Are we talking babies now?" I chuckle. "Since you bring it up, I've given a lot of thought to my baby options. Sure. I'd consider adoption. There are so many babies and kids out there who need homes and good parents. Destiny is forever in the back of my mind. And I'd worry about passing the BRCA mutation onto a child of mine. But more and more, I'm thinking I'd like to go another way."

Adam pulls back so he can look into my eyes.

"I want to bear your child. Use my eggs that are frozen, do the IVF procedure where the embryos can be biopsied to identify which carry the BRCA mutation."

"The designer baby method you mean," Adam says. "You do realize this could mean we might even be able to select the baby's sex."

"Is that important to you?" I say.

"Not at all. I'd love any child we make together."

"It's just that with 50-50 odds of the gene being passed on to a child of mine, it's a risk I don't want to take. I was a mess before Simon got tested, thinking my niece could have inherited it."

Adam leans his forehead into mine. "Sounds like you've been doing a lot of thinking about this."

"I've been reading up on it a lot. More and more patients like me are choosing preimplantation genetic diagnosis so doctors only transfer BRCA-free embryos to the mother's womb. Perhaps one day, future generations will no longer carry the harmful gene." I pull back trying to read the expression in Adam's eyes. "How do you feel about all this?"

"As long as our family begins with you and me, we'll figure out the rest. Sounds to me like you've made your mind up."

"I think I have."

Adam grins. "When do we start?"

"As soon as we get back from the Keys." Our December destination wedding will be taking place on the beach in Key Largo, where the honeymoon will follow.

"That's in two months," Adam says, sounding surprised.

"Yeah. I know. My doctor's already given me the green light. I'm the big three-oh, Adam. I want to do this. I'm ready to do this."

"Okay then," Adam says before he kisses me on the forehead. "But you know thirty is the new twenty."

Leaving Adam with Simon and the other men at the bar, I take my drink over to join my girlfriends. "It's just us women now," I say.

"I don't know when I've had this much fun," Lynne says.

"And great drinks," a tipsy Carol chimes in.

"So glad I came." Teagan nods. "And in a couple of months . . . your and Adam's wedding. Yay! A private sunset cruise, a floating tiki bar, snorkeling . . . Mike and I can't wait."

"Yeah," Carol says. "About that. You won't hold it against me if I don't do the snorkeling thing, will you? I'm kind of spooked by sharks and riptides."

"Nah. I get it," I say. "Another girlfriend went snorkeling with me a few years ago. One day I lobster and never flounder again."

Lynne and Teagan crack up while Carol feigns a smile.

I look around at the faces of these women, my friends, my other family. "All right, it's that time," I say.

"What time is it?" Carol says.

Taking my glass, I raise it in their direction.

"I feel a toast coming," Teagan says.

With glasses lifted I start, "To good times."

Carol's glass is almost at her lips when Teagan adds, "to lasting friendships."

"And . . . " I drag this out because I'm having way too much fun watching Carol squirm. "Here's to the ladies who lunch."

"Hear! Hear!"

Don't miss the next *Lunch Tales* **book:** *Teagan*
Lucille Guarino

• • •

For news on all upcoming books, sign up for Lucille Guarino's
Newsletter: https://lucilleguarino.substack.com/
Or check out her website at: https://lucilleguarino.com/

AFTERWORD

Dear readers,

Three facts:

- Second to skin cancer, breast cancer is the most common cancer in the world.
- Breast cancer incidence has been slowly rising in the United States.
- Early detection saves lives.

We hear about the importance of self-breast exams and getting mammograms often and yet we can never hear it enough. Even before you experience signs and symptoms, mammograms can detect abnormalities. They play a key role in the screening for breast cancer and should be part of your regular checkup.

As American women with a one in eight chance of getting breast cancer, we all know someone who's had it. Sometimes it's genetic. Mostly, it's random. Almost four million women in the United States are walking around with a history of breast cancer. Ask any one of them. They will tell you, "Don't be afraid. Don't put it off."

Live bravely. And please, take care of yourselves.

Lucille Guarino

ABOUT THE AUTHOR

Lucille Guarino is an award-winning author of three novels. An avid reader of most genres, Lucille loves emotion-heavy stories with strong female characters who are as realistic as they are inspiring. She holds the record in her family for reading the most books, writing the most stories, and giving them some of the funniest fall fails. Having lived most of her life in northern New Jersey, she now lives in Lexington, South Carolina, with her husband and close to her two daughters and grandchildren. She delights in embarrassing her kids . . . and now her grandkids. She loves road trips, touring the countryside, and talking to the locals. If there was ever any doubt about her fear of heights, standing before the almighty Grand Canyon clinched it.

NOTE FROM LUCILLE GUARINO

Word-of-mouth is crucial for any author to succeed. If you enjoyed *Lunch Tales*, please leave a review online—anywhere you are able. Even if it's just a sentence or two. It would make all the difference and would be very much appreciated.

Thanks!
Lucille Guarino

We hope you enjoyed reading this title from:

www.blackrosewriting.com

Subscribe to our mailing list – *The Rosevine* – and receive **FREE** books, daily deals, and stay current with news about upcoming releases and our hottest authors.
Scan the QR code below to sign up.

Already a subscriber? Please accept a sincere thank you for being a fan of Black Rose Writing authors.

View other Black Rose Writing titles at www.blackrosewriting.com/books and use promo code **PRINT** to receive a **20% discount** when purchasing.